Also by Danielle Steel

Country

For years, Stephanie Adams has protected her children from her unhappy marriage. Then Stephanie's husband dies suddenly, and her whole life changes . . . After a chance meeting with country music megastar Chase Taylor, an exciting new world is opened up to her. By seizing the day, Stephanie has found a way to be happy. But can her family find it in their hearts to let her go?

Property of a Noblewoman

An abandoned safe-box is opened to reveal a treasure trove. But there is no will in the box. Clerk Jane Willoughby is charged with discovering more about the box's owner, the late Marguerite Wallace Pearson di San Pignelli. And when Christie's auctioneer Philip Lawton joins Jane's quest, neither of them could have imagined where the contents of the box would leave them . . . or how it will change their lives forever.

The Apartment

Four young women are sharing a loft apartment in New York City. They also share an ambitious streak: they are all determined to reach the top of their fields. Throughout thick and thin – and the ups and downs of their romantic relationships – the apartment is always a safe haven. But when life begins to change for each of the women in ways they could never have predicted, will their bonds of friendship survive?

Precious Gifts

Veronique Parker's world is turned upside down when her former husband dies suddenly, leaving her and their daughters astonishing inheritances: a painting, a French château, the freedom to pursue their dreams, and a revelation from the past. These gifts will lead them on a journey certain to change Veronique and her daughters' destinies in the most surprising of ways . . .

Prodigal Son

In a matter of days, Peter McDowell loses everything – including his marriage. Returning to the home he left twenty years ago, he comes face to face with his brother Michael. But to his surprise their reunion is tender. Only later, as Peter mulls over his late mother's journals, does he begin to question what lies beneath Michael's perfect surface . . .

Undercover

After a job gone wrong shatters undercover agent Marshall's world, he flees to Paris. Meanwhile, Ariana knows that, as the daughter of an American Ambassador, her safety is always at risk. Even when she is relocated to Paris, trouble is never far behind. Paired together, Marshall and Ariana must trust each other if they are to find freedom from their past . . .

Danielle Steel is one of the world's most popular and highly acclaimed authors, with over ninety international bestselling novels in print and more than 600 million copies of her novels sold. She is also the author of *His Bright Light*, the story of her son Nick Traina's life and death; *A Gift of Hope*, a memoir of her work with the homeless; and *Pure Joy*, about the dogs she and her family have loved.

To discover more about Danielle Steel and her books visit her website at www.daniellesteel.com

And join her on Facebook at www.facebook.com/DanielleSteelOfficial or on Twitter: @daniellesteel.

Also by Danielle Steel

MAGIC
THE APARTMENT
PROPERTY OF A NOBLEWOMAN
BLUE
PRECIOUS GIFTS
UNDERCOVER
COUNTRY
PRODIGAL SON
PEGASUS
A PERFECT LIFE
POWER PLAY
PURE JOY: *The Dogs We Love*
WINNERS
FIRST SIGHT
UNTIL THE END OF TIME
A GIFT OF HOPE: *Helping the Homeless*
SINS OF THE MOTHER
FRIENDS FOREVER
BETRAYAL
HOTEL VENDÔME
HAPPY BIRTHDAY
44 CHARLES STREET
LEGACY
FAMILY TIES
BIG GIRL
SOUTHERN LIGHTS
MATTERS OF THE HEART
ONE DAY AT A TIME
A GOOD WOMAN
ROGUE
HONOUR THYSELF
AMAZING GRACE
BUNGALOW 2
SISTERS
H.R.H.
COMING OUT
THE HOUSE
TOXIC BACHELORS
MIRACLE
IMPOSSIBLE
ECHOES
SECOND CHANCE
RANSOM
SAFE HARBOUR
JOHNNY ANGEL
DATING GAME
ANSWERED PRAYERS
SUNSET IN ST. TROPEZ
THE COTTAGE
THE KISS
LEAP OF FAITH
LONE EAGLE
JOURNEY
THE HOUSE ON HOPE STREET
THE WEDDING
IRRESISTIBLE FORCES
GRANNY DAN
BITTERSWEET
MIRROR IMAGE
HIS BRIGHT LIGHT:
The Story of my Son, Nick Traina
THE KLONE AND I
THE LONG ROAD HOME
THE GHOST
SPECIAL DELIVERY
THE RANCH
SILENT HONOUR
MALICE
FIVE DAYS IN PARIS
LIGHTNING
WINGS
THE GIFT
ACCIDENT
VANISHED
MIXED BLESSINGS
JEWELS
NO GREATER LOVE
HEARTBEAT
MESSAGE FROM NAM
DADDY
STAR
ZOYA
KALEIDOSCOPE
FINE THINGS
WANDERLUST
SECRETS
FAMILY ALBUM
FULL CIRCLE
CHANGES
THURSTON HOUSE
CROSSINGS
ONCE IN A LIFETIME
A PERFECT STRANGER
REMEMBRANCE
PALOMINO
LOVE: POEMS
THE RING
LOVING
TO LOVE AGAIN
SUMMER'S END
SEASON OF PASSION
THE PROMISE
NOW AND FOREVER
GOLDEN MOMENTS*
GOING HOME

* Published outside the UK under the title PASSION'S PROMISE

For more information on Danielle Steel and her books, see her website at www.daniellesteel.com

Danielle Steel

Blue

CORGI BOOKS

TRANSWORLD PUBLISHERS
61–63 Uxbridge Road, London W5 5SA
www.penguin.co.uk

Transworld is part of the Penguin Random House group of companies
whose addresses can be found at global.penguinrandomhouse.com

First published in Great Britain in 2016 by Bantam Press
an imprint of Transworld Publishers
Corgi edition published 2016

A CIP catalogue record for this book
is available from the British Library.

ISBN
9780552166256 (B format)
9780552166263 (A format)

Book design by Virginia Norey
Typeset in 12/15.5pt Adobe Garamond by Falcon Oast Graphic Art Ltd.
Printed and bound by Clays Ltd, Bungay, Suffolk.

Penguin Random House is committed to a sustainable
future for our business, our readers and our planet. This book
is made from Forest Stewardship Council® certified paper.

1 3 5 7 9 10 8 6 4 2

To my Beloved Children,
Beatie, Trevor, Todd, Nick,
Samantha, Victoria, Vanessa,
Maxx, and Zara,

Life is made up of special moments,
moments of joy, or of sorrow, of great
good fortune, incredible thoughtfulness,
moments you never forget, and that impact
an entire lifetime, moments you treasure.

May all your special moments be precious,
happy ones, change your life in fortunate ways,
and turn out to be great blessings.

May your impact on others be kind,
theirs on you always loving,
and may you always, always know
and remember how infinitely I love you,
with all my heart, now and forever

With all my love,
Mommy/d.s.

Blue

Chapter 1

The trip by jeep from the small village near Luena to Malanje in Angola, in southwest Africa, followed by a train ride to Luanda, the capital, had taken seven hours. The drive from Luena was long and arduous due to unexploded land mines in the area, which required extreme diligence and caution to avoid as they drove. After forty years of conflict and civil war, the country was still ravaged and in desperate need of all the help outside sources could provide, which was why Ginny Carter had been there, sent by SOS Human Rights. SOS/HR was a private foundation based in New York that sent human rights workers around the globe. Her assignments were usually two or three months long in any given location, occasionally longer. She was sent in as part of a support team, to address whatever human rights issues were being violated or in question, typically to assist women and children, or even to address the most pressing physical needs in a trouble spot somewhere, like lack of food, water, medicine, or shelter. She frequently got involved in legal issues, visiting women in prisons, interfacing with attorneys, and trying to get the women fair trials. SOS took good care of their workers and was a responsible organization, but the work was dangerous at times. She had taken an in-depth training course before they sent her into the field initially, and had been taught about everything from digging ditches and purifying water, to extensive first aid, but nothing had prepared her for what she had seen since. She had learned a great deal about man's cruelty to man and the plight of people in underdeveloped countries and emerging nations since she'd started working for SOS/HR.

As she cleared customs at JFK airport in New York, Ginny had been traveling for twenty-seven hours, after the flight from Luanda to London, the four-hour layover at Heathrow, and then the flight to New York. She was wearing jeans, hiking boots, and a heavy army surplus parka, her blond hair shoved haphazardly into a rubber band when she woke up on the plane just before they landed. She had been in Africa for four months, since August, longer than usual, and was arriving in New York on December 22. She had hoped to be back out on assignment by now, but her replacement had not gotten to them on time. Ginny had tried to orchestrate her absence from New York at this time, but now she had to face Christmas alone in New York.

She could have gone to Los Angeles to spend the holiday with her father and sister, but that sounded even worse. She had left L.A. nearly three years before, and had no desire to return to the city where she had grown up. Since leaving L.A., she had lived the life of a nomad, as she put it, working for SOS Human Rights. She loved the work, and the fact that it was all-consuming, and most of the time kept her from thinking about her own life, a life in which, in her wildest dreams, she had never imagined she would be living and working in the countries that were familiar to her now. She had helped midwives to deliver babies, or done it herself when there was no one else at hand. She had held dying children in her arms, and comforted their mothers, and cared for orphans in displacement camps. She had been in war-torn areas, lived through two local uprisings and a revolution, and had seen anguish, poverty, and devastation that she would otherwise never have encountered in her lifetime. It put everything else in life into perspective. SOS/HR was grateful for her willingness to travel to some of the worst areas it serviced, no matter how desolate or dangerous, or how rugged conditions were. The more rugged the conditions, and the harder the work, the better she liked it.

She cared nothing about the potential dangers to herself. She had actually disappeared for three weeks in Afghanistan, and the home office had thought she had been killed. Her family in Los Angeles feared it might be the case, but she had come back to camp weak and sick, having been taken in and cared for by a local family who had nursed her through a high fever. She seemed to welcome and embrace the worst SOS/HR had to offer. And they could always count on her to show up and stick it out. She had been in Afghanistan, several parts of Africa, and Pakistan. Her reports were accurate, insightful, and helpful, and twice she had made presentations to the office of the High Commissioner for Human Rights at the United Nations, and once to the Human Rights High Commissioner in Geneva. She was impressive in describing, in all its poignancy and pathos, the plight of those she served.

She was worn and tired when she landed in New York. She had been sad to leave the women and children she had been caring for in a refugee camp in Luena, Angola. The human rights workers had been trying to relocate them, despite a web of red tape that prevented them from accomplishing their mission. She would have liked to stay for another six months or a year. Their three-month assignments always seemed too short. They just became familiar with the conditions in the country when they were replaced, but their job was to report accurately on local conditions as much as to change them. They did what they could while they were there, but it was like emptying the ocean with a thimble. There were so many people in desperate need, and so many women and children in dire circumstances around the world.

And yet Ginny was able to find joy in what she did, and couldn't wait to leave again on another assignment. She wanted to spend as little time as possible in New York, and she was dreading the holidays. She would have preferred to spend them working to the point of exhaustion in a place where Christmas didn't exist, as it didn't now to her. It was rotten luck that she had landed in New York three days before Christmas, the worst days of the year for her. All she wanted to do was sleep when she got back to her apartment, and wake up when it was over. The holidays meant nothing to her except pain.

She had nothing to declare in customs except a few small wooden carvings the children in the refugee camp had made for her. Her treasures now were the memories she carried with her everywhere, of the people she met along the way. She had no interest in material possessions, and everything she traveled with was in a small battered suitcase and the backpack she wore. She never had time to look in a mirror when she was working, and didn't care. A hot shower was her greatest luxury and pleasure, when she was able to take one; the rest of the time she took cold showers, using the soap she brought with her. Her jeans and sweatshirts and T-shirts were clean but never pressed. It was enough that she had clothes to wear, which was more than many of the people she cared for had, and she often gave her clothes away to those who needed them more. Except for a Senate hearing where she spoke eloquently, she hadn't worn a dress, high heels, or makeup in three years. And when she made her presentations to the United Nations or the Human Rights Commission, she did so in a pair of old black slacks, a sweater, and flat shoes. The only thing important to her was what she had to say, the message they needed to hear, and the atrocities she had seen on a daily basis in the course of her work. She had a front-row seat to the cruelties and crimes committed against women and children around the world. And she owed it to them to speak on their behalf when asked to do so when she came home. Her words were always powerful and well chosen and brought tears to the eyes of those who heard her.

She walked out of the terminal and took a deep breath of cold night air. Holiday travelers were rushing to buses and taxis or greeting relatives outside the terminal, as Ginny silently watched them with deep blue eyes the color of a lake. They were almost navy blue. She looked serious for a moment, debating whether to take a shuttle or a cab into the city. She was bone tired, and her body ached from the long trip, and from sleeping in cramped quarters in coach. She felt guilty spending money on herself after what she saw in the course of her missions, but she decided to spoil herself. She walked to the curb and hailed a taxi, which swerved and rapidly approached to pick her up.

She opened the door and put her bag and backpack

into the back seat, climbed in, and closed the door, as the young Pakistani driver checked her out and asked where she was going. She saw his name on the license on the partition between them as she gave him her address, and an instant later they took off, darting through the airport traffic, and headed toward the highway. It felt strange to be back in civilization after the desolate area where she'd been living for the past four months. But she always felt that way when she returned, and by the time she got adjusted to it, she left again. She always asked that they reassign her quickly, and most of the time they did. She was one of their most valuable workers in the field, both for her willingness and for her expertise after almost three years.

'Where are you from in Pakistan?' she asked him as they joined the flow of traffic moving toward the city, and he smiled at her in the rearview mirror. He was young and looked pleased that she had guessed.

'How did you know I'm from Pakistan?' he asked her, and she smiled back.

'I was there a year ago.' She guessed his region then, and he looked amazed. Few Americans knew anything about his country. 'I was in Balochistan for three months.'

'What were you doing there?' He was intrigued by her as traffic slowed them down. It was going to be a long, slow ride into the city in holiday traffic, and talking to him kept her awake. He seemed more familiar to her than the people she would meet in New York, who seemed like foreigners to her now.

'I was working,' she said quietly, glancing out the window at what should have been a familiar landscape but no longer was. She felt like a woman without a home, and had felt that way since she left L.A. She sensed now that that would be the last real home she'd ever have, and she preferred it that way. She didn't need a home anymore – whatever tent or camp she was living in was enough for her.

'Are you a doctor?' He was curious about her.

'No, I work for a human rights organization,' she said vaguely, fighting waves of fatigue as she sat in the warm, comfortable cab. She didn't want to fall asleep until she got back to her apartment, had a shower, and could climb into her bed. She knew that the fridge would be empty, but she didn't care, she had eaten on the plane. She didn't want to eat that night and could buy whatever she needed the next day.

They drove on in silence then, and she watched the skyline of New York come into view. It was undeniably beautiful, but it looked like a movie set to her and not a place where real people lived. The people she knew lived in old military barracks, refugee stations, and tents, not brightly lit cities with skyscrapers and apartment buildings. With the passing years, she felt more and more separate from this way of life each time she returned, but the organization she worked for was based in New York, and it made sense for her to keep an apartment here. It was a shell she crawled into briefly once every few months, like a hermit crab needing a place to stay. She had no attachment to it, and had never considered it home. The only personal things she had were still in boxes she had never bothered to unpack. Her sister, Rebecca, had packed them for her when Ginny sold her house and left L.A., and shipped them to her in New York. Ginny didn't even know what was in them, and didn't care.

It took them just over an hour to reach her apartment, and she paid the driver with a generous tip. He smiled at her again and thanked her, as she looked for her keys in a pocket of her backpack, then stepped out into the frigid air. It felt like it was going to snow. She stood fumbling with the lock to her building for a moment, with her bags on the pavement beside her. The facade looked faintly battered, and there was a chill wind coming from the East River a block away. She lived in the upper eighties near East End, and she had rented the apartment because she liked walking along the river in warmer weather, and watching the boats drift by. After living in a house in L.A. for years, living in an apartment seemed less oppressive and more impersonal, which she preferred.

She let herself into the building and pressed the button of the elevator to the sixth floor. Everything in the building had a dreary look to it. She noticed that several of her neighbors had Christmas wreaths on their doors. She didn't bother with Christmas decorations anymore, and this was only the second time she'd been there for Christmas since she'd moved to New York. There were so many more important things to think about in the world than putting up a tree or a wreath on the door. She was anxious to get to the office, but knew that it would be closed for the next several days. She was planning to do some reading, work on her latest report, summing up her mission, and catch up on sleep. The report would keep her busy for the next week, and all she had to do was pretend that it wasn't the holidays.

She turned on the lights when she walked in, and saw that nothing had changed. The beaten-up old couch she had gotten at a garage sale in Brooklyn looked as tired as it had before. She had bought a well-used, secondhand leather recliner, and it was the most comfortable chair she'd ever owned. She often fell asleep in it while she was reading. There was another large chair facing the couch in case she had a guest, which she never did. But if so, she was prepared. Her coffee table was an old metal trunk with travel stickers on it that she had bought when she got the couch. There was a small dining table and four unmatched chairs, and a dead plant on the windowsill that she had meant to throw away in July, had forgotten, and it had become part of the décor. The person who cleaned her apartment didn't dare throw it away. She had a few old lamps that cast a warm light around the room, and a television she almost never used. She read the news on the Internet, which she preferred. And the décor in her bedroom consisted of the bed, a chest she had also bought secondhand, and a chair. There was nothing on the walls. It wasn't a cozy place to come home to, but it was a place to sleep and keep her clothes. She had a cleaning woman who came once a month when she was away, and once a week when she was there.

She dropped her suitcase and backpack in her bedroom, came back to the living room, and sat down on the couch, which was welcoming, despite the way it looked. She leaned her head back, thinking about how far she'd come in the past twenty-eight hours. She felt as though she had been on another planet, and had just returned to Earth. She was still thinking about it when her cell phone rang. She couldn't imagine who it was since the SOS/HR office was closed, and it was ten o'clock at night. She fished it out of the pocket of her parka and answered it. She had turned it on in customs, but there was no one she wanted to call.

'You're back! Or are you still on the road?' the voice said in a cheerful tone. It was her sister, Rebecca, in L.A.

'I just walked in,' Ginny said with a smile. They sent each other text messages regularly, but hadn't spoken in a month. And she had forgotten that she'd told her when she was coming back.

'You must be exhausted,' Becky said, sounding sympathetic. She was the family nurturer, and the older sister Ginny had relied on all her life, although she hadn't seen her now in three years. But talking to each other, e-mail when it was possible, and texting kept them close. Becky had just turned forty, and was four years older than Ginny. Becky was married, with three kids, and lived in Pasadena, and their father, with slowly but steadily developing Alzheimer's, had lived with her for two years. Her father couldn't live alone anymore, but neither Becky nor Ginny wanted to put him in a home. Their mother had been dead for ten years. He was seventy-two years old, but Becky said he looked a decade older since he got sick. He had worked in a bank, and retired when their mother died. He had lost his lust for life after that.

'I'm tired,' Ginny admitted, 'and I hate coming back this time of year. I was hoping to be here before this and out again by now, but my replacement showed up late,' she said, closing her eyes, and fighting not to fall asleep as she listened to her sister's voice. 'I'm hoping they send me out again pretty soon, but I haven't heard anything yet.' It cheered her up thinking that she wouldn't be in New York for long. It wasn't the apartment that depressed her, it was having nothing to do between assignments, and being useful to no one in New York. There was nothing she wanted to do, except leave again.

'Why don't you relax? You just got home. And why don't you come out here for a visit before they ship you out?' She had already asked Ginny to spend the holidays with them, but she had said no, yet again.

'Yeah,' Ginny said, sounding noncommittal, as she pulled the rubber band out of her hair, and her long blonde hair cascaded down her back. She was much prettier than she knew, and didn't care. Her looks were no longer important in her life, although they had been before, in a distant faraway time that had ceased to exist three years before.

'You should come out before Dad gets more confused,' Becky reminded her. Ginny hadn't seen the slow but steady deterioration and didn't realize how bad it had gotten in the last few months. 'He got lost two blocks from the house the other day – one of my neighbors brought him home. He couldn't remember where he lives. The kids try to keep an eye on him, but they forget, and we can't watch him all the time.' Becky hadn't worked since her second child was born. She'd had a promising career in public relations, which she gave up to raise her kids. Ginny was never sure she'd done the right thing, but Becky seemed to have no regrets. Her son and two daughters were teenagers now, and were keeping her busier than ever, although Alan was always helpful to her, and with their dad. He worked in electronics, and was an engineer, and provided Becky and their kids a solid, stable life.

'Should we get Dad a nurse, so it puts less burden on you?' Ginny asked, sounding concerned.

'He'd hate that. He still wants to feel independent. I don't let him walk the dog anymore, though – he lost him twice. I guess it's going to get a lot worse, and the medication isn't helping as much as it was.' The doctors had warned them that the medication would only slow things down for a while, and after that there was nothing they could do. Ginny tried not to think about it, which was easier when she was far away. Becky lived with the realities of his situation every day, which made Ginny feel guilty, but she did try to sympathize with Becky when she called. She couldn't go back to L.A. It would have killed her to move back. She hadn't even been there for a visit since she left, and Becky had been amazingly understanding about it, in spite of having to deal with their father by herself. All Becky wanted now was for her sister to visit him before it was too late. She tried to convey that to Ginny without making her feel guilty or terrifying her. But the prognosis for their father was poor, the disease was progressive, and Becky could see changes in him every day, particularly in the last year.

'I'll visit one of these days,' Ginny promised, and meant it when she said it, but they both knew it wouldn't happen before she left on her next trip. 'What about you? Are you okay?' Ginny asked her. She could hear the kids in the background – Becky didn't have a moment to herself all day.

'I'm fine. It's nuts right before Christmas, the kids are all over the place. We wanted to take them skiing, but I don't want to leave Dad, so the girls are going with friends, and Charlie has a new girlfriend he can't tear himself away from, so he's thrilled we're not going away. He has to finish his college applications, so I'll be riding his ass all through the holidays.' The thought of her nephew going to college woke Ginny out of her stupor and made her realize how fast time had flown.

'I can't believe that.'

'Neither can I. Margie will be sixteen in January, and Lizzie is turning thirteen. Where the hell did my life go while I was driving car pool? Alan and I will be married twenty years in June. Scary, isn't it?' Ginny nodded, thinking about it. She remembered their wedding as though it were yesterday. She'd been their maid of honor at sixteen.

'Yes, it is. I can't believe you're forty, and I'm thirty-six. Last time I looked you were fourteen and had braces, and I was ten.' They both smiled at the memory. Then Alan walked in from work, and Becky said she had to go.

'I have to burn him something for dinner. Some things don't change, I'm still a lousy cook. Thank God we're having dinner at Alan's mother's on Christmas Eve. I couldn't deal with the turkey again. Thanksgiving nearly did me in.' They were the all-American family, and everything Ginny had never been.

Becky had always done everything that was expected of her. She had married her high school boyfriend while they were still in college. After they graduated, with their parents' help, they bought a house in Pasadena. They had three terrific kids, and she was the perfect mom. She was head of the PTA and had done Cub Scouts with their son, she got the girls to all their after-school classes and helped them with their homework, kept a beautiful home, and was a great wife to Alan. They had a solid marriage, and now she took care of their father, while Ginny trotted around the world to war zones and desolate places, trying to cure the ills of the world.

The contrast between the two sisters seemed more marked than ever before, and yet they respected and loved each other. Still, the path Ginny had chosen in recent years was hard for her older sister to understand. She knew the reasons for it, but it seemed too extreme a reaction to her, and Alan agreed with her. They both hoped Ginny would come home and settle down, and start living a normal life again. In spite of everything that had happened, they thought it was time, before she became too different, to the point of strange. Becky was afraid that Ginny was getting there, although she admired what she did. But they felt she should give up her travels and the risks she took every day, before she got herself killed. Becky was convinced that Ginny was punishing herself, but enough was enough. It all sounded very noble, but two and a half years in the wilds of places like Afghanistan was just too much. It was hard for her and Alan to imagine what she did there. And Becky never said it, so as not to put pressure on her younger sister, but she needed help with their dad. With Ginny gone so much and so far away, all the hard decisions and difficult moments rested on Becky. Ginny had left before their father started to decline, and now with the work she did, she wasn't around to participate.

'I'll call you tomorrow,' Becky promised before she hung up. They both knew it would be a bad day. It always was – it was the anniversary of the day Ginny's life had changed forever, and everything she cherished and held dear had disappeared. It was a day she would have liked to forget or sleep through every year, but she never could. Ginny lay in bed that night wide awake, running the film over and over again in her head, as she always did, thinking of all the ways it could have been different, and why it should have been, and what she should have done and didn't. But it always turned out the same way. She was alone, and Mark and Chris were dead.

She and her husband had gone to a holiday party given by friends two days before Christmas. There were going to be children and a Santa Claus, so they had taken Christopher with them. Ginny had never seen the photographs of that night, but the pictures of him on

Santa's lap had been heartbreaking for Becky to look at when she packed them for her sister, along with all Chris's baby albums and her wedding photographs with Mark. They were in the boxes Ginny had never opened that were stacked in the unused second bedroom of her New York apartment. She had no idea what Becky had sent her as souvenirs of her lost life, and had never been able to face them.

Ginny and Mark had been the golden couple, network stars. She was an on-air reporter, and he was the most popular anchorman in the business. Handsome, beautiful, and madly in love, they had married when Ginny was twenty-nine, with a blossoming network career, and Mark was already a star. Chris had been born the following year. They had a gorgeous home in Beverly Hills and everything they had ever wanted, and a marriage and life that were the envy of their friends and all who knew them.

They went to the party that night, with Chris in the back seat in a little red-velvet Christmas suit with a plaid bow tie. He was three, and couldn't wait to get on Santa's lap. While Ginny watched him, Mark had headed for the bar and had a glass of wine with some of the men. He'd had a long day, and Ginny had a glass of wine, too. Most of the parents had a glass in their hand and were in a festive holiday mood. None of them were drunk, and Mark seemed fine to Ginny when they left the party to get Chris home to bed. She had said it a thousand times afterward, that Mark appeared sober to her, as though that would make a difference and would change everything, but it never did. The autopsy showed that his blood alcohol level was over the limit, not shockingly so, but just enough to affect his reflexes and slow his reactions. He'd obviously had more than one glass, while she had been watching Chris and talking to the other mothers. And knowing how responsible Mark was, Ginny was sure Mark hadn't felt as though he drank too much that night, or he would have asked her to drive or call a cab.

They took the freeway to get home, flipped over the divider when it started to rain, and had a head-on collision with a sixteen-wheeler, which crushed their car. Mark and Chris were killed instantly. Ginny had been in the hospital for a month with a broken vertebra in her neck and two broken arms. They had to use a Jaws of Life to pry her out of the car. Becky had gone to the hospital as soon as they called her, but they hadn't told Ginny what had happened to Mark and Chris. Becky told her the next day. Three lives had ended in an instant, Ginny's as well as theirs. She never went back to the house afterward, and had Becky get rid of everything, except the few things she packed up to save for her and later sent to New York.

Ginny had stayed with Becky while her neck healed, and she had been incredibly lucky. The break was high enough that it didn't paralyze her, although she wore a neck brace for six months. She resigned from her job at the network, avoided all their friends, and couldn't face anyone. She was convinced that her letting Mark drive home that night was what had killed them, and that it was her fault that he drove. She had assumed they'd each had a single glass of wine, since Mark rarely drank more than that, and she didn't like driving on the freeway at night. It had never occurred to her to ask him how many glasses he'd had, since he looked sober to her. If she'd asked him, she told herself later, she could have driven, and maybe Mark and Chris would still be alive. Becky knew that her sister would never forgive herself no matter what anyone said to her. And nothing would change the fact that Ginny's husband and three-year-old son were dead.

Ginny had moved to New York in April, without calling anyone to say goodbye, and spent a month looking for work with a human rights group. All she wanted to do was get as far away as she could from her old life. Becky never said it, but she was certain she had a death wish and was trying to get herself killed on the assignments she signed up for, at least for the first year. It broke Becky's heart, knowing how she felt, and no one could help her. All she hoped for her sister was that time would ease her wounds and help her live with what had happened. She was no longer a wife or a mother, and had lost the two people she loved most in the world. And she had given up a career she had worked hard to build. Ginny had been a good reporter and done well at the network. She had been a happy, successful, totally fulfilled woman, and her life had turned into everyone's worst nightmare overnight. Ginny never talked about it, but her sister knew and could sense how agonizing it all was for her. It was why Becky didn't press her about their father. Ginny already had enough to deal with, with loss and tragedy. Becky didn't have the heart to ask her to take on more, so she took care of their father, while Ginny risked her life around the world.

But one day she would have to stop and face it, no matter how hard she ran, or how far, the two people she had lost were gone and always would be. Becky just hoped she didn't get herself killed before then, and she was always relieved to know that she was back in New York, even for a short time. At least she was safe when she was home. It was hard for either of them to believe they hadn't seen each other in almost three years, but the time had flown. Becky was busy with her family, and Ginny was always in some remote, troubled country, risking her life and atoning for her sins.

Becky seemed sad when she hung up, as Alan bent down to kiss her. Becky was a pretty woman, but had never been as spectacular looking as her sister, particularly when Ginny was at the network getting her hair and makeup done every day. Even without it, Ginny had always been better-looking than Becky. Ginny was the showstopper, and Becky the girl next door.

'Are you okay?' Alan asked his wife with a look of concern.

'I just talked to Ginny. She's in New York. Tomorrow is the anniversary,' she said with a meaningful look, and he nodded.

'She should come out and see her father if she's back in the States,' he said in a disapproving tone. He was tired of seeing Becky shouldering all the burden, and Ginny none. There was always some excuse why she couldn't. Becky was more understanding about it than he was. It didn't seem fair to him.

'She said she will,' Becky said quietly. Alan said nothing, took off his jacket, sat down in his favorite chair, and turned on the TV to watch the news, while Becky went out to the kitchen to make their dinner, thinking about her sister. They had always had very divergent goals, but the differences between them had gotten more extreme in the past three years. Now they had nothing in common, except the same parents and their childhood history. Their lives were a million miles apart.

Ginny was thinking the same thing as she walked into her bathroom in New York, turned on the shower, and took off her clothes. Becky had a husband, three teenagers, a house in Pasadena, and an orderly life, while she had no material possessions she cared about, an apartment filled with secondhand furniture, and no one in her life, except the people she took care of around the world. When the water was hot enough, she got into the shower and let it run down her long, lean body, and on her face as it washed away her tears. She knew how painful the next day would be for her. She'd live through it as she had every year, but sometimes she wondered why. Why did she fight to hang in and stay alive? For whom? Did it really matter? It was getting harder and harder to find an answer to that question as time went by, and nothing changed, and Mark and Chris were still gone. She found it difficult to believe that she had managed to live without them for three interminable years.

Chapter 2

The next day when Ginny woke up, it was bright and sunny, and she could tell from the chill of the room that it was bitter cold outside. It was the day before Christmas Eve, the day she hated most in the year, and she was dealing with culture shock and jet lag after her trip. She turned over and went back to sleep. When she woke again four hours later, the day had turned gray and it was snowing. She found some instant coffee in the cupboard and a can of stale peanuts, which she threw away. She was too lazy to go out into the cold to get something to eat. She wasn't hungry anyway, she never was on this day, and she wandered into the living room in her pajamas and tried not to notice the photograph of Mark and Chris in a silver frame on her battered desk. She had only two photographs of them in the apartment. The one she was trying to avoid was of Mark with Chris at his second birthday party. She sat down in the recliner and closed her eyes, thinking inevitably of the day three years before when they had gone to the party, with Chris in his little red-velvet suit with short pants and the plaid bow tie. She tried to push the image out of her mind but couldn't. The memories were just too strong, of the party, waking up in the hospital after the accident, and then Becky telling her what had happened. They both had sobbed and everything after that was a blur. They had held the memorial service after she got out of the hospital a month later, she could hardly remember it she had been so hysterical. She had stayed in bed at Becky's afterward for weeks. The network had been wonderful about it and asked her to take a leave of absence instead of quitting, but she knew she could never go back without Mark. Working in network news without him made no sense and would have hurt too much.

She lived on their savings, his life insurance, and the proceeds from the house sale ever since. She had enough to continue the kind of work she was doing for a long time, despite a meager salary from SOS/HR. She spent almost nothing and wanted no trappings of a fancy life. She had no needs, other than new hiking boots when hers wore out. All she needed now were rough clothes for her trips. She didn't care what she wore, how she dressed, what she ate, or how she lived. Everything that had mattered to her before was gone. Her life was an empty shell without Mark and Chris, except for the work she did, which was the only thing that gave meaning to her existence. She had no tolerance for the injustices she saw committed every day, in different cultures and countries around the world. She had become a freedom fighter, defending women and kids – perhaps, she realized, to assuage her own guilt for not having been more aware on that fateful night, and letting her husband put all three of them at risk. All she wished was that she had died with them, but instead, cruelly, she had survived. Her punishment was to live without them for the rest of her life. The thought was almost more than she could bear when she allowed herself to contemplate it, which she rarely did, but she could never avoid it on this day. The memories came rushing at her like ghosts.

After dark, she stood at the window, watching the snow fall gently onto the streets of New York. There were already three or four inches sticking to the ground. It was beautiful, and made her suddenly want to go outside and take a walk. She needed to get some air and get away from her own thoughts. The visions in her head were oppressive, and she knew the cold and snow would distract her and clear her head. She could stop and get something to eat on the way back, since she hadn't eaten all day. She wasn't hungry but knew she had to eat. All she wanted now was to get out of the apartment and away from herself.

Ginny put on two heavy sweaters, jeans, hiking boots with warm socks, a knitted cap, and her parka. She pulled the hood over the cap and grabbed a pair of mittens out of a drawer. Everything she owned now was functional and plain. She had put all her jewelry from Mark in a safe deposit box in the bank in California. She couldn't imagine wearing it again.

She put her wallet and keys in her pocket, turned off the lights, left the apartment, and took the elevator downstairs. And a moment later she was walking through the snow on Eighty-ninth Street, heading east toward the river, taking deep breaths of the freezing air as the snow continued to fall around her. Long plumes of frost sailed into the air when she exhaled. She walked along the overpass to the river, then stood at the railing looking at the boats drifting by – a tugboat and two barges, and a party boat all lit up for someone's Christmas party. It looked festive as it went by, and she could hear music and laughter in the crisp night air.

There was almost no traffic on the FDR Drive while she stood looking down at the water, as images of Chris and Mark forced their way into her mind again and she thought about what her life had become since their deaths. It was a life that she had dedicated to others, a life that served someone at least, but, as her sister had guessed, she hadn't cared if she lived or died, and had lived accordingly, taking outrageous risks. People thought she was brave, but only she knew how cowardly she was, hoping to get killed so she wouldn't have to spend the rest of her life without her husband and son.

As she looked down at the water shimmering beneath her, she thought about how easy it would be to climb over the railing and slip into the river. It would all be so much simpler than living without them. Feeling strangely calm, she wondered how long it would take her to drown. She was sure that there were currents in the river, and with her layers of clothing on, she would be pulled under quickly. And suddenly the idea seemed immensely appealing. She didn't think of her sister or father. Becky had her own life and family, they never saw each other, and her father wouldn't understand that she had died. As she mused about it, it seemed like the perfect time to make an exit.

She was considering climbing over the railing when a sudden movement in her peripheral vision at her left caught her eye and startled her, and she turned her head to see what it was. The hood of her parka partially blocked her vision, and all she saw was a flash of white dashing into a small utility shed as she heard the door slam. Clearly, someone was hiding inside it, and she wondered if whoever it was had been intending to attack her. Jumping into the river and drowning seemed simple and reasonable to her in her current state of mind – getting mugged by a hoodlum hiding in a utility shed seemed more unpleasant and she'd still be alive, presumably, at the end of it. But she didn't want to leave. She had her plan to carry out, to jump into the river, and she didn't want to wait until the next day. There was something poetic that appealed to her about dying on the same day they had, even if it was three years later. Her sense of good order dictated that she should kill herself tonight. It never occurred to her that her thinking was distorted, her judgement paralyzed by grief. It all made perfect sense to her. And she didn't want to run away and give up her plan just because someone was hiding in the shed. In fact, it was annoying her that whoever was in there didn't come out but continued to hide. She stood waiting for someone to emerge, so they couldn't startle her or attack her. And she refused to leave and stood her ground, determined to carry out her plan. Having made the decision gave her a sense of relief from pain. She had chosen a way out.

It seemed very silent in the shed, and then she heard some shifting around and muffled coughing. Her curiosity got the best of her. If they were coughing, maybe whoever it was in there was sick and needed help. That hadn't occurred to her before. She stared at the shed for long minutes, and then boldly walked up to it and knocked on the door. She wondered if it was a woman after all, although she thought she'd seen a man out of the corner of her eye, but whoever it was had moved very quickly into the shed and closed the door.

She stood in front of the shed for a minute, then knocked cautiously on the door again. She didn't want to pull it open and startle them. There was no answer, so she knocked a third time. She was going to offer help if the person was sick. And once she had tended to their needs, she would address her own. She had it all worked out in her head. She was a classic suicide about to happen. She knew people did things like it every day, and it no longer seemed shocking to her.

'Are you all right?' she asked in a firm voice. There was still no answer, but, as she started to walk away, a small voice finally spoke up.

'Yeah, I'm okay.' The voice sounded very young. It could have been male or female, she couldn't tell. Her instincts took over then, and she forgot about herself.

'Are you cold? Do you want something to eat?' There was a long, long pause, as the person in the shed thought about it, and finally answered again.

'No, I'm fine.' It sounded like a boy that time, and then he added, 'Thank you.' Ginny smiled. Whoever it was, was polite. She started to walk away, and thought about her plan again, although the interruption had slowed her momentum and distracted her. She didn't feel quite as determined as she had a few minutes before, but she started to walk back to the railing, wondering who was in the shed and what they were doing there, when she heard a voice in the distance behind her shout 'Hey.' She turned in surprise and she saw a boy who looked about eleven or twelve in a T-shirt and torn jeans, and high-top sneakers, with his hair uncombed and a little wild. He was looking at her with wide eyes, and even from the distance she could see that they were a bright, almost electric blue in a pale light-coffee-colored face. 'You got food?' he asked her, as she stood looking at him, shocked at how little he was wearing in the snow.

'I could get some,' she answered. She knew there was a McDonald's nearby. She bought breakfast or dinner there often herself.

'Nah, that's okay,' he said, looking disappointed and shivering in the cold, standing near the shed. It belonged to the city, but clearly someone had left it unlocked, and he was using it as shelter and a place to sleep.

'I could bring you something,' she offered. He hesitated, then shook his head, and disappeared back into the shed, as Ginny went back to the railing to gaze down at the river. By then she was beginning to feel awkward about what had seemed so right only moments before. She was about to go home when he was suddenly standing beside her with his bright blue eyes and jet-black hair.

'I could come with you,' he suggested, in answer to her earlier offer of dinner. 'I've got money to pay.' It was a clear sign, as she looked at him, trying hard not to shiver, that she wasn't meant to leap into the river and die that night. She was meant to feed this child instead. She started to take off her parka to offer it to him, but he bravely declined. They began walking away from the river side by side. She had intended to die moments before, as the final escape from her sorrows, in a bout of cowardice that was rare for her, and now she was going to dinner with this unknown boy.

'There's a McDonald's about two blocks away,' she said to him as they walked. She tried to walk quickly so he wouldn't get too cold, but he was shaking visibly when they got to the restaurant and she got a good look at him in the bright lights. He had the bluest eyes she'd ever seen, in a sweet, still childish face that gazed at her full of innocence. It felt as though their paths had been meant to cross that night. It was warm in the restaurant, and he jumped up and down to warm himself. She wanted to put her arms around him to help him but didn't dare.

'What would you like?' she asked him gently. He hesitated. 'Go for it,' she encouraged him. 'It's almost Christmas, live it up.' He grinned and ordered two Big Macs and fries and a large Coke, and she ordered a single Big Mac and a small Coke. She paid for it, and they went to a table to wait for their order, which was ready a few minutes later. By then he'd warmed up and had stopped shivering. He dove into the food with a vengeance, and was halfway through the second burger before he stopped to thank her.

'I could have paid for it myself,' he said, looking mildly embarrassed, and she nodded.

'I'm sure you could. My treat this time.' He nodded.

She watched him, wondering how old he was, still

startled by how blue his eyes were. 'What's your name?' she asked cautiously.

'Blue Williams,' he answered. 'Blue is my real name, not a nickname. My mama named me that because of the color of my eyes.' She nodded. It made perfect sense.

'I'm Ginny Carter,' she said, and they shook hands. 'How old are you?' He looked at her suspiciously then, suddenly afraid.

'Sixteen,' he said instantly, and she could tell that he was lying. He was obviously worried that she'd report him to Child Protective Services. At sixteen he would have been exempt.

'Do you want to go to a shelter tonight? It must be cold out there in the shed. I could drop you off, if you want,' she offered. He shook his head vehemently in answer and drank half the Coke, having already finished both burgers and most of the fries. He was starving and ate as though he hadn't had a meal in a while.

'I'm fine in the shed. I have a sleeping bag. It's pretty warm.' She considered that unlikely but didn't challenge him.

'How long have you been out on your own?' She wondered if he was a runaway someone might be looking for. But if so, whatever he had run away from had to be worse than what he was experiencing on the streets, or he'd have gone home.

'A few months,' he answered vaguely. 'I don't like

shelters. There's a lot of crazy people in them. They beat you up, or rob you, and a lot of them are sick,' he said knowledgeably. 'It's safer where I am.' She nodded, willing to believe it – she'd heard stories about violence in shelters before. 'Thank you for dinner,' he said, smiling at her, looking more than ever like a little boy, and nowhere near sixteen. She could see that he didn't shave yet, and despite the life he was leading, he had the appearance of a child, a very wise child, but still a child.

'Would you like something else?' she offered, and he shook his head, and they left the table. She stopped to order two more Big Macs and fries and another Coke, and handed the bag to him when she got it, to take with him. 'In case you get hungry later.' His eyes were wide with gratitude as he took the bag, and they left the restaurant and walked back the way they had come, hurrying along the street in the cold. It was still snowing, but the wind had died down. They got back to the shed quickly, and when they did, she unzipped her parka, took it off, and handed it to him.

'I can't take that from you,' he objected, trying to refuse it, but she gave it to him, standing in her two thick sweaters in the falling snow. It was freezing, and she could only imagine how cold he was in the thin T-shirt and nothing else.

'I've got another one at home,' she reassured him, and he slowly slipped it on gratefully. It was thickly padded and insulated and he smiled as he looked at her.

'Thank you, for dinner and the coat.'

'What are you doing tomorrow?' she asked him, as though he had a heavy social schedule, and wasn't just trying to stay alive in the shed, and she wondered if he really did have a sleeping bag as he claimed. 'Can I interest you in breakfast? Or drop something off for you?'

'I'll be around. I usually go out in the daytime, so they don't see me here.'

'I could come by in the morning, if you want,' she suggested, and he nodded, with a puzzled look.

'Why are you doing this? Why do you care?' he asked, looking suspicious again.

'Why not? See you tomorrow, Blue.' She smiled, and waved. She walked away and headed toward her apartment, as he disappeared into the shed, wearing her parka and carrying the extra meal she had given him. She had completely forgotten about wanting to jump into the river. And as she thought about it, it no longer made sense. She was smiling to herself as she walked along in the snow. It had been a strange encounter. She wondered if he'd be there when she came back the next day. She realized that he might not be, but whether he was or was not, he had given her far more than she had given him. She had given him a parka and dinner, and she knew with absolute certainty that, were it not for Blue suddenly appearing out of nowhere, she would have been at the bottom of the river by now. And as she walked into her apartment, she realized with a shiver how close she had come to ending her life that night. It had seemed so easy for a minute, and such a simple thing to do, to just climb over the railing, let the waters close over her, and disappear. And instead she had been saved by a homeless boy called Blue with brilliant blue eyes. She thought of him as she fell asleep that night, and she slept peacefully for the first time in months. She had survived the anniversary thanks to him, and he had saved her life.

Chapter 3

Ginny woke up early the next day, and saw that it had stopped snowing. There was a foot of snow on the ground, and the sky was still gray. She showered and dressed quickly, and was back at the shed at nine o'clock. She knocked on the door of the shed politely and a sleepy voice answered. It sounded as though she had woken him up. He poked his head out a moment later, wearing her parka and holding his sleeping bag.

'Did I wake you?' she asked apologetically, and he nodded with a grin. 'Do you want to go to breakfast?' He smiled at the question and rolled up his sleeping bag, to take with him. He didn't want to leave it in case someone invaded the shed and took it away. And he had a small nylon gym bag with all his worldly possessions in it. He was ready in two minutes, and they walked back to McDonald's. He headed for the bathroom as soon as they got there, and when he came out, she could see that he had brushed his hair and washed his face.

They ordered breakfast and went back to the table where they'd had dinner the night before.

'Merry Christmas, by the way,' she said as they dug into breakfast. She had coffee and a muffin, and he had two Egg McMuffins with bacon and fries. He had a healthy appetite like any growing boy.

'I don't like Christmas,' he said softly as he drank hot chocolate with whipped cream on top.

'Neither do I,' she admitted with a distant expression.

'Do you have kids?' He was curious about her.

'No,' she said simply. 'I used to' would have been more information than he needed or she wanted to say. 'Where are your mom and dad, Blue?' she asked him, as they finished eating and she sipped her coffee. She couldn't help wondering how he had wound up on the streets.

'They're dead,' he said quietly. 'My mom died when I was five. My dad died a few years ago, but I hadn't seen him in a long time. He was a bad guy, my mom was a really good woman. She got sick.' He looked at Ginny carefully. 'I lived with my aunt, but she's got kids and she doesn't have room for me. She's a nurse.' Then he looked at Ginny suspiciously again. 'Are you a cop?' She shook her head in answer, and he believed her. 'A social worker?'

'No. I'm a human rights worker. I fly to countries a long way from here, to take care of people in war zones or bad places where they need help. Africa, Afghanistan, Pakistan, places like that. I work in refugee camps, or where people have gotten hurt or are sick, or are being treated badly by their governments. I work with them for a while, and then I go someplace else.'

'Why do you do that?' He was intrigued by what she'd said. It sounded like a hard job to him.

'It seems like a good thing to do.'

'Is it dangerous?'

'Sometimes. But I think it's worth it. I just got back two days ago. I was in Angola for four months. That's in southwest Africa.'

'Why'd you come back?' Her job sounded mysterious to him.

'Someone else took my place, so I came home. The foundation I work for moves us around every few months.'

'Do you like doing it?'

'Yes, most of the time. Sometimes I don't like it so much, but it's only for a few months at a time, and even if it's scary or uncomfortable, you get used to it.'

'Do they pay you a lot?'

She laughed at that. 'No, very little. You have to do it because you love what you're doing. It's pretty rugged most of the time. And sometimes it's very scary. What about you? Do you go to school?'

He hesitated before he answered. 'Not lately. I used to,

when I lived with my aunt. I don't have time now. I do odd jobs when I can.' She nodded, wondering how he survived on the streets, with no family and no money. And if he was as young as she suspected, he had to avoid being reported to Child Protective Services if he didn't want to be taken to juvenile hall or put in the state system. It made her sad knowing he wasn't in school and was on the streets fending for himself.

They talked for a few more minutes and then walked out of the restaurant. He said he was going back to the shed later, after it got dark. It seemed like a depressing place to spend Christmas Eve, and as she looked at him, she made a decision.

'Do you want to come to my apartment for a while? You can spend the day there before you go back to the shed tonight. You can watch TV if you want. I have nothing to do today.' She was planning to volunteer to serve dinner at a homeless shelter that night. It seemed like a good way to spend it, serving others instead of feeling sorry for herself and waiting for the holiday to pass. Blue hesitated when she asked him, still not sure if he could trust her, or why she was being kind to him, but there was something about her that he liked, and if everything she said was true, she was a good person.

'Okay. Maybe I'll come for a while,' he agreed, and they walked down the street together.

'I live a block away,' she explained, and they were there

a few moments later. He followed her into the hallway when she unlocked the door, and they went up in the elevator. She opened her apartment door with her key, and they walked in. Blue looked around as they did, and he took in the tired furniture and bare walls, and then grinned at her in surprise.

'I thought you'd live somewhere nicer than this.' She laughed at what he said. He was polite but truthful, with the honesty of youth.

'Yeah, I haven't done much decorating since I moved here. I'm away a lot,' she explained with a sheepish smile.

'My aunt has three kids in a one-bedroom apartment uptown.' By uptown she could guess that he meant Harlem. 'And her place looks better than this.' They both laughed at what he said, Ginny even harder than he did. It was the ultimate damning statement when a homeless boy thought her apartment looked like a dump. And looking around, she couldn't disagree.

'Try the recliner, it's pretty comfortable.' She pointed to it and handed him the remote for the TV. She felt totally at ease having him there. There was nothing dangerous about him, and she felt the connection of a kindred soul. They were both homeless in their own ways. He walked around the room for a minute before he sat down, and noticed the photograph of Mark and Chris on her desk. He looked at it for a long moment and then glanced back at her.

'Who are they?' He could sense that they were important to her and there was a story behind the photo. He had surprised her with the question, and it took her breath away for a minute before she answered as calmly as she could.

'My husband and son. They died three years ago. The anniversary was yesterday.' She tried to keep her voice even as she said it.

Blue didn't answer for a beat and then nodded at her. 'I'm sorry. That's really sad.' But it was no sadder than losing his parents and winding up homeless on the streets. She wasn't officially homeless, but Mark and Chris's deaths had changed her life forever, too, and left her adrift.

'Yes, it was. It was a car accident. That's why I travel so much now. I have no one to come home to.' She hated how pathetic it made her sound. 'Anyway, I like what I do, so it works out.' She didn't tell him that they'd had a beautiful home in Los Angeles, with decent furniture, that she'd had a great career that she'd abandoned, and that she actually used to dress up every day in real clothes, not army surplus. It didn't matter anymore. All of that was over and history now. Now she lived in this tiny apartment with threadbare mismatched furniture she'd found abandoned on the sidewalk or at Goodwill, as though to punish herself for what had happened. It was her version of sackcloth and ashes. But he was too young to understand that, so she said nothing while he turned on the TV and channel-surfed for a while. She saw him glance at her laptop, too. Someone else might have worried that he'd steal it. The thought never crossed her mind. And after he'd watched TV for about an hour, he asked her if he could use her laptop, and she told him he could.

She saw him check several Web sites for homeless youth where they could pick up messages people left for them. He didn't write anything, but she had the impression he was looking for something as he scanned the screen.

'Do friends leave you messages on there?' she asked with interest. His was a world she knew nothing about. He seemed to know his way around the Web sites as well as the streets.

'My aunt does sometimes,' he said honestly. 'She worries about me.'

'Do you ever call her?'

He shook his head. 'She's got too much on her mind already. Her kids, her job. She works nights at a hospital, and she has to leave the kids alone. I used to baby-sit for them at night.' But from what he said, four people living in a one-bedroom apartment sounded difficult. But at least he kept in contact with her on the Internet, Ginny thought.

He went back to watching TV then, while Ginny checked her own e-mail and had none. A little while later her sister called her, and apologized profusely for not calling her the day before, on the anniversary. She had meant to but never got around to it.

'I'm so sorry. The kids drove me crazy all day, and Dad had a bad night the night before. I never got a moment to myself. He was agitated all day yesterday, he wanted to go out, and I didn't have time to take him. It makes him nervous being in the car with the kids. They play their music too loud, and they talk all the time. He does better when things are quieter and he can rest. He has trouble sleeping at night, though, and I worry that he'll go outside in the middle of the night. He gets worse after dark, more confused and angry sometimes. They call it sundowning. He's better in daytime hours.'

Listening to her sister made Ginny realize how little she knew about his illness, and how much Becky had to do to cope with it. It made her feel guilty hearing about it, but not enough that she wanted to share the burden of taking care of him. She felt overwhelmed just listening to her.

'What are you doing tonight?' Becky asked her. She hated knowing that Ginny was alone on Christmas Eve.

Ginny didn't tell her that she had picked up a homeless boy, fed him twice, and brought him to her apartment for the day. She had done it for him, but he was company for her, too. But she knew that Becky would be panicked if she told her. The idea of a homeless boy she didn't know in her apartment would have sent Becky into a tirade of warnings, worry, and fear. But Ginny felt confident, and was convinced he would do no harm. She had gotten much braver and more adventuresome in the past few years, after her many experiences in strange places abroad. It wasn't something Ginny would have done a few years earlier, either, but in the context of how she lived now, she was at ease, and he had been very polite, respectful, and well behaved.

She told Becky about her plan to serve meals at a homeless shelter that night, and a few minutes later, they hung up. Ginny and Blue both got hungry around three o'clock, and she asked him what he'd like to eat. His eyes lit up when she suggested Chinese food, and she ordered them a feast that was delivered in an hour. They sat down at her table in two of the ugly, unmatched chairs and devoured most of it, and then sat back, too full to move. Blue headed back to the recliner, watched some more TV, and fell asleep, while Ginny moved quietly around the apartment, putting things away from her trip. He woke up at six and saw that it was dark outside. He stood up with a grateful look at her. They had spent a nice day together, and she had enjoyed having him there. It added a warm feeling to the apartment, which usually seemed cold and impersonal to her. And it had been a godsend for him. He didn't have to hang around the bus terminal or Penn Station, looking for a warm place to sit and wait for the day to go by so he could go back to the shed for another night. That was his home now, as it had been for several weeks. He knew he'd have to give it up eventually when some city worker discovered him, but for now he was safe in the small shed where he spent his nights.

'I've got to go now,' he said and stood up. 'Thanks for all the food and the nice day.' He looked as though he meant it and seemed sad to leave.

'Do you have a date?' she asked, teasing him with a wistful smile. She was sad to see him leave, too.

'No, but I should get back. I don't want anyone taking my shed,' he said as though fearing squatters in a palatial home. But he knew that safe, cozy spots like that, where he could be undisturbed and undiscovered, were hard to come by on the streets.

He put her parka on as she watched him, and it tore at her heart as he went to the bathroom and then came back and put his sleeping bag under one arm. 'Will I see you again?' he asked her sadly. Most people were transitory in his life. This was the longest he had spent with anyone in months, since he'd been on the streets. People disappeared, went to shelters or other cities, or found shelter somewhere else. It was rare to meet up with someone again.

'Are you sure you don't want to go to a shelter for the night?' She had checked the Internet while he was sleeping, and had found that there were several for young people that offered bed space, free meals, and even job opportunities, and reunification with their families if they wanted, which she knew Blue didn't. At least he could have a real bed in a warm place, but he was adamant about not going to a shelter.

'I'm fine where I am. What are you doing tonight?' he asked her as though they were friends.

'I'm going to volunteer to serve dinner at a homeless shelter. I've done it before when I was in New York. I thought it would be a good way to spend Christmas Eve. Do you want to come with me?' He shook his head. 'The food is pretty good.' He had eaten a lot of the Chinese food and said he wasn't hungry. 'Breakfast tomorrow?' she offered, and he nodded and walked to the door. He thanked her again, and then he left.

She thought about him while she got dressed. She knew it would be hard work carrying heavy pots and ladling out hundreds of dinners. The shelter served thousands every night, and she welcomed the opportunity to exhaust herself so she wouldn't think about how things used to be.

She took a cab downtown to the West Side, and signed up when she got there. They assigned her to the kitchen for the first two hours, carrying the heavy pots full of vegetables, mashed potatoes, and soup. It was hot, back-breaking work, and then they put her on the front lines, helping to plate and serve meals. There were mostly men that night and a few women, and people were in good spirits, wishing each other merry Christmas. All she could think about was Blue as she worked, and how cold he must be in the shed. It was nearly midnight when she finished and signed out again. The last stragglers had left by then, and volunteers were setting up the long tables for breakfast. She wished everyone merry Christmas and left, and stopped at a church on the way home, to catch midnight mass and light candles for Mark and Chris, Becky and her family, and their father. And at one in the morning, she took a cab the rest of the way home. But as soon as she got out at her address, she knew what she wanted to do.

She walked the short distance to the shed. There was no one around, and she kept an eye out for anyone who might attack her. It was late, but there was no one in sight. The wind had come up again, and it was freezing. The cabdriver had said that it was ten degrees with the wind chill factor. She saw the railing where she had stood trying to get up the courage to jump the night before, and she walked straight to the shed and knocked softly, but loud enough to wake him up, since he was probably asleep. She had to knock several times before he answered, and he sounded sleepy when he did.

'Yeah? What?'

'I want to talk to you,' Ginny said, loud enough so he could hear her, and a moment later he stuck his head out the door, and made a face in the bitter wind.

'Shit, it's cold out here,' he said as he squinted at her, still half asleep.

'Yes, it is. Why don't you spend the night on my couch? It's Christmas. And it's a lot warmer in my apartment than it is here.'

'No, I'm fine,' he said. He had never thought about staying with her, and he didn't want to take advantage of her, she had already been so nice. He didn't want to abuse it, but Ginny had a determined look in her eye.

'I know you're fine. But I want you to come home with me. Just for tonight. They say it's going to be even colder by tomorrow. I don't want you to turn into an icicle out here. You'll get sick.' He hesitated, and then as though he didn't have the strength to resist, he opened the door wide, stood up with all his clothes and shoes on, rolled up his sleeping bag, and followed her down the street to where she lived. He was too tired to argue with her, and didn't want to anyway. The thought of a warm place to sleep was appealing, and she seemed like a good person, with good intentions.

They went back to her apartment, and she made him a bed on the couch with two pillows, sheets, and a blanket. It was the closest he'd had to a bed in months. She handed him a pair of her own pajamas, and told him he could change in the bathroom. And when he came out, he looked like a little kid in his father's pajamas, as he stared at the neat bed she had made him on the couch.

'Will you be okay here?' she asked, looking concerned, and he grinned.

'Are you kidding? This is a lot better than my sleeping bag.' He couldn't understand what had happened to him, and why she had appeared to shower bounty on him. It was beyond his wildest imagination. But he was going to enjoy it while he could. She watched him slip under the covers, and then she turned off the lights and went to her own room to change and read for a while in bed. It was strange how comforting it was to know that there was someone in the apartment with her, another human presence, even if she couldn't see him from her bedroom, but she knew he was there. She peeked out once, and saw that he was sound asleep, and then she went back to bed, smiling to herself. It had turned out to be a very nice Christmas Eve after all, the best in years. And for him, too.

Chapter 4

Ginny was making herself a cup of coffee the next morning, when Blue wandered into the kitchen, still wearing her pajamas, and looking like one of the Lost Boys from *Peter Pan*. She turned and smiled when she saw him.

'Did you sleep okay?' she asked him.

'Yeah, like a baby. Did you wake up really early?'

She nodded. 'I'm still on some other time zone. Are you hungry?' She hadn't stopped feeding him since they met, but he looked as though he needed it, and he was a growing boy.

He looked embarrassed when he answered. 'Kind of. But I'm okay. I usually only eat one meal a day.'

'Out of necessity or choice?'

'Both.'

'I make fairly decent pancakes, and I have some mix here. Do you want some?' She had bought it one day in a fit of nostalgia and never used it. She tried not to think of the Mickey Mouse pancakes she used to make for Chris. The last time she'd made pancakes had been for him. She knew she'd never make the Mickey Mouse ones again.

'That sounds good,' Blue admitted, and she got out the mix and made them for him. She had butter in the freezer and maple syrup in the cupboard. And when they finished them, she called Becky to wish them all a merry Christmas at the house in Pasadena. Alan answered and she talked to him for a few minutes, and then Becky got on.

'Should I speak to Dad, or will that just confuse him?' Ginny asked her sister. She wasn't sure her father would know who she was, and if he did, she didn't want him to get upset, asking her to come out.

'He's a little scrambled today. He keeps thinking I'm Mom, and that Margie and Lizzie are you and me. He won't know who you are on the phone, or even if he saw you today.'

'That must be tough to deal with,' Ginny said, feeling instantly guilty that she wasn't there.

'It is,' Becky said honestly. 'What about you? What are you going to do today?' She could only imagine how rough Christmas was for her, with no one to spend it with, and the ghosts of Christmas past.

'I think I'm going to spend it with a friend,' Ginny said pensively. She had told Blue he could use the shower, and she could hear him in her bathroom. She was going to run his clothes through the washing machine and dryer in the building, so he'd have clean clothes.

'I thought you didn't have friends in New York.' Becky sounded puzzled. She had given up encouraging Ginny to meet people – she never did and didn't want to. She said she met enough people on her assignments and didn't need to know anyone in New York, since she was always there so briefly, only weeks. And her situation was always too hard to explain. She didn't want anyone's pity, nor to share her story with them. It was none of their business, and you couldn't have friends if you weren't willing to be open with them, which she wasn't. She was sealed tight like an oyster. She had said more to Blue about Chris and Mark than to anyone in years.

'I don't have friends here. I just met him,' Ginny said vaguely.

'A guy?' For an instant, Becky was shocked.

'Not a guy, a boy,' Ginny explained and wondered if she should have.

'What do you mean, "a boy"?'

'He's a homeless kid. I let him spend the night here.' And as soon as she said it, she knew she shouldn't have. She and Becky hadn't been on the same wavelength for years. Becky had a life, a family, and a home, and a lot to risk. Ginny had nothing, and didn't care.

'You let a homeless boy spend the night there?' Becky said, horrified. 'Are you sleeping with him?'

'Of course not. He's a child. He slept on the couch. He was living in a shed near my apartment, and it's ten below here. You can die of exposure on nights like that.' She didn't think he would, he was young and strong, but anything was possible.

'Are you insane? What if he kills you in your sleep?'

'He's not going to do that. He's about eleven or twelve, and a very sweet boy.'

'You have no idea who or what he is, and maybe he's older than he says, and a criminal of some kind.' The vision of Blue as a criminal in the too-big pajamas was beyond absurd. She hadn't even bothered to lock her bedroom door the night before. She had thought about it, and dismissed the idea. Nothing about him scared her.

'Trust me. He's a sweet kid. He's not going to hurt me, and I'm going to try and talk him into going to a youth shelter. He can't stay on the streets in this weather.'

'Why should he agree to that, if you let him stay in your apartment?'

'For one thing, because I'm leaving in a few weeks, and he can't stay here.' Blue had appeared in the doorway of her bedroom, back in the oversize pajamas, and he was carrying his clothes for her to wash, as she had suggested. 'Anyway, I can't talk to you about it now. I have to do laundry. I just called to wish you a merry Christmas. Give Alan and the kids and Dad my love.'

'Ginny, get that boy out of your apartment!' Becky almost shrieked at her. 'He's going to kill you!'

'No, he's not. Trust me. I'll talk to you tomorrow. Kiss Dad for me.' She got off the phone a minute later, and in Pasadena Becky looked at her husband with an expression of panic.

'My sister has lost her mind,' she said, nearly crying. 'She let a homeless boy sleep in her apartment.'

'Holy God, she is insane.' He was equally worried and strongly disapproving. 'She has to get back to some kind of normalcy before she gets herself killed.'

'Yeah, but what can I do about it? I'm here, trying to keep Dad from getting lost or run over by a truck crossing the street. Now I'm supposed to keep my sister from being murdered by homeless boys she lets sleep in her apartment? She should be locked up.'

'It could come to that one day,' Alan said with a grim look. He had always worried that she would eventually lose her mind over the death of her son and husband. But Becky was right, they couldn't do anything about it.

And in New York, Blue was just as worried. 'Who was that?'

'My sister in California,' Ginny said as she took his clothes from him to put in the washing machine in the basement. 'I used to live in L.A.,' she explained, as he stared at her unhappily.

'You're leaving again soon?' he asked with a sorrowful

look. He had heard what she had said to Becky. He had just met her, and now he was about to lose her, too.

'Not for a while,' she said calmly. She could see fear of abandonment on his face and in the deep blue eyes. His hair was clean, and he looked immaculate in her pajamas, as they sat down on the couch. 'I might go sometime in January, but I don't know yet. But then I'll come back. I always do.' She smiled at him.

'What if you get killed?' She was about to say 'no one will miss me,' but she could see in his face that he would, although they hardly knew each other. He looked panicked at the thought of her leaving.

'I won't get killed. I've been doing this for two and a half years. I'm good at it. And I'll be careful. Don't worry. Now let's talk about what we're going to do today. We both hate Christmas, so let's do something that has nothing to do with the holiday. What do you like to do? Go to movies? Go bowling? Do you ice-skate?'

He shook his head in answer, still worried. 'I used to bowl with my aunt Charlene, before . . . before she got too busy.'

Ginny could tell that there was something he wasn't telling her, but she didn't want to pry. 'Want to try it?'

'Okay,' he said, smiling slowly.

'And then we can go to the movies, and have dinner.' It sounded like a slice of heaven to him. She wanted him to have a good time while he was with her. She had no idea what would happen after that. All they had to do was get through the day, and make it a decent Christmas for both of them. She had been planning to stay in bed and read and finish her report, but that wasn't in the cards now. She could do it later.

After she took them to the machines in the basement, Blue's clothes were clean and dry an hour later, and they went downtown to a bowling alley that she called to make sure was open. Neither of them was good at the game, but they had a ball playing, and then they went to a movie. She picked an action film in 3D she thought he'd like, and he loved it. He had never seen 3D before, and he was mesmerized by it. And then they had hot dogs for dinner at a deli, and stopped at a small grocery store for food before they went back to her apartment. It was dark and snowing again when they got back to her place. She asked if he'd like to sleep on the couch again, instead of going back to the shed, and he nodded. She made the bed up for him, and she left him there, watching TV, and went to her bedroom. Becky called her as soon as she lay down.

'You're still alive? He hasn't killed you yet?' She was only half-kidding. She had been worried sick about her all day, about her mental state and poor judgement to have done something so dangerous.

'No, and he's not going to. It's Christmas, Becky, give the kid a break.' She had given him more than a break, she had given him a great time, and they had both loved it.

'Will you get him out of there tomorrow?'

'I'll see. I want to get him to the right place. He's afraid of shelters.'

'Oh, for chrissake. I'm afraid for your life. Who cares if he's afraid of shelters? Where's his family?'

'I don't know yet. His parents are both dead. He used to live with his aunt, but something went wrong there.'

'This isn't your problem, Ginny. There are millions of homeless people in the world. You can't take them all in. You can't heal all the broken and wounded in the world. Just take care of yourself. Why don't you look for a job in New York? I think all this humanitarian work you do gives you a Mother Teresa complex. Instead of picking up homeless orphans off the street, come and visit your father.' Ginny ignored the tart remark. Becky sounded tired.

'I don't have a family to come home to, Becky,' Ginny reminded her. 'It allows me to dedicate my life to others.'

'You have us. Move back to L.A.'

'I can't. That would kill me,' Ginny said sadly. 'And I don't want a desk job in New York. I like what I'm doing. It fulfills me.'

'You can't run around the world for the rest of your life. And if you want a family to come home to, you have to stay somewhere for more than ten minutes and stop going to war zones, and working in refugee camps. You need a real life, Gin, while you can still have one. If you do that stuff for long enough, you won't be able to settle down again.'

'Maybe I don't want to,' she said honestly. Then Becky had to drive her younger daughter to meet a friend, and mercifully got off the phone, and Ginny spent the rest of the evening reading, while Blue watched TV in the living room. She went to check on him at ten o'clock, and he was sound asleep in his bed on the couch, with the remote still in his hand. Ginny gently took it from him and put it on the trunk in front of him, covered him with the blanket, and turned off the light. Then she went back to her bedroom and closed the door, and read until midnight. She thought about what Becky had said to her, and she knew they were convinced she was crazy for taking Blue in, but it felt right to her for now, at this moment. She would figure it out later. She wanted to convince him to contact his aunt, and let her know he was okay. And then she wanted to get him into a good shelter where they could help him. For now, he was her mission. And by the time she left again, she wanted to know he was in good hands. She was convinced there was a reason their paths had crossed, and she was sure that was it. She was meant to get him to safe harbor, and she vowed to herself that she would. She turned off the light, and two minutes later she was sound asleep.

* * *

While Ginny cooked Blue breakfast the next day, he went on the Internet again and logged onto various sites. She noticed him on several youth and homeless sites again, where people posted messages for each other. And she saw him frowning as he read one of them more carefully than the others. As she set his plate of scrambled eggs down next to the computer, she saw that it was from someone named Charlene, who was asking him to call her, and it was obviously his aunt, since he had mentioned her name. Ginny looked at the site carefully without seeming to, so she could get back to it if he went out. Ginny wanted to contact her to learn more about Blue, and figure out what to do with him when she left New York.

She said something to Blue after breakfast about where he was going to stay in the future.

'You can't go back to the shed, Blue. It's too cold. And sooner or later someone from the city will lock it up again.'

'There are other places I can stay,' he said, jutting out his chin defiantly. Then he looked at her and the expression in his eyes grew soft. 'Not as nice as this, though.'

'You can stay with me as long as I'm here,' she said generously. She didn't realize how agonizingly lonely she had been before he arrived. Now she knew. 'But I have to go back to work next month, and I'll be gone for a while. Let's find a good place for you to stay before I go.'

'Not a shelter,' he said, looking stubborn again.

'There are long-term places for homeless kids. Some of them sound pretty good – you can come and go as you want.' She had been checking them out on the Internet. It wouldn't be an ideal situation, but it would afford him shelter, a place to stay, meals, counseling, and job placement if he wanted that. But he wasn't really old enough to work.

'You just get ripped off in shelters, and most of the kids are on drugs.' She could tell that he wasn't, which was remarkable given his hard life.

'Well, we'll have to figure something out. I can't take you with me.' It was as though she had adopted him, and was determined to solve his housing situation, when in fact he was a fragile bird who had come to light on her branch, and was perched next to her for now. But he had no choice but to fly away again when she did, and she wanted him to be safe after she left.

'I just want a room somewhere and a job,' he said. It was a tall order for a boy his age, no matter how bright he was. No one hired eleven- or twelve-year-old boys, except as drug runners in bad neighborhoods, and Blue seemed to have stayed clear of that.

'How old are you, Blue? Honestly this time,' she said with a serious expression, and he didn't answer for a while, clearly deciding whether or not to tell her the truth. And then finally he spoke up.

'I'm thirteen,' he growled at her, 'but I can do a lot of

stuff, I'm good on the computer, and I'm strong.' He was slight from lack of food, but he was willing.

'When was the last time you were in school?' She was afraid it might be years.

'September. I'm in eighth grade.'

'That means you could go to high school next year.' She thought about it for a minute and looked him in the eye. If Christopher had been alive, he would have been six. She had no experience with teenage boys, except her nephew, whom she had been too busy to pay much attention to while he was growing up. Her sister knew a lot more about kids than she did, but she couldn't ask her about Blue. 'I'll make a deal with you,' Ginny said quietly. 'If you go back to school, I'll pay you for odd jobs you can do for me.'

'Like what?' He looked suspicious of the deal.

'There's plenty you can do for me. The apartment needs regular cleaning. I want to move some stuff around. I guess I could get rid of my lovely furniture, and upgrade it a little.' She glanced around, and he grinned.

'Yeah, maybe we could burn it,' he quipped, and they both laughed.

'Let's not be that extreme. You can do errands for me. We'll figure it out.'

'How much do you pay?' he asked seriously, and she laughed again.

'Depends on the job. How about minimum wage?'

He considered it and nodded. It sounded good to him.

'Why do I have to go to school? I always get bored there.'

'You're going to be bored for the rest of your life if you don't graduate. You're a smart boy – you need to go to school. You can't get a decent job unless you at least go to high school, and maybe one day you can go to college.'

'And then what?'

'That's up to you. But without school, you'll be dishing up fries at McDonald's. You deserve better than that,' she said, convinced.

'How do you know that?'

'Trust me, I do.'

'You don't even know me,' he challenged her.

'That's true, but I know you're smart, and you could go far if you wanted to.' She could see that he was a good kid. He was resourceful and enterprising – all he needed were some decent breaks. 'Will you do it, go back to school, I mean? I'll help you register in the public school near here. We can say you were away for a while.' It seemed like a lifetime before he answered, and then slowly he nodded and looked at her. He didn't look happy about it, but he agreed.

'I'll try it,' he compromised, 'but if it's boring and full of dummies, or the teachers are mean, I'm out of there.'

'No. Dummies or not, you stick it out till June, and go to high school in the fall. That's the deal.' She stuck out her hand, wanting him to shake it, and finally he put his hand in hers.

'Okay. So when do I start work for you?'

'What about now? You can do the dishes, and vacuum the apartment. And we need some more groceries.' He had already finished the milk they bought the night before and she'd forgotten to buy fruit. 'How about going to the store for me? I'll make a list. What do you like to eat?' She grabbed a piece of paper and a pen off her desk and wrote down the basics, and he added his wish list of too-sweet cereals, fruit roll-ups, potato chips, cookies, beef jerky, peanut butter, all the things kids like to snack on, and sodas of every kind. 'Your dentist is going to love me,' she said, rolling her eyes as he dictated to her, and then she realized he probably didn't have one, but she didn't want to ask. First things first, and getting him into school was top of her list. If nothing else, if she could get him off the streets, to a safe place, and get him back to school, her mission would be accomplished.

She sent him to the store a few minutes later with three twenty-dollar bills and the grocery list. And as soon as she heard the elevator doors close, she went to the laptop to the site he'd been on, and found the message to Blue from Charlene. It was dated the day before. Ginny responded quickly, hoping it was his aunt – she remembered that he had referred to her as Charlene when they talked about bowling.

'I have information about Blue. He is safe, well, and in good hands. Please call me, Virginia Carter,' and she added her cell phone number.

Ginny was sitting on the couch, innocently reading a magazine, when he got back, carrying the bag of groceries, and he diligently gave her the change. And then he started a list of the time he was spending doing errands, so she could pay him for his time. She smiled when she saw him do it and nodded. 'Very businesslike,' she said approvingly, and she was surprised to see that his handwriting was steady, legible, and neat.

He spent part of the day vacuuming and cleaning her apartment, and helping her move furniture, and he threw out her long-dead plant with a look of disgust. And that afternoon they went for a walk. They walked past the public school she had in mind for him, it wasn't far away, although they didn't know where he'd be living, and he made a face. They walked past a church then, and the face he made was even worse. He looked angry and venomous.

'You don't like churches, either?' She was surprised. He had very definite ideas. She wasn't deeply religious, but she had an ongoing sense of communication with God, in a loose form that worked for her.

'I hate priests,' Blue said, nearly snarling.

'Why?' She wanted to know more about him, but he was very private about his life. Like a flower, she had to wait for the petals to unfurl on their own. She didn't want to push, but she was intrigued by what he said about the clergy.

'I just hate them. They're jerks. And really fake. They pretend to be good people and they're not.'

'Some are,' she said quietly. 'Not all priests are bad or good. They're just people.'

'Yeah, but they like to pretend they're God.' He seemed agitated as he said it, and she didn't want to upset him, so she didn't argue the point. Blue clearly had total contempt for them all.

They went to another movie after dinner, this time not in 3D, but they enjoyed it anyway, and talked about it on the way back to her apartment. It was beginning to feel familiar walking along with him and talking, almost as though they had known each other for longer than they had. He had a good sense of humor, and was very articulate, and as soon as they got back to the apartment he asked her how much he'd made that day, helping her. They added it up, and he was pleased at the amount. He grinned happily at her and turned on the TV. She kept checking her phone for messages from Charlene, but she had none so far. She wondered if she'd call back and hoped she would.

She did some work that night on her laptop and saw that Blue had been on the kids' homeless site again. She wondered if he was looking for a message from someone in particular.

And in the morning, while Ginny was still in bed, Charlene called on her cell phone. She was indeed his aunt.

'Who are you?' she asked Ginny immediately. 'Are you a social worker, with an agency for kids? Are you a cop?' She sounded both suspicious and relieved. Ginny explained how they had met and that Blue was sleeping on her couch.

'How long has it been since you've seen him?' Ginny asked, curious about her and what had happened, and she wondered if the woman on the phone would tell her the truth. She had a pleasant, intelligent voice.

'Not since September. It just wasn't working out here. I've got three kids in a tiny apartment with one bathroom and no space to move around. My kids sleep in the bedroom. I sleep on the couch, and Blue was sleeping on the floor. That's no way for a boy to live. It would break his mama's heart if she knew he has no home.' She regarded his situation with Ginny as temporary, as Ginny did herself. 'And he doesn't like my boyfriend,' she added cautiously, once she knew that Ginny had no official capacity. 'He drinks a bit, and they fight all the time. Blue doesn't like the way he talks to me. He's very protective, a little too much so at times. They got in a bad argument, and my guy took a swing at him. Blue left after that. There really is no room for both of them here, and Harold stays here sometimes. When he does, Blue was sleeping in the tub, and we only have the one bathroom. Blue's father was a lot like Harold – he beat Blue up a bunch of times, and his mama, too. She was such a good woman, and she loved that boy to death. There was nothing she wouldn't have done for him – it was all she was worried about when she died. I took him in, I promised her I would, but I only had one baby then. With three, I just can't. No money, no space, no time. He needs to get in the foster care system and get a decent home.'

'He doesn't seem to want that, and he might be too old for people to want to foster him. At thirteen, kids can be tough.'

'He's a good boy, and smart,' his aunt said lovingly. 'He's had some bad breaks with his mama dying. And his daddy was never around. He went to prison for dealing drugs, and died there three years ago, but Blue hardly ever saw him anyway. I'm the only blood relative he's got.' It sounded like a sad situation to Ginny, and her heart ached for him. She knew there were thousands of kids like him, but there was something special about Blue, which had touched her heart.

'I'd like to get him into an adolescent homeless shelter, and he's agreed to go back to school,' Ginny said hopefully.

'He won't stick at either,' his aunt said knowingly. She knew him too well, far better than Ginny. 'He always runs away, from everything. He'll run away from you, too. He's like a wild thing now – if you get too close to him, he runs. I think he's scared, or maybe he thinks we're all going to die like his mama and daddy.' It was a valuable insight into him. 'But he's a nice kid,' she said again.

'Do you want me to try to get him to come and see you?' Ginny offered.

'He won't want to. And if Harold shows up, it'll be a mess. Just let me know where he is. I can't do anything for him myself.' She had basically given up on him – he was one more mouth to feed, and a problem she didn't want, particularly if it upset her boyfriend. Her allegiance was to Harold, not to Blue. It was obvious she didn't want to see him. He really had no one in the world. He was an orphan in every sense of the word.

'I'll let you know if I get him into a shelter. I'm leaving town in a few weeks, and I'll be gone for several months. I'd like to get him situated before I leave,' Ginny said, but she was even more worried about him now. He had no one to fall back on, no support system, and not a friend in the world, other than her.

'Wherever you put him, he won't stay. He'll be back out on the streets again. He knows how to make it there. And I don't think he'll ever go back to school.' It sounded like a dismal fate to Ginny, which his aunt was all too willing to accept. 'I'm a nurse's aide at Mount Sinai Hospital. I tried to get him interested in nursing for a while. He said it sounded like filthy work. He dreams a lot, and thinks he's going to get a good job one day because he's smart. You and I know that's not enough.'

'That's why I'd like to get him back in school,' Ginny said doggedly. 'He agreed for now.'

'He always does,' his aunt Charlene said with resignation. 'Don't let him break your heart,' she warned. 'He doesn't get attached to anyone since his mama. I think he just lost her too young.' Ginny was surprised that Blue's aunt was willing to accept that he was damaged forever, and to let him seek his own fate on the streets, without at least trying to turn the tide. Ginny was willing to do that, just the way she did for the people in the areas where she worked, to change their situation. And Blue was a bright thirteen-year-old boy, living in a civilized city and country. She wanted him to have a chance. He deserved it.

'I'll let you know where he is and what he's doing before I leave,' she promised, but his aunt didn't sound nearly as worried about him as she was. Charlene knew him well, and his strong drive to detach and run away.

Ginny was thinking about it as she made breakfast for them that morning. She wanted to tell him that she had spoken to his aunt, but she didn't dare. She didn't want him to think they were in some kind of conspiracy against him.

'How about we look at some of those youth shelters today?' she suggested after breakfast, and saw his eyes get cold and stony.

'I'd rather do work for you and make some money,' he said, dodging the issue. He didn't want to face that she would be leaving soon, and she could see that it upset him. But she was determined to find him a safe place to live and to enroll him in school before she left. It was all she could think of now.

Without saying anything to him, she bought him some binders and notebooks, pens and pencils, a calculator, and all the things he'd need for school. She left them in a bag in her closet, and didn't say anything about them.

They spent New Year's Eve watching TV and saw the ball in Times Square fall, and all the crowds of people there. He looked excited about it, and they had fun together.

And on the Monday afterward, she and Blue went to the school she'd shown him and met with the vice principal about enrolling him. Ginny gave them her address and didn't say the arrangement was temporary – she wanted to give him the best shot she could of getting him into the school. They asked where his last school had been, and he explained that he had been living with his aunt then and no longer was. The school was used to kids moving around and asked no questions about it.

'You're his legal guardian?' the vice principal asked her, and Ginny paused before she answered.

'No, I'm not. His aunt still is, although he doesn't live with her.'

'Then we'll need her signature on the forms,' he said, handing them to her. 'Once she signs them, we'll enroll him in eighth grade. He's got some catching up to do, if he's been out of school since September.' Blue looked morose at that, and they left a few minutes later. He glanced at Ginny in despair.

'Do I really have to?'

'Yes, you do. And we need to get those forms signed by your aunt. Can I call her?' He hesitated for a long time and then nodded.

'Yeah, I guess so. She doesn't care if I go to school or not.'

'I'm sure she does,' Ginny said firmly. She knew he was right but couldn't say so, since he didn't know she'd spoken to his aunt. 'And I care. You have no choice, Blue, unless you want to work at the lowest-level jobs all your life. You can't get a decent job without even finishing eighth grade.'

He knew she was right and hated to hear it, and that night they called his aunt. She had no problem about signing the papers. She warned Ginny again that he'd drop out and run away, and she agreed to sign the forms if Ginny brought them to the hospital that night, which she agreed to do. Charlene's shift started at eleven, and before Ginny left, she asked Blue if he wanted to come, and he shook his head from where he sat on the couch.

'I'll just wait here,' he said softly. He seemed to have no ties that meant anything to him. He had been set adrift and was swimming on his own. Ginny just didn't want him to drown in the process, and even though they hardly knew each other, she had made a commitment to help him and intended to see it through. It was why she was good at what she did in her current work. She never gave up on anyone, and was willing to keep plodding until she got results. Her motto was 'Nothing is impossible,' as she had already said several times to Blue. And it made her heart ache for him that he felt so alone and disenfranchised that he didn't even want to see his aunt. She suspected that the final scene with Harold had been a bad one, probably worse than Charlene had said, for him to be so reluctant to see her now.

Ginny met Charlene at Mt. Sinai Hospital as promised – she was wearing her nurse's aide uniform. She was a pretty African American woman about Ginny's age, in her mid-thirties. When they talked Charlene mentioned randomly that Blue's father was white, and had the same dazzling blue eyes. The combination of his parents accounted for the light café au lait skin. Both women agreed that he was a beautiful boy.

'Thank you for what you're doing for him,' Charlene said with a sigh after she signed his school forms. 'I hope he doesn't let you down.'

'He might,' Ginny said practically, 'and if he drops out

of school, I'll just drag him back in again. I don't intend to lose this fight.'

'Why? Why do you care about him so much?' Charlene looked puzzled. Ginny was white, lived in a good neighborhood, sounded like she had a good job, and must have had a life before she met him. Charlene couldn't figure out why she was concerned about the boy.

'He deserves a decent chance in life,' Ginny said with determination. 'We all do. Some of us get luckier than others. He has a right to an amazing life, just like everyone else. He's still young. It can happen. He needs someone to go to bat for him, and believe in him. You've got your own kids to worry about. All I have is me, so I can spend some time on Blue.' There was something in Ginny's eyes that made Charlene wonder, it was a look of deep pain, but she didn't question her further. She just said that Blue was a lucky boy. But he hadn't been until then, Ginny knew, and just as she had done for others, she wanted to turn his luck around and give him a fighting chance at a better life than the one he had, sleeping in a sleeping bag in a utility shed on the streets, with no one to care about him.

Charlene thanked her again, and Ginny left, and hailed a cab on upper Fifth Avenue to go back to her apartment, where Blue was waiting for her.

Her cell phone rang when she was in the cab. She thought it might be Blue, but when she looked, she saw it was Becky.

'Where are you?' Becky sounded tired. At nine p.m. for her, it had been a long day, chasing all three kids and her father.

'I'm on my way back to the apartment. I just had to meet someone to get some papers signed.'

'For what?' Becky was half curious and half worried.

'For Blue. We got him enrolled back in school today. He's supposed to start tomorrow.' Ginny sounded victorious.

'What is it with you and this kid?' Becky asked, in an irritated tone. He had been in Ginny's life for exactly two weeks, and suddenly her whole life revolved around him.

'Everyone deserves a chance, Becky. Sometimes it takes a village to get there. I'm part of that village for him. And actually, other than an aunt who has no time or room for him, for now all he has is me. I'm used to cutting through red tape and tilting at windmills. This boy needs someone to believe in him, and at the moment I'm it.'

'He's lucky to have you on his team. I just don't see why you're doing it. What's the point? In a couple of weeks you'll be halfway around the world in some refugee camp again, getting shot at by rebels, and he'll probably be back on the streets. You pick all the unwinnable battles,' she said, with an edge to her voice. She wanted Ginny to have an ordinary life again.

'Yes, I do,' Ginny said quietly, not denying what her sister said. 'Someone has to do it, and sometimes you win.'

The cab was at her address by then, and she got off the phone. The minute she walked through the door, Blue turned to look at her with a lifetime of worry in his eyes.

'So did she sign it?' he asked. Ginny nodded and hung up her coat.

'She did and she sent you her love,' which wasn't entirely true. Charlene had actually never said that word to her. 'You start school tomorrow,' she said firmly as Blue rolled his eyes and glared at her.

'Do I have to?' She glared right back at him and said he did, and he harrumphed off to the bathroom to brush his teeth, like the thirteen-year-old boy he was.

The next morning was slightly frantic as she made breakfast for him and he got ready for school. She handed him the supplies she'd bought, and she walked him to school. He didn't say anything, and she wondered if he was nervous about it. And when they got to the corner, she wished him a good day, and stood and watched him disappear into the building. She knew there was the possibility that he could walk out again as soon as she left. But she had done all she could to get him headed in the right direction. After that it was up to him, just like the children she helped take care of in refugee camps. But this was different. For some reason that even she didn't understand, she cared about this boy. Between the night she had first seen him dart into the shed and that morning, he had embedded himself into her heart. She had sworn to herself three years before that she would never love anyone again. And she sensed that Blue had made the same decision as a little boy when his mother died. And now here they were, two lost souls who had found each other and were swimming toward shore together side by side. It was a strange feeling, as she walked back to the apartment, and got to work on her laptop. She had let her work slide for the last few days, and she had to go into the office the next day. And soon she'd be leaving again. But at least Blue was on his way and back to school. Now all she had to do, before she left, was find him a place to live.

Chapter 5

When Ginny went to the SOS/HR office, she found that they were considering two possible assignments for her. One in the north of India, where young girls were being sold into slavery by their fathers; a center there was offering them refuge if they were able to escape. Many of them had been severely abused, and all were in their very early teens. And the other location was in the mountains in Afghanistan, at a refugee camp where she had worked before. She was familiar with the area, and the work had been dangerous, exhausting, and rewarding. She was more inclined to go there, and it was more typical of the assignments she'd had before. The dangers there were obvious, and SOS/HR was extremely protective of their workers, ran their camps and programs with military precision, and worked in areas with a Red Cross and international presence. So Ginny knew that particularly in troubled areas, she wouldn't be out in the field alone. And in most instances, even the countries they were assigned to respected the humanitarian work they did, and their effectiveness in helping the local populace. Ginny rarely felt unwelcome in the countries where she went. Conditions were rigorous, and sometimes risky, but it was a first-rate operation, which was why she had signed on with them.

'You're not ready to give up the rough stuff yet?' her supervisor, Ellen Warberg, asked her with a sharp look. 'Most people burn out after a year. You've taken all the toughest assignments for almost three years.'

'I like the challenge,' Ginny admitted quietly. Without exception, she had accepted hardship posts, and was known for it in the New York office. But thus far her work had been flawless and above reproach. And she showed no signs of slowing down. By the end of the conversation, they had agreed on the post in Afghanistan, and they wanted her to leave in two weeks. As she left the office, she thought about how little time it gave her to find a place for Blue.

When she got home, she looked on the Internet again, and found three possibilities. Before he came home from school, she made appointments at all three that week. She wanted to tie up all the loose ends before she left. If she managed to, it would make her brief hiatus in New York a success. She hadn't wasted her time.

Blue was doing fine at school. He had only been there for two days, and did his homework in an hour on her dining table every night. He said the courses and teachers were boring, but he showed no sign of dropping out yet, contrary to his aunt's prediction, but it was still early days. Ginny's fear was that he would drop out after she left. She thought that as long as she was there, he would stick with it, at least for now. But nothing about what he was doing in class inspired him. He said he had heard it all before, and she suspected that might be true. He was both bright and mature for his age, and his sphere of interests was broader than most kids. He seemed to know a lot about world events, and he was interested in music. The public school system was not set up, and didn't have the funds, to add to the general curriculum. It catered to the lowest common denominator in the classroom, not the highest. By the end of the week, he was being tested for the gifted program, and had been approved for special classes.

She hadn't told him about Afghanistan yet, but she planned to in the next few days. She wanted to see the adolescent shelters first. By the weekend, she had seen all three, and there was one she thought was perfect for him. The clients they accepted were between the ages of eleven and twenty-three. Some were reunified with their families after counseling, but it was rare. Most of the residents were in situations like Blue's, from broken homes where parents had died or disappeared or were in prison. The shelter encouraged everyone to go to school, helped them find part-time or full-time jobs, and offered counseling, medical care, and housing on a drop-in basis, or they could stay for as long as six months. It operated on a harm-reduction model, which meant that some of the residents were still on drugs, but had to meet certain criteria for behavior, and be using the drugs on a diminishing basis and never at the shelter. The program was practical and realistic, and the shelter had a bed available for Blue, but he had to want to be there – no one was going to force him to stay. He would live in a dorm room with five other boys close to his age, and he would get free meals every day. The entire program was free, funded by private foundations and government grants. It was tailor-made for Blue.

Ginny explained Blue's situation to the director, and how she had met him. The director, a woman Ginny's age, commented that he was lucky to have found a mentor in her.

'I'm going to be gone for three months. He can stay with me again when I get back, but I really want him to be here while I'm away,' she said hopefully.

'That's up to him,' Ann Owen, the director, said philosophically. 'The entire facility is voluntary, and there are lots of other kids who want a place here if he doesn't.'

Ginny nodded, hoping Blue would agree to stay there, and not decide to fend for himself on the streets. He always had that option, and his aunt said he preferred it to living with rules and structure. He had been on his own too much, but so had most of the other kids at Houston Street, as the facility was called. Ginny told Blue about it after she saw it, and he looked glum.

'I don't want to stay there,' he said, looking sullen.

'You can't go back to the shed. This place will feed you, house you, and give you a bed. There are other kids your age and older to hang out with. If you get sick, they'll take care of you. Be smart, Blue. Don't put yourself at risk on the streets. That's a shit life and you know it.'

'I can do whatever I want out there,' he said stubbornly.

'Yeah, like freeze and starve, and get mugged and ripped off. Great choice if you ask me.' She was as wise as he was to what he'd have to face on the streets. 'I'll be back at the end of April, and you can stay here again then if you want to. But you have to make it till then.' It sounded like a lifetime away to both of them, and he was still worried she'd never come back at all. 'At least take a look at it with me on Saturday, then decide. It's up to you,' she reminded him. Ultimately, the choice was his, no one could force him. And it wasn't going to be as comfortable as her apartment, but he had only been there for a short time, and it was a lot better than the shed, and other places he'd stayed where he had to fend for himself. Ginny couldn't help wondering if he would be able to live with structure long term, and if he ever had.

His life till now had been independent and free-form.

He looked like he had lead in his shoes when they went to see Houston Street on Saturday, and he almost crawled up the chipped steps to the main house. They had three facilities on the same block, one for women and two for men, as they referred to their young clients. Blue said not a word as they looked around. A few of the clients waved, and he ignored them. And he was stone-faced when they talked to the resident adviser, Julio Fernandez, who was warm and welcoming, with lots of information to impart. Blue listened to all of it and looked like he was about to cry.

'When would you want to come in, Blue?' Julio asked him directly.

'I don't,' he said bluntly, to the point of rude.

'That's too bad. We have a bed for you right now, but we won't for long. We get pretty full.' There was also a subway nearby that would get him to his school in minutes. And as Julio and Ginny talked about the facility, Blue drifted away. A moment later she noticed that someone had put some classical piano music on, which seemed a little ambitious to her. She paid no attention until Julio stopped talking and stared at something behind her. She turned to see what it was, and her mouth nearly fell open when she saw that it was Blue playing the piano, with an intense look on his face. As they watched him, he switched to jazz and continued playing. He paid no attention to them, and was intent and in another world as he played.

'That's quite a talent,' Julio said to her softly, as she continued to stare. Blue had never said that he played the piano. Nor had his aunt. He had simply said he liked music, but he was masterful at the keyboard. Some of the residents stopped and listened, too, and several people applauded when he finished, closed the piano, an old upright, and walked back to where Julio and Ginny were standing. He looked unimpressed by what he had just done, unlike everyone who had heard him play.

'So when do I have to move in?' he said to Ginny.

'You don't,' Julio interjected. 'You don't have to do anything you don't want to do. This isn't jail. It's home to a lot of kids like you who want to be here, but everyone is here by choice. We don't take assignments from the courts.' They had room for four hundred and forty residents on any given day or night, and most of the time they were at capacity.

'When are you leaving?' Blue asked Ginny with a miserable expression.

'In ten days. You should probably move in next week before I leave, so I know how you're doing for a few days. We can still see each other once you're here.' She tried to sound encouraging, but he looked desperately unhappy.

'Okay, I'll come next week,' he said with a blank look. He seemed totally without emotion. They thanked Julio then and left, after confirming a bed there for Blue the following week, and the moment they left the building, Ginny looked at him in amazement.

'You never told me you play the piano,' she said, still stunned by how well he had played. It was masterful, he had an extraordinary gift, and she couldn't imagine how or where he'd learned.

'I don't. I just fool around,' he said with a shrug.

'That's not fooling around, Blue. That's real talent. Can you read music?' He was full of surprises.

'Sort of. I taught myself. I just kind of do it.'

'Well, you "just kind of do it" extremely well. You knocked me and everyone else on our asses.' He smiled at that then. And she didn't ask him how he liked the place – she could tell. And there was no point making an issue of it since he had agreed to go. But what she had just heard from him on the piano had seriously caught her attention. He had a talent that couldn't be ignored, even more so if he'd taught himself. He was a boy of many facets, as she was only just beginning to discover. 'Where did you learn to play?' she asked him on the subway back uptown.

'There was a piano in the basement of the church my aunt goes to. The priest there used to let me play.' His face tightened as he said it, and she saw a strange look come into his eyes. 'He was a jerk, though, so I stopped. I just play now whenever I see a piano. Sometimes I go into music stores, until they throw me out.' She wondered why his aunt hadn't said anything to her about it – it certainly was worth mentioning. Blue explained her silence on the subject a moment later when he said, 'She doesn't know.'

'Why didn't you ever tell her that you play like that? She never heard you?'

'The priest said he'd get in trouble if anyone knew he let me play there, so we had to keep it a secret. I did.' And then he added a moment later, 'My mama used to sing in a choir, and play the organ at church. I sat next to her sometimes during the services, but she never taught me to play. I just watched. I guess I could probably play the organ, too.' Ginny realized that she must have been a talented woman if she had a son with a musical gift like that.

And that night after dinner, she had an idea that came to her and she shared with Blue. 'What if you apply to a music and art school for high school next fall? LaGuardia Arts is a public school. I could check it out if you want.'

'Why would they take me?' he said glumly. He was still depressed about the shelter he was moving into, although it didn't look bad to her.

'Because you have enormous talent,' she reassured him. 'Do you know how rare it is to teach yourself to play like that?' He had bowled her over.

'I play the guitar, too,' he said vaguely, and she laughed.

'Any other abilities you're hiding from me, Blue Williams?'

'No, that's it,' he said, looking like a kid again. 'But I'll bet I could learn to play drums. I've never tried, but I'd really like to.' She grinned, and he cheered up as the evening wore on. He gave her a neat list of the money she owed him for the odd jobs he'd done for her. He'd kept careful track. She paid him, and he was very pleased. Most of all she could feel how sad he was that she was leaving, and how worried he was about her. 'What if you never come back?' he asked her, panicked.

'I will,' she said quietly. 'Trust me. I've never gotten hurt, and I always come back.' She had reassured him before, but he was still worried. In his world, you lost people forever.

'You'd better come back,' he said with a dark look, and she hugged him before he went to bed that night. There were times when he really seemed like a child to her, and at others he was streetwise way beyond his years. He had seen too much at his age.

The time for him to move into Houston Street came too soon for both of them. The day before he left, he bought her flowers with his own money at the grocery store. Ginny helped him move with a heavy heart, but she knew it was the right thing for him. Still, for the first time, she was sad to leave New York for an assignment. Until then she had always been happy to go.

Blue was very quiet on the ride downtown in the cab. She had gotten him a few things, some T-shirts and new jeans, as well as his school supplies, and a bag to carry them in. And he looked bereft as he walked up the steps. And she stunned him totally when she left him in his dorm room. She gave him a laptop as a gift, and his eyes nearly fell out of his head when he saw it.

'You'd better write to me and stay in touch,' she said seriously. 'I want to know that you're okay.' He nodded, speechless for a moment, and threw his arms around her neck and hugged her, and she could see that there were tears in his eyes. No one had ever done anything like that for him, but she had wanted to. It was an important tool for him. And she had no one to spoil anymore. She promised to visit him that weekend before she left, and they were going to go out for dinner together.

But when she saw him on that last day, he looked miserable. They had missed each other's company all week, and had Skyped several times, which he loved, and she enjoyed it, too. But losing someone, even for a few months, was all too familiar to him, and no amount of reassurance could convince him that she was coming back. He was too scarred by his earlier losses, and his mother's death at five, to have faith that he'd see Ginny again. Everyone had abandoned him till then.

His mother and father by death, and his aunt by choice.

She hugged him tight when she left him on the front steps of Houston Street on Sunday night, and she went home to finish packing her bags. She was leaving for Kabul in the morning, and she promised to e-mail him whenever she could. In the farthest outposts she often didn't have Internet access, but when she traveled to less remote areas, she did. She said she'd stay in touch with him, and two agonizing tears rolled down his cheeks when she left. She cried on the subway all the way uptown.

Becky called her that night to say goodbye, and had a knack for saying all the wrong things. Ginny's heart already ached after saying goodbye to Blue. The time they had spent together and the relationship they had formed so unexpectedly had been a rare gift to both of them, and Ginny was intending to continue it when she got back. And she'd been researching LaGuardia Arts high school for him, and wanted to convince him to apply when she got back.

She'd called the school and they had told her that students applied in fall and winter for the following year, and auditioned in November and December, and he was already two months past when final applications were due. Acceptances were being mailed that month. She had explained his unusual circumstances and been told that a special review of his situation might be possible, as a hardship case, particularly if he was as gifted as she said. They promised to explore the possibility of making an exception for him, while she was away, and would be in touch. She didn't want to disappoint Blue, so she hadn't told him yet.

'Thank God you finally got that kid out of your house,' Becky said when Ginny told her he was at a youth shelter. 'I thought you'd never get rid of him. You're lucky he didn't kill you.'

'You don't know what you're talking about,' Ginny answered, in an irritated tone that masked her sorrow at saying goodbye to him hours before. She had her own issues about losing people, too.

'No, you have to stop doing crazy things like that. One of these days, someone will do you in, and no one will be surprised. And you didn't come out to visit Dad,' she said with obvious reproach in her voice.

'I'll come out next time, I promise,' Ginny said unhappily, her guard down for a minute, despite her sister's acerbic comments. 'It's just hard for me.'

'It's harder taking care of him,' Becky said bluntly, 'and he's getting worse. Next time might be too late – he may not recognize you at all. Sometimes he doesn't recognize me, and he sees me every day. He got lost again this week, and went out with no clothes on yesterday after his bath. I can't do this forever, Gin. We have to figure something else out soon. It's hard on Alan and the kids.' What she said was true and made Ginny feel guiltier than ever for not helping her.

'We'll talk about it when I get back.'

'When? In three months? Are you kidding? He goes downhill faster and faster every day. And you're going to feel like shit if he dies before you come home.' Her sister's words hit Ginny like a punch in the stomach.

'Let's hope he doesn't,' Ginny said miserably, feeling like the worst daughter and sister on the planet. She already felt like the worst wife and mother, for having allowed Mark to drive them when he'd had too much to drink and she hadn't seen it. And now she might miss her chance to say goodbye to her dad. But she could only withstand so much loss. She was a little bit like Blue that way, after losing Chris and Mark.

'Well, I hope that's the last of that homeless kid at least. That's one headache you don't need.' Ginny said nothing, Becky had said more than enough. She was depressed when she got off the phone, and already missed Blue. She hoped he'd be all right while she was away. She had done the best she could, getting him back into school, and living at Houston Street. It was up to him now to stick with it, and hang in until she got back. And then they could think about his future and high school in the fall.

She hardly slept that night, thinking about him, and he Skyped her the next morning before she left. He looked as sad as she did and thanked her for the fantastic laptop again. He was sleeping with it under his pillow, and even one night between his legs, so no one could take it from him. It was never out of his sight or his hands, even in school.

'I'll see you soon, Blue,' she said gently as they looked at each other on the screen.

'Just make sure you come back!' he said, scowling at her, and then slowly he smiled. It was a smile she knew she would remember every moment that she was away. And then as she looked at him, without another word, he pressed the button to disconnect Skype, and he was gone.

Chapter 6

As often was the case to reach the places where she was assigned, Ginny flew from New York to London, and had a layover there. She hated the massive size and chaos of Heathrow, but knew it well. And she Skyped Blue while she waited. He was on a break at school, so they talked for a few minutes, and after that she dozed in a chair for several hours, and then caught the flight to Kabul. She slept for most of the trip and then took another plane to Jalalabad in eastern Afghanistan where an SOS/HR worker would pick her up to drive her through the Hindu Kush, through the town of Asadabad on the border of Pakistan, to a village along the Kunar River, where the camp was located.

Conditions were more rigorous at this camp than she remembered. For five years, they had functioned without the help of Doctors Without Borders, but they had started working there again, so they had good medical assistance, but the camp was more crowded than when she'd been there before. They had limited supplies, no comforts whatsoever, and, trying to meet everyone's needs, the atmosphere of the camp was stressful for the workers. But SOS/HR functioned as efficiently as it could in what was essentially a war zone, and had been for over thirty years.

Ginny's driver was a young worker in his early twenties, who was doing his master's thesis on the camp she'd been assigned to. His name was Phillip, and he had been studying at Princeton, and was full of innovative new theories and naïve ideals about what they should be doing there and weren't. She listened patiently while he talked to her about it, but she had far more experience than he did, and was more realistic about what they could achieve. She didn't want to discourage him but knew that most of what he was suggesting was twenty years away, if that. The situation in Afghanistan was intense, and had been for many years. Women were subjected to appalling abuses, and one in ten children died.

Ginny could hear gunfire in the distance as they approached the camp. Her driver told her that the camps in Jalalabad itself were even worse than here. There were more than forty camps in the city, mostly made up of mud huts and shanties, where people were dying from lack of food. Children seemed to be the hardest hit, and many families had gone there to escape the fighting in the provinces, only to die from lack of food and irregular medical care at the refugee camps in the city. It was hard to know which was worse.

After nearly three years in the field, Ginny knew that sometimes it was just about helping the locals survive the hardships that they faced, not teaching them a new way of life or changing the world. She was used to dealing with women who'd been severely wounded, children who had lost limbs or were dying of terrible diseases, or of simple ailments they had no medicines for. And sometimes their clients died just from having been through too much. Her work was about supporting them in whatever way she could, and doing what was needed.

As Ginny stepped out of the truck, she felt an enormous wave of relief wash over her. Being here, in a place like this, where nothing mattered except human life and the simplest of survival skills, brought everything down to the value of human dignity and life. And everything else that she had been through disappeared the moment she arrived. She felt needed and useful and could at least try to make a difference in these people's lives, even if the results would be less than they hoped for.

There were children wandering through the camp in barely more than rags, in plastic sandals or bare feet, despite the freezing cold, and women wore burqas. She had put one on herself the moment the plane landed in Jalalabad, so as not to offend anyone or cause a problem at the camp. She had lived and worked in burqas and with her head covered before. She had thought about Blue several times on the long flights, but faced with what she had to do here, he was all but forgotten. She had done what she could for him, but she had more important work to do now, and she needed her wits about her to focus on her job. The country was in a constant state of civil war. And she knew from Phillip that many of the insurgents were living in caves nearby, which didn't surprise her, either.

There was a medical station at the edge of the camp, and wounded civilians were frequently brought there. A shocking number of them died, too badly injured by the time they were brought in, and often with festering wounds that had received little or no medical treatment until then. Everything was as basic and rudimentary as it could get. Their supplies were brought in by helicopter once a month, and they had to make do with what they'd been given until the next drop. Doctors Without Borders came regularly to tend to the more seriously ill, and the rest of the time, the workers did the best they could with the materials at hand.

Ginny and Phillip were among the few nonmedical personnel in the camp. And in the past, on similar assignments, Ginny had been brought into the operating tent to hold bowls filled with evil dressings and bloody rags. You had to have a strong stomach to work there, and a strong back to do heavy work, often helping to unload trucks full of supplies and equipment, and above all you had to have a willing spirit and a loving heart. She couldn't change their living conditions, or the state of the country, but she could make them a little bit more comfortable in some way, and give them solace and hope. By being willing to live with them in the camp, and experience the same dangers, she told them through her actions how important they were to her.

Two little girls holding hands stared at her, then smiled as she walked across the camp to the main tent. Most of their equipment and supplies were old military surplus, but were functional and served them well. She was wearing heavy army surplus gear and rugged boots with a man's parka, and it was freezing, and had been snowing earlier that day. She was wearing the burqa over her heavy clothes, and whenever she removed it, she had an armband that identified her as a human rights worker, with SOS/HR's logo printed across it, and there were two men in the camp wearing the armband of the Red Cross. SOS/HR worked closely with them.

Ginny went to report her arrival and introduce herself to a burly redheaded Englishman with a huge mustache. He was sitting at a makeshift desk in the main tent with butane heaters around him. At night, they slept in tents, or in the trucks. The man in charge of the camp was ex–British military, and his name was Rupert MacIntosh.

He was new since she'd been there, but he had been working in the field for years and was well known for his competence. Ginny was delighted to meet him.

'I've heard about you,' he said to Ginny when he shook her hand. 'You have quite a reputation as something of a daredevil. I want no accidents here, I warn you. We do all we can to avoid them. I'd like to keep it that way.' He looked at her sternly and then grinned. 'Fetching outfit, I must say.' She laughed at that, too, with her burqa over her heavy clothes, with hiking boots. He had also been told that she was very pretty, but it was hard to tell with everything she had on. She was even wearing a wool cap under the burqa. They dressed for the weather there and the heavy work they did, and nothing else.

He described the missions they had been concentrating on so far. A number of women and children had found their way to the camp, and the locals didn't like it when they refused to return home, to be mistreated again. But sooner or later they would have to. He told Ginny there had been a stoning in a nearby village two days before, of a woman who had been raped. She had been blamed for the rape, by 'tempting' her attacker, and killed. The man had gone free, to return to his home. It was typical of the situations they had all encountered many times.

'Do you ride?' he asked her, and she nodded. She had noticed horses and mules tethered in a roped-off area, for when they went into parts of the mountains where there were no roads. She had also ridden while on assignment in similar places.

'Well enough.'

'That'll do.'

When she joined the others in the mess tent later, she noticed how many nationalities there were – French, British, Italian, Canadian, German, American – all human rights workers from organizations that were combining their efforts. The mix of nationalities made it more interesting to be in the camp, although everyone spoke English, and she spoke a little French.

The food was as bad and scarce as she had expected it to be, and she was nearly falling asleep in her plate, at the end of the meal after the long trip.

'Get some sleep,' Rupert said, patting her on the shoulder, and a German woman led her to their tent, where she was assigned a cot, one of six, just like Blue at Houston Street. Ginny found it comforting to be down to basics and living in such a rudimentary way. It put everything else into perspective, and one's problems ceased to exist. She had discovered that the first time she came here, on her first assignment. She was too tired to take off her clothes that night, and fell asleep as soon as she crawled into her heavy sleeping bag on the cot, and didn't wake up until dawn.

The next day she went to work in the tent she'd been assigned to, taking case histories of the children, with the help of a translator. They never got involved in local politics and had strict orders not to, and none of the insurgents had bothered them in the past year, although that could change at any time, as they all knew.

She'd been there for a week when they went up into the mountains on mules, snaking on narrow paths along a cliff, to find out if anyone needed their assistance, or to be brought down for medical care. They brought two unridden mules for that purpose, and brought a six-year-old boy back with them, and his nineteen-year-old mother. The boy had been badly burned in a fire and was disfigured but had survived. The girl left five other children in their hut with her own mother. Her husband and father hadn't wanted her to leave their village, but had finally agreed for the sake of the child. Her face was heavily veiled, and she spoke to no one on the way, and kept her eyes downcast. And she was quickly absorbed into the group of local women when they returned to the camp.

Ginny was busy from dawn to nearly midnight every day, but she never had a sense of danger. The people in the area weren't hostile to them, and the number of women and children in the camp kept growing. It was another month or so before she went to Asadabad, the capital city of Kunar Province, in one of the trucks with one of the German women, an Italian man, and a French nun.

Rupert had asked her to send several e-mails from Asadabad, where they had Internet reception, since at the camp they had none. There was a Red Cross office that they were allowed to use. She walked in with Rupert's list of communications and reports to send. They gave her a desk and a computer to work at, while the others walked around town. After she sent Rupert's messages, she decided to check her own e-mail, rather than join the others for lunch.

She had three messages from Becky, reporting on their father's deteriorating condition, and asking her to call when she could. She had been in Afghanistan for six weeks by then, and Becky's last message was two weeks old. She had finally given up trying to reach Ginny, and sounded exasperated by her silence since Ginny couldn't receive e-mails, a fact Ginny had warned her of before she left. And there was an e-mail from Julio Fernandez at the Houston Street Shelter, and one from Blue that was only three days old. She decided to read Blue's first and opened it quickly. She had thought of him since she'd been there, but most of the time she had had more pressing things on her mind. Her days were very full.

Blue's e-mail began with an apology, and as soon as she saw it, she could guess the rest. He said that the people at Houston Street were very nice, but he hated all the rules. He wasn't crazy about the other kids, either. Some were okay, but one of his roommates had tried to steal his laptop, and it was so noisy at night he couldn't sleep. He said it was like living in a zoo, so he had written to tell her he had left. He didn't know where he was going, but he told her he'd be fine, and said he hoped that she was safe and would be back soon, in one piece.

After she read it, she saw there was another one from his school. It advised her that Blue had dropped out two weeks after she left. And the last one from Julio Fernandez said that they had tried to convince Blue to stay, but he had been determined to leave. He said that Blue didn't do well with their routine and was too used to doing what he wanted on the streets. He said it wasn't unusual, but it was incompatible with what they expected of their residents. So Blue had done exactly what Charlene had said he would, he had run away from the shelter and dropped out of school. And now she had no idea where he was and couldn't do anything about it. And she would be there for another six weeks. With so little communication available to them, and none at the camp, her hands were tied. And there was no way to track him down from here.

She answered Blue's e-mail first, and told him that she hoped he was okay. She made a point of telling him that she was fine. And she begged him to go back to the shelter and the school. She reminded him she was planning to come back at the end of April, and told him that she expected to see him at the apartment as soon as she did.

She tried to reassure herself, remembering he had managed without her for thirteen years, and she was sure that he would survive on the streets for another six weeks, although she wasn't pleased with what he'd done. She was very disappointed that he hadn't managed to stick with it, particularly at school. But she'd see what she could do when she went back. In the meantime, he was on his own, and would have to live by his wits, as he had before. And she knew that he knew life on the streets well.

After that, she thanked Julio Fernandez for his efforts and said she'd be in touch when she got back. She wrote to his school and asked if they would consider it a leave of absence, and promised that Blue would catch up on the work when he returned. It was all smoke and mirrors, but it was the best she could do for now. And then she wrote to Becky and told her they had no means of communication at the camp, except radios that were used only for emergencies and weren't long range. She kept her e-mail to her sister short, then called her on the phone from the Red Cross office. Becky answered her cell on the second ring.

'Where the hell are you?' she asked, sounding worried.

'In Afghanistan. You know where I am. We don't have e-mail from the camp. This is the first time I've come to town since I got here, and I probably won't come in again. What's up with Dad?' She was terrified to hear that he had died.

'Actually, he's better. They're trying a new medication, and it seems to work. He's a little clearer, in the mornings at least. He's always a mess at night. But we're giving him a sleeping pill now, so I'm not as worried about his getting up at night and wandering out of the house while we're asleep.' Her fear of that had kept her awake at night for months.

'Well, that's a relief.' Ginny had been panicked for a minute but felt better when she heard what Becky said.

'I wish to hell you'd come back and lead a more reasonable life. This is just too crazy, especially now with Dad. I have no way to reach you if he gets really bad, or if he dies.'

'You have my emergency contact number at the local Red Cross. I gave it to you before I left,' she reminded her. 'If it's an emergency, they'll send someone to the camp to find me. Otherwise, I'll be home in six weeks.'

'You can't keep doing this, Ginny. You're thirty-six years old. You're not some kid in the Peace Corps with no responsibilities, and I can't make all the decisions all the time. You need to be part of this, too.'

'I told you, I'll come to L.A. when I get back.'

'You've been saying that for almost three years.'

Ginny didn't tell her sister that she was a lot more useful here than she would have been in L.A. And she felt as though this was where she was meant to be for now.

'I can't stay on long. This is the local Red Cross phone. Give Dad a kiss from me.'

'Take care of yourself, Gin. Do us all a favor, don't get shot or killed.'

'I'll try not to. You're a lot more likely to get shot in L.A. than I am here. It's been peaceful at the camp.'

'Good. I love you.'

'I love you, too,' Ginny answered, although her sister drove her insane sometimes, and she couldn't imagine herself leading a life like Becky's, or even the one she'd had, ever again. That meant married, with kids, and living in Pasadena. Before, when Ginny had been married to Mark, Becky had thought their life was superficial and too glitzy. Now she thought her sister was insane. Their lives had never run parallel or been the same, or even remotely similar, and Becky had never approved of what she did. Knowing that took some of the sting out of what she said. But in Ginny's mind, Becky was always the disapproving older sister, and had been since they were children.

After she made the call, Ginny printed out the incoming messages for Rupert, and went to find the others, finishing lunch at a restaurant nearby. The food looked and smelled awful, and she was glad she had skipped lunch to do her e-mails instead from the Red Cross office.

'What did you guys have? The typhoid special?' Ginny wrinkled her nose and made a face at whatever they were eating. She had a cup of tea with them at the end of the meal, and they walked around town for a while, then got back in the truck for the drive back to camp.

She brought Rupert his messages, and they sat and chatted for a while. It was still cold, and freezing at night, as it had been since she arrived. It was still winter there in early March. She and Rupert talked about some of the medical problems they'd been dealing with, and he said that they'd be going back up into the mountains in a few days. He asked her to come with him, as he liked the way she handled the locals, and she was especially good with the children. She had a warm, gentle way with them.

'You should have some of your own one of these days,' he said with a warm smile. He was married but was known to be something of a womanizer, with a wife in England he hardly ever saw. He knew nothing of Ginny's history and was startled by the frozen look on her face in response to his comment.

'I . . . actually I did have a little boy,' she said, hesitating. 'He died in an accident with my husband.' *Which was my fault,* she thought, but didn't say.

'I'm so sorry,' he said, looking mortified. 'Stupid thing for me to say. I had no idea. I thought you were one of those American single women, who put off marriage and having children until they're forty. There seem to be a lot of them these days.'

'It's all right.' She smiled pleasantly at him. The words were always hard to say, and she hated how pathetic they made her sound, and the implication of tragedy that went with them. But it seemed wrong not to acknowledge Mark and Chris's existence. It reminded both her and Rupert of how little they all knew of each other or what had led them to this kind of work. In his case, he had dropped out of medical school when he was young, and had a wife he was happy to see only a few times a year.

'I take it you have no other children?' He looked genuinely compassionate as she shook her head.

'That's what got me into this kind of work. I can be useful to someone instead of sitting home and feeling sorry for myself.'

'You're a brave woman,' he said admiringly.

The memory of looking into the East River on the anniversary of their deaths flashed instantly into her head. The only thing that had stopped her that night was meeting Blue, and she had felt differently about her life ever since. She felt more hopeful for the first time in a long time, and now she wanted to help him, too.

'Not always brave,' she said honestly. 'There have been some pretty rocky moments, but I don't have time to think about it here.'

He nodded and walked her back out into the center of the compound, well aware that even in her burqa and layers of warm clothes, she was a beautiful woman. He'd had his eye on her since she arrived, but having heard of his reputation from the others, she'd been careful not to encourage him, since he was married, and she didn't want complications in her life. She was there to work.

The comings and goings in the camp kept things interesting, and occasionally brought in new people. There was a delegation from the Human Rights High Commission in Geneva, and a group of German doctors, who were very welcome while they were there. Ginny and a few of the others rode up into the mountains with them. They delivered a baby, and examined a number of sick children. They brought two of them back to the camp with their mothers for additional medical treatment.

Two weeks before she was scheduled to leave, she went back up to the mountains again with some other members of the medical team at camp. Everything had gone smoothly so far, and her replacement was due to arrive from the New York office in another week. She was relaxed and chatting with Enzo, a young Italian medic who had arrived the week before. As they rode up the steep, rocky path on horses and mules, she and Enzo were talking about everything they wanted to eat when they got home, since food was scarce and barely edible. They passed a tricky bend in the road and rode past one of the caves where they'd always been told rebels were hiding. She and Enzo were laughing about something he had said, when a shot rang out nearby, and her horse reared up.

Ginny clutched his mane, praying he wouldn't go over the edge of the path into the steep ravine. She managed to calm him, and backed him away from it, but the horse was skittish. The Italian tried to grab the bridle and help her, just as another shot rang out closer still. Ginny looked instantly toward the leader of the group, who signaled to them to go back the way they came. And the moment he did, Enzo slumped forward on his horse with a bullet hole in the back of his head and his brain exploding from it. As soon as she looked at him, she saw that he was dead.

One of the Germans in their group swiftly grabbed his horse's reins, and led the others back down the mountain, with the entire team in hot pursuit. No other shots were fired, but Enzo had become the first casualty they'd had in nearly a year. And they didn't slow down until they reached the camp. One of the men pulled Enzo's lifeless body from his horse. They had managed not to let him fall off on the way back, and all of them were in shock at his sudden death.

The entire team met in Rupert's tent shortly afterward to discuss what security measures they would take that night. None of them had the sense that they'd been followed on the way back, and their assessment was that it had been a random lucky shot, though not lucky at all for

Enzo, whose body had been wrapped in a tarp and put on a truck, to be driven into town and sent back to Italy by the Red Cross.

Rupert warned them all to be especially careful, and he assigned the male members of the camp to stand watch that night. They had contacted the local authorities by radio, and the police had promised to come out. There was tension throughout the camp while Ginny and the others tried not to alarm the women and children. But the atmosphere had changed instantly, from easy confidence to vigilance and fear. It made Ginny realize again how dangerous their work was, and that the risks were not to be taken lightly.

Rupert called her into his tent after that. He looked somber as he sat at his makeshift desk.

'I'm sending you and some of the other women home next week. I've just been told that there was another sniper a few miles away last night. I think things may heat up here again.' Ginny knew that the worker replacing her was a man. And Rupert was very protective of all of them, male and female, and efficient and professional when he needed to be. 'I'd just be more comfortable sending some of you girls home. You've been here for two and a half months, almost your full tour of duty for the assignment. You've done your job here, that's long enough.' And the camp had been running smoothly for the past two months, more so than ever before, with Ginny's help.

'I'm willing to stay on,' Ginny said quietly. 'We just won't go back up into the mountains.' The insurgents and soldiers of the opposition rarely came down from the caves.

'I know you are. You're always willing. But it's time to go home,' he said firmly, and Ginny could see that there was no point arguing with him. He had made up his mind. She thanked him and left. It was a little bit like being in the army – you did what you were told. Rupert was very military about the way he ran the camp. You could tell that he was a retired army officer and accustomed to having his orders followed. She went back to her tent and told the other women that they were being sent home. He was keeping the men there, but wanted as many women as possible shipped out of the camp. He didn't feel right keeping them there. And the women seemed relieved when she told them. Only Ginny had said she was willing to stay, and she would have if he'd let her.

Enzo's death cast a pall over the camp for the next several days. There were no further incidents, but Rupert was adamant about sending the women home, and Ginny was at the top of that list since she was waiting to be replaced. And the day her replacement arrived, Rupert called the women into his tent again.

'You're going tomorrow,' he said quietly. 'There are strong rumors that there might be an increase in violence here soon. In fact, I think we're going to move the camp, but you're out of here.' He thanked all of them then for the fine work they'd done, and he chatted with Ginny for a few minutes when the others left the tent. 'It's been a pleasure working with you,' he told her. 'I'd heard good things about you before you got here, but the reality far exceeded the advance press.' He smiled at her. 'You're a hell of a brave woman, and you do a terrific job.' It was high praise coming from him, because he was so competent himself. 'I hope everything goes well for you when you go back. And I hope we meet again sometime in one of these crazy places. There are certainly easier areas to be in.' He had always preferred the most dangerous ones himself. He missed the adrenaline rush of combat, and he never worried about the risks to himself. He was a true warrior, and he admired that in Ginny, too. She wasn't afraid of anything. Even when Enzo was shot, she hadn't panicked, and had been strong and steady all the way back to camp, helping the rider on the other side keep Enzo's body on his horse. She had never worried about getting shot herself.

'Will you stay in New York for a while?' he asked her, making idle chitchat before she went to pack.

'I never stay for long,' she said to him with a smile. 'I'm like you. This is where I want to be. I come alive here, doing this kind of work. I get bored in New York.'

'Yes, admittedly, no one is shooting at you from caves there. That's the bit you ought to avoid.' But they both knew that it came with the territory for them, and was part of the job.

They all had a quiet but convivial dinner that night in the mess tent. And Rupert was on hand to see them off the next day. Five other women left with her, two French girls from Lyon who had arrived together six months earlier from an organization in France, an English girl, and two Germans. Ginny had gone around to the women and children she had cared for, to say goodbye to them. And as they pulled out of camp, she already missed the easy camaraderie that she enjoyed so much while she was there. And the six women chatted all the way to Asadabad, and then on to Jalalabad to catch their flight to Kabul. Only the two French girls were relieved to leave. The two Germans and the Englishwoman were as sad as Ginny to go. They all knew that it would be hard to adjust to their off-duty lives again.

They discovered while they were talking that Ginny had been doing it for three years. No one they knew had continued to do fieldwork for as long, but Ginny wouldn't have had it any other way. The last thing she wanted was a desk job in New York. This had become her life.

Only when they landed at the airport in Kabul, after the flight from Jalalabad, did she begin thinking of her life in New York again. Usually, she dreaded going home to her lonely apartment and non-existent life there. But this time she couldn't wait to get to New York. She had to find Blue. She hoped he would turn up at her apartment on the day she was meant to return. But if not, she had every intention of looking for him, and turning the city upside down to locate him. She had a strange sensation of panic, like a wave washing over her, as she worried about what would happen if she never saw him again. She knew that she'd be devastated. Whatever it took, she was going to find him.

She tried Skyping him in the airport in Kabul, got no answer, and e-mailed him before her flight took off. She tried again during her layover in London. But he wasn't answering on Skype, and had sent no response to her e-mails. Wherever he was, he was keeping very quiet. She wondered if he was back in the shed. It was early April, and it wouldn't be too cold, so she wasn't panicked. But she wanted to find him as soon as possible, and to know how he was, and why he had left school. And after she found him, she had promised Becky she would visit her father in L.A.

She fell asleep thinking of Blue on the flight back to New York, and still was when she woke up. She could see him in her mind's eye, with his mischievous glance and his most serious expression. She was wide awake when they landed. And as soon as she got to her apartment, she dropped off her bags, and then walked to the shed. But he wasn't there. The city had reclaimed it and put a padlock on the door. And with the shed no longer an option, she had no idea where he was.

She went to Houston Street the next day, without stopping for breakfast, and met with Julio Fernandez. He said Blue had never really adjusted, and had gone back to the streets, as some of the kids did. That life was familiar to them, and, in some cases, easier for them to deal with, despite the discomforts and the risks. He wished her luck trying to find him.

She called his aunt Charlene, who didn't know where he was, either. She hadn't heard from him while Ginny was away, and hadn't spoken to him now in seven months. And she reminded Ginny that she had warned her he would run.

Ginny looked for him in other shelters, and in places where she was told homeless kids hung out. She went to drop-in centers, and finally, at the end of the week, she gave up. All she could do was wait to see if he'd show up at her apartment. She had sent him several e-mails telling him she was back, all of which had gonc unanswered, and she posted a message for him on the site for homeless kids, in case his laptop had been stolen or got lost. There was nothing else she could do. And she was upset when she went to the SOS/HR office to turn in her report. They knew all about the sniper and were relieved that she hadn't gotten hurt. So was Becky, who had heard about it on the news. Their father was continuing to do better on the new medication, although they knew it was only a temporary reprieve. Eventually, he'd get worse again. The medication would keep the Alzheimer's in check for only so long. Ginny had offered to talk to him on the phone when she got back to New York, but Becky said he still got confused on the phone.

Ten days after she got back, she was shuffling aimlessly around her apartment, wondering if she'd ever see Blue again, when the office called her. They said they needed her to attend a Senate hearing in Washington, D.C., about the situation of women in Afghanistan, and they felt she was the perfect person to speak since she'd been there so recently. Normally, she would have been enthusiastic about doing it, but after her fruitless search for Blue, she wasn't in the mood. She had lost one more person that she cared about, and although he hadn't been in her life for long, he had a place in her heart now and she was depressed about not finding him, and hoped he was all right, wherever he was, and hadn't gotten hurt, or worse.

The Senate hearing was the following week, and she spent the weekend preparing her speech about the plight of women in Afghanistan. Very little had changed despite the many human rights organizations that had been there. The old customs were nearly impossible to change, and the punishment for violating them severe, often including death. She was going to report on two women who had been stoned to death, in both cases for crimes men had committed against them. Their culture was a prime example of what needed to change. But effecting those changes was a battle they had not yet won, and probably wouldn't for years.

She was due to make the speech on Monday afternoon at a subcommittee hearing on human rights. There were to be two other speakers, and she was going to be the last one. She was planning to take the Acela to Washington, and would arrive shortly after noon.

Ginny went to Penn Station and was wearing a dark blue suit and high heels, a radical change of dress for her. She was carrying a briefcase with her speech in it and her laptop, so she could work on it some more on the way down and make last-minute changes. She was just boarding the train when she happened to turn around on the platform, and saw a group of young kids run past her. They jumped off the platform and headed across the tracks to a cutout in the tunnel. She could see other kids camped out there in sleeping bags. It was a dangerous place to be if they crossed the wrong set of tracks, but the kids were clever about concealing themselves, and the security guards in the station were unaware of them.

And suddenly in their midst, she saw a familiar figure. He was wearing the old parka she had given him the night they met. And glancing to see that no one was looking, she jumped off the platform, stumbled and nearly fell, and called to him as she made her way across the tracks.

He turned at the sound of his name, and when he saw

her, he looked like he'd seen a ghost. Everything in that look told her that he had never believed she was coming back. He had thought he would never see her again, and now she was shouting his name, and making her way across the tracks toward him in high heels. He stood rooted to the spot and then walked slowly toward her. His expression was blank as they stood face-to-face next to the tracks. There was no train coming, and she was breathless from running after him, and unsteady in her shoes.

'I've been looking everywhere for you for two weeks,' she said, looking at him intensely, as his bright blue gaze met hers. 'Where were you?'

'I was here,' he said simply, waving toward the platform where the others were gathered. They were a nest of homeless kids living together.

'Why did you leave Houston Street and drop out of school?'

'I didn't like it. And school is dumb.'

She wanted to tell him that he was, too, if he thought he could get by with an incomplete eighth-grade education for the rest of his life, but she didn't say it. He knew what she thought.

'It was a stupid thing to do,' she said angrily. 'And why didn't you answer my e-mails and tell me where you were? Do you still have the laptop?'

'Yes. I thought you'd be mad at me.' He looked sheepish.

'I am, but that doesn't mean I don't care about you.' She heard them announce her train for the final call, and she couldn't stay, but at least now she knew where he was. 'I have to leave. I'm going to Washington. I'll be home late tonight. Come to the apartment tomorrow, and we'll talk.'

'I'm not going back there,' he said stubbornly, and she didn't know if he meant school or Houston Street, but she didn't have time to discuss it with him. She looked at him a last time, then reached out and hugged him, and he hugged her back.

'Come and see me. I'm not going to yell at you,' she reassured him. He nodded as she took off across the tracks. When she got back on the platform, she turned to wave at him, and he waved back, and then she ran to the Acela as fast as she could, and got in just as the doors closed. She stood watching as they pulled out of the station, and she saw him in the tunnel with the other kids. He was talking and laughing with them in the strange life that was familiar to him. He had been back on the streets for over two months while she was away, which was a long time at his age. She wondered if he'd come to her apartment. Maybe he had decided that he didn't want to be part of her life.

She was feeling disheveled as the train picked up speed. Her jacket had come unbuttoned, and she had scraped one of her shoes. She tried to calm down as she read her speech again, but her heart was pounding. She was elated that she had found him, and all she could think of now was Blue.

Chapter 7

The senator who had invited her to speak to the subcommittee on international human rights had arranged for a car and driver to meet her at Union Station in Washington. She had just enough time to stop for a sandwich on the way. She wanted to hear the other speakers, and she was ushered into the building when she got there. They were expecting her. She took her seat in the audience, and was deeply moved by the first two speakers. Both reported on atrocities against women in Africa and the Middle East. The chairman called a recess, and she had time to comb her hair and put on lipstick.

Then it was her turn, and she was led to a podium facing the committee, who were seated on a raised platform. She read the speech she had prepared about the deeply troubling state of human rights for women in Afghanistan. None of it was new information, but her delivery was powerful, and the examples she gave upset everyone in the room. She spoke for forty-five minutes, and when Ginny was finished, there was total silence as people tried to recover from what she'd said.

It felt good to do something well, and for an instant it reminded her of her years at the network, when she had enjoyed her career as a reporter. She had put all those skills away and buried them, and now she was someone else, a person who went to troubled countries, lived in miserable conditions while she was there, and tried to heal the ills of the world to the degree that it was possible. But for those few minutes in her navy blue suit and high heels, she was part of a different world again. And as she left the podium, it felt good. She was sorry Blue hadn't been there to see it. It would have been interesting for him to experience the excitement of the Senate in action and see how it worked. And speaking in front of a Senate hearing wasn't something she did every day. It even impressed her.

The chairman of the subcommittee thanked her, and she went back to her seat. A few minutes later, he thanked everyone for being there, and they were all dismissed. Several press photographers took her picture as she left the room. Outside the building she found the car waiting to take her to the station, where she boarded the Acela for New York.

She fell asleep on the train, and was back in her apartment at ten o'clock that night. It had been an exhausting day, and after she took a bath, and thought about everything that happened, she climbed into bed, wondering if Blue would show up the next day. She was afraid he wouldn't, and she was considering if she should go back to the station to talk to him again if he didn't, or just let him be. He had a right to the life he wanted, and she couldn't force him into a better one. The final choice was his.

The next morning, she was drinking a cup of coffee and reading the news online, when the bell from downstairs rang. She had been reading coverage in *The New York Times* about her speech the day before. It had gone over very well. She walked over to the intercom, hoping it was Blue, and she was thrilled to hear his voice. She buzzed him in, and the elevator brought him up a moment later. She was waiting at the door for him. He was still wearing her parka, and he looked taller to her, and slightly more mature than he had three months ago. Going back to the streets had changed him. He looked slightly less boyish and more adult. He hesitated for a minute, and she waved him to the couch where he had slept. She could see that he felt awkward in the apartment, as he took off her parka and sat down.

'Have you eaten?' He nodded, and she wondered if it was true, but she didn't insist. 'So how have you been?' she asked politely, searching his eyes for the truth. Life wasn't easy on the streets. She saw that he had brought his schoolbag, and she assumed he had the laptop in it. He had nowhere to leave his valuables now, so he had brought them with him.

'I'm okay,' he said quietly. 'I read about the human rights worker getting shot by the sniper in Afghanistan. I'm glad it wasn't you,' he said earnestly.

'I was with him. He was a really nice man,' she said, remembering Enzo. 'They sent some of us home early because of it. I've been back for almost two weeks, looking for you.' Her eyes met his, and then he looked away, avoiding her gaze.

'I'm fine,' he said again. 'It didn't feel right at Houston Street. I didn't like some of the kids.'

'I wish you had stayed there. And what about school? What are you going to do about that now? You know what I think.' He nodded.

'I don't know. Even the teachers didn't care if we did our homework. It just seemed so stupid, sitting there and wasting time every day.'

'I know it feels that way, but it's an important thing for you to do.' He almost groaned as she said it, although he knew it was true.

'I want to come back,' he said softly, barely loud enough for her to hear him as he met her eyes again.

'To stay with me?' She looked startled. She thought he had given her up, too, but he was here.

He nodded in answer, and then spoke more clearly. 'I

thought you were never coming back so it didn't matter what I did.'

'It matters a lot,' she confirmed to him. 'I told you I would come back.' He shrugged in answer.

'I didn't believe you. People always say they're coming back and never do.' And he'd been terrified she might be killed, so he'd given up on all of it and gone back to the streets.

'And what do you want to do if you stay with me again? You can't just sit here and watch TV and play games on your laptop.'

'I don't know.' He hung his head for a minute and then looked up at her.

'If you stay here, you'd have to go to school, and not drop out again. You'd have to stick with it. I'll be going away again in a month. I'd want you at the shelter while I'm gone, so I know you're okay, and not in danger living on the streets. You can come back here, Blue, but only if we agree on those things, and you live up to the commitments you make. I don't want you lounging on my couch and doing nothing, because you're too bored and lazy to go to school.'

'I hate it there, the shelter and the school. But if you make me, I'll go.'

'You have to make yourself go to school. I can't run behind you like the police, and I don't want to do that anyway. If I "make" you do any of it, you'll just run away again. You have to want what it's going to get you in the end. And if we team up here, I don't want you loose on the streets while I'm away. I'd worry myself sick about you. I did this time, and there's nothing I can do from that far away and in the kind of places that I go to. I need to know that I can count on you to do what you say you will. Just like I do, when I tell you I'll come home.' He nodded with a serious expression, and she could see that he knew she meant it. She wanted to help him, and she was willing to have him stay with her, she wanted him to, but not if he was going to run away and drop out of school when she was gone. She needed him to be more reliable than that. 'So what do you think?'

'I think I'll hate going back to school and staying at Houston Street,' he said seriously, then grinned at her. 'But I'll do it for you, because you're a good person, and I don't want to give you any trouble. Now can I come back?'

The look of gratitude on his face made her smile at him, with tears in her eyes. She was all he had in the world. She thought she had lost him when he disappeared, but now she had an idea.

'Yes, you can come back. But you can't sleep on my couch anymore.'

'That's okay,' he said matter-of-factly. 'I slept on the floor at my aunt's, and in the bathtub when her boyfriend was there. He was an asshole,' he added for good measure, which was the first time he had mentioned him. What Ginny knew about him, she had heard from Charlene. 'I can sleep on the floor here.'

'That's not what I have in mind.' She beckoned to him, and walked him back to the second bedroom that had been full of unpacked boxes since she moved in. 'I have a job for you – minimum wage of course. We're going to take this room apart, unpack the boxes, and set up a proper room for you, for when you're here. How does that sound?' His eyes lit up like a child at Christmas as he stared at her in disbelief.

'I've never had my own room before,' he said in an awed whisper. 'Not even with my mama. We slept in the same bed, but I was little then. When can we do it?' There was urgency and excitement in his eyes.

'Well, let's see,' she said, pretending to think about it. 'I've already read the newspaper. I've had a shower. I need to go to the grocery store later. Why don't we start now?' He let out a shout and threw his arms around her, and then she asked him where his things were. He said he'd left his little rolling suitcase and sleeping bag with a friend at the station, but he could pick them up anytime.

'Why don't we go out for breakfast to celebrate, pick up your things, and then come back and get to work? Tomorrow we can go out and get you a bed and a dresser and whatever you need.' She was thinking about IKEA, or a place she knew downtown that had decent furniture at reasonable prices, and she wanted to upgrade some of her own things as well. She was getting a little tired of the secondhand look, and she had already gotten three years' use out of what she'd bought for nearly nothing when she moved to New York. Suddenly, she wanted to warm the place up and turn it into a home for them.

They walked down the street together to McDonald's on a balmy April day, and the world felt like a good place to both of them. She had found him, and he was going to have his own room for the first time in his life. Both their wishes had been granted. And she told him about the camp in Afghanistan while they ate Egg McMuffins, and she mentioned the art and music high school to him again.

'Do you want me to check it out? Applications for the fall were due in September, and you're late for auditions, but I talked to them before I left. If you're serious about it, they might be willing to apply special circumstances, and accept an application now. It's a big deal if they do that. If they do, and they accept you, you have to be responsible about it, you can't drop out or run away. I'd be putting my word on the line to vouch for you,' she said solemnly, and Blue looked impressed. 'And you'd have to audition, if they let you. That shouldn't be a problem for you. Maybe you'd enjoy school if you were doing something you love.'

'If I can play the piano every day, I'll like it,' he said,

stuffing another muffin into his mouth. He was eating as if he hadn't seen food in three months.

After breakfast they took the subway to Penn Station. She followed him down the stairs, then waited on the platform while he went to find his friends on the ledge where they all slept at night. No one was there except a boy who looked about sixteen. Ginny watched Blue pick up his things, and talk for a few minutes with him. Blue had told her that there were no girls in the group, and they'd been sleeping there all winter. No one bothered them, and it was a good place to stay when it was cold. He was back with her a moment later, with his bag in his hand, and his sleeping bag under his arm. It was looking tattered and dirty, and she suggested they get a new one. With that, he ran back and gave it to his friend, which touched her, as the other boy took it gratefully from him.

Then they went back to her apartment and got to work. Ginny turned an overhead light on and looked at the markings on the boxes. She had never bothered to before, and she suddenly realized how much of it was sentimental. There were boxes marked 'baby pictures,' another one marked 'wedding,' and other boxes Becky had packed that weren't labeled at all. She started with those, and was shocked to see photographs of herself, Chris, and Mark in silver frames, and some knick-knacks from their living room, some of which had been wedding presents. There were some fur cushions and a beautiful cashmere throw. They were things Becky had thought she might use again. There was a beautiful antique tortoiseshell dresser set that Mark had given her for her birthday, leatherbound books she had given him, and a box of Chris's teddy bears and favorite toys, which made her gasp when she opened it, and she closed it immediately. Some things were still too painful to see even now. There was an empty closet she had never used in the front hall, where she was planning to put the things she wouldn't use, or was saving only out of sentiment, like the baby pictures and wedding album. But a lot of the other things she was happy to see again. Becky had chosen well.

They sifted through all of it by early afternoon, and among other things, she knew she wanted to buy a bookcase for her favorite books. She had taken several of the framed photographs out and put them around the living room. She felt as though she could live with them again. Blue's lively presence was a buffer against her loneliness and grief when she looked at them. He picked up each of the photographs carefully and stared intently at Mark and Chris's faces, as though trying to get to know them through the photos.

'He was really cute,' Blue said softly, as he set a photograph of Chris down gently on her desk.

'Yeah, he was,' Ginny agreed with tears in her eyes, and as she turned away, Blue patted her shoulder, and she turned to smile at him as tears rolled down her cheeks. 'Thank you. I'm okay. I just miss them a lot sometimes. That's why I keep running away to crazy places like Afghanistan and Africa. I don't have time to think when I'm there.' Blue nodded as though he understood. He had his own way of escaping the memories, like dropping out of school and running away. But they both knew that you could never run far enough or fast enough to get away from the pain completely. It was always waiting nearby, and a sound, a smell, or a memory could bring it back to mind.

She looked at her watch then and decided they had time to go downtown. She had a sense of what they needed, and had measured the room. There was enough space for a single bed, a desk, a dresser, and a chair. She wanted the bookcase, too, and whatever else they could find. The place she wanted to go to was on the Lower East Side.

'How're we going to get the stuff back uptown?' Blue asked worriedly.

She smiled. 'They deliver,' she answered with a straight face, and he laughed. It had been hard going through her boxes, and he hated to see her cry, but she'd seemed happy to find a lot of her old stuff.

As soon as they got to the store, they got busy picking new things. Ginny found a bookcase she liked for the living room that looked like an antique, and she bought a new desk to replace the ugly one she had. Her dining table was fairly decent, but she bought four matching chairs, and a slightly battered leather one that would go with the recliner. The pièce de résistance was a couch covered in dark gray flannel that was part of a sample sale. She hadn't bought that much furniture at once since they'd decorated the house in Beverly Hills, and this was a far cry from what she'd had there, but it suited her life now. And then they looked at bedroom furniture for Blue. He stood, seeming paralyzed as he looked around.

'What do you like? Old-looking stuff? Modern? White? Wood finish?' It touched her heart to see him so overwhelmed, and he gravitated almost immediately to a masculine-looking set that was painted navy blue. It had a desk, a chest, and a headboard for the bed. Then his face lit up when he saw a red leather chair. Ginny picked out a couple of lamps for the room, and a small red area rug that matched the chair. All put together, it was almost grown-up, but not quite. It had the right feeling for a boy his age.

She had some prints and posters in the boxes, from her old kitchen, that she was going to hang on the walls. And the fur pillows Becky had salvaged for her were going to look great on the new couch. Her living room was going to be mostly beiges and grays now. She had decided to keep her own bedroom the way it was, since the furniture was in decent condition and all of it was white. And she had found a white Mongolian lamb rug in one of the boxes that she was going to use in her bedroom. Her whole apartment was about to get a major lift. She paid for all of it, and arranged for delivery the next day, and for an additional charge they were going to haul away whatever she no longer wanted, which was most of what she had. They had done a good day's work.

They stopped in Chinatown after their shopping expedition, ate a delicious meal at a restaurant she loved, and then headed back to the apartment. Blue wanted to watch a movie on TV when they got home, but Ginny reminded him that he had school the next day. He groaned when she said it, and then at a look from her, he held up both hands in surrender.

'Okay, okay, I know.'

And when he went to sleep on the couch that night, after she made it up as a bed for him, she told him to kiss it goodbye, since it would be gone the next day when he came home from school.

He dragged his feet when he left in the morning, but he went. And Ginny printed out an application to LaGuardia Arts high school, as they had told her to do, while she waited for the furniture to come. She read the application carefully, and saw again that Blue would need to audition. They were several months past all the deadlines, but if they did allow him to apply and audition, he had a chance. The principal, whom Ginny had spoken to, had said that the exception they might make for him involved timing, but they would make no allowances for poor testing or a bad audition. He had to be qualified, like everyone else, and Ginny thought that was fair. She left the form sitting on her desk, and sent Charlene an e-mail that he was staying with her again, just so she knew.

And as soon as the furniture arrived, Ginny was busy, telling them where to put it, watching them move the old things out. The overall effect was magical when the pieces were all in place. After the deliverymen left, she put the fur pillows on the gray couch, which was perfect, and the lamb rug in her bedroom. She had a few other velvet cushions that she put on the couch, too, and a soft beige mohair one in the leather chair. She took out more photographs of her parents, Becky, Mark, and Chris, and put them around, then hung some art photographs and posters. The trunk she was using as a coffee table still looked all right, with the old travel stickers on it, and she set some magazines down on it. The four new dining chairs were a vast improvement, and she filled the bookcase with her books.

Then she went to work on Blue's room. All the dark blue pieces looked beautiful, and the red rug and chair added just the right amount of color. She hung three bright posters in the room, plugged in the lamps she'd bought, and made the bed. The apartment looked like a different place by that afternoon.

When Blue came home from school, she let him in, and his eyes widened in amazement.

'Whoa! Whose house is this? It's like one of those decorating shows where the people leave home and a decorator comes in and makes it all look good, and then everyone cries when they see it again.'

'Thank you, Blue,' she said, touched by what he said. And then he went to check out his bedroom and there was silence in the room. She glanced in, and he was standing still in the middle of the room, staring at it all in disbelief. The posters she had hung looked great, the lamps were lit, and the bed was made with clean sheets, a blanket, and a bedspread, waiting for him. He turned to look at her then.

'Why did you do this for me?' he said, suddenly realizing how much she had done. It had all looked different in the furniture store. Now it felt like a home, and for now anyway, he lived there with her.

'You deserve it, Blue,' she said softly, patting his shoulder, as he had done to comfort her the day before. 'You deserve an amazing life.' He had improved her life immeasurably, and now she had a home, too, not just an apartment full of mismatched ugly furniture where she stayed between trips. It had taken her three years to open the boxes full of familiar things. Blue had given her the strength to do it and inspired her. Some of it was still painful to see, but she had put just the right number of photographs out – without feeling overwhelmed. And she was ready to live with them again.

They made dinner together that night, and she put candlesticks on the table, and lit the candles. And then she showed Blue the application to LaGuardia Arts. He glanced at it nervously.

'I don't think I could get in,' he said, looking defeated as he flipped through it.

'Why don't you let them decide that?' she said calmly. She had checked back with them that afternoon and they were willing to let him apply and audition late. It was an extraordinary opportunity. She didn't push him about it, or want to overwhelm him. He had homework to do after dinner. She left him to it while she did the dishes, and thought about how drastically her life had changed since he had come into it. She looked into the living room from the kitchen while she dried her hands, and saw him working at the dining table, with his head bent over his books. The new furniture was perfect in the room. There was a homey feeling to it, and as she stood admiring it, he glanced up and smiled at her.

'What are you looking at?' he asked her, suddenly self-conscious.

'The place looks nice, doesn't it?' It was so great having someone to talk to and share things with, and do projects with. Their lives had collided at just the right time, for both of them. She hadn't once thought of throwing herself into the river since that awful night of the anniversary, the night before Christmas Eve, and now she had familiar objects around the apartment, and a boy who needed her and, more than anything, needed a chance in life and a lucky break. All she could do was hope that she was it. Just thinking about it made her life worthwhile.

She put the kitchen towel back on the rack and turned off the light. And Blue went back to doing his homework. That night he slept in his own bed and bedroom for the first time. She was just drifting off to sleep when he pounded on the wall, and she wondered if something was wrong as she leaped out of bed and heard him shout to her.

'Thank you, Ginny!'

She smiled and sat back down. 'You're welcome. Sleep tight!' she called, and slipped into her bed with a smile.

Chapter 8

It took some time to get his old transcripts together, and the recommendations he needed, but she and Blue finally filled out the application to LaGuardia Arts for the fall with an essay about how much it meant to him. And the next day, Ginny dropped it off to the admissions office herself. And he had an appointment for an audition the following week. He was nervous about it. She was doing all she could to reassure him so he wouldn't panic, and she had promised to go with him. She had called the vice principal at his current school, and made every possible excuse for him and explained his home situation. She told him about the application to LaGuardia Arts and practically begged him to do what he could to help Blue get in. He said it would be a stretch, given Blue's poor attendance record, but he admitted that his grades were good, and that he was capable, and he had written a strong recommendation for him. He told Ginny that if Blue kept his grades up in his final exams, and turned in the papers he hadn't finished yet, he'd graduate in June. Ginny impressed on Blue the importance of that if he wanted to go to LaGuardia, which would be a lot more fun and interesting than a regular school.

They were walking down the street talking about it, and she asked him which term papers he still had due. She had suddenly become the substitute mother of a teenager, with all that it entailed, although it was part-time duty for her, since she was away for three months out of four and had only known him for four and a half months, but it was still a learning process for them both.

They walked past a church then, and she stopped, as she often did. She liked lighting candles for Chris and Mark. Blue waited patiently outside for her. He wouldn't set foot in the church. And this time, when she came out, he looked bothered.

'Why do you do that? It just gives money to the priests, and they're a bunch of liars and crooks. They don't need the money.' He sounded harsh as he said it.

'It makes me feel good,' she said simply. 'I'm not praying to the priests. It gives me comfort to light candles. I've been doing it since I was a kid.' He didn't comment as they walked along, and she decided to be brave and ask him about his contempt for priests and churches and all things religious. His anger toward all of it was obvious, and his evident hatred for the priests was almost rabid at times. She knew his mother had sung in a choir, so religion couldn't be completely foreign to him. 'Why do you hate priests so much, Blue?'

'I just do. They're bad people. They make everyone think they're good, but they're not.'

'Like who?' She was curious now, he was so adamant about it. 'Did you know a bad priest when you were a little kid?' She wondered if it was some kind of association with his mother's death.

'Yeah, Father Teddy,' he answered, with a look of fury on his face that surprised her. 'He's the priest at my aunt's church. He used to play with me in the basement.' She nearly fell over when he said it, and tried not to seem panicked or overly impressed.

'What do you mean, "play with you"?' she asked, trying to sound casual about it, but suddenly a flashing red light went off in her head. And it was a measure of his trust in her that he brought it up.

'He kissed me,' Blue said, looking straight at her then, with his piercing blue eyes that went straight to her soul. 'He made me kiss him, too. He said God would like that and wanted me to.'

'How old were you?'

'I don't know. It was after my mom died, maybe nine or ten. He let me play the piano they had in the basement for church socials, but he said he'd get in trouble if I told, so I had to keep it a secret. I couldn't tell anyone he let me go there. I played all afternoon sometimes – that's when he'd make me kiss him. I'd probably have done damn near anything to play that piano. Sometimes he'd sit on the bench with me, and once he kissed me on the neck, and then he . . . you know . . . he did stuff . . . I didn't want to do it, but he said I couldn't come back anymore if I didn't let him.' Ginny felt almost faint as she steeled herself. The vision of the scene he was describing was making her feel sick. She wanted to ask him a vital question, but she didn't know how to phrase it so it wouldn't make him feel ashamed.

'Did he . . . did you do it with him?' she asked, trying to look as bland and non-judgemental as she could, while feeling rage at the priest who would do such a thing to him, and abuse a child.

Blue shook his head. 'No, I didn't do it. I think he wanted to. But I stopped going before he could. He just touched me, a bunch of times . . . you know . . . there . . . and put his hand down my pants while I was playing. He said he didn't mean to do it, but my playing was so good that it tempted him. He said it was my fault, and I'd be in a lot of trouble if I told anyone, for tempting a priest like that. He said I might even go to jail like my daddy. He scared me.

'I didn't mean to tempt him, or get in trouble with God, or go to jail, so I stopped going to play the piano. He whispered to me after church and asked me to come back, but I never did. He used to visit my aunt on Sundays after church. She thought he was the best thing that ever happened, and said he was a saint.'

'Did you ever tell her what he did to you?'

'I tried to once . . . I told her that he kissed me, and she said I was a liar and I would go to hell for saying bad things about Father Teddy. Between hell and jail, I never told her the rest. She wouldn't have believed me anyway. I've never told anyone except you.' He sensed how much faith she had in him, and he had felt comfortable sharing the secret he had carried for four years.

'You know that what he did was wrong, don't you, Blue? That *he* was wrong, and none of that was your fault. You didn't "tempt" him. He's a very sick person, and he was trying to blame you for what he did.'

'Yeah, I know,' Blue said, looking like a child again, as his eyes bored into hers. 'That's why I told you priests are liars and crooks. I think he just let me play the piano so he could do that.' He was dead on with that, Ginny knew. It had been a hideous plot to seduce an innocent child, and a total violation of his position of trust in the boy's life. It was horrifying. She was just grateful that he hadn't raped him. He could have easily in the church basement with no one else around. It occurred to her that other little boys in the parish might not have been as lucky. Thank God the lure of the piano hadn't been enough for Blue to allow the priest to abuse him further. And she hoped for Blue's sake that that was true.

'He's a terrible person, Blue. People go to prison for doing things like that.'

'Nah, they'd never send Father Teddy to jail. Everybody loves him, including Charlene. I always went out when he showed up on Sundays. I didn't want to be around him. And I told Charlene I was sick every time she went to church. After a while, she stopped asking and just let me stay home. I've never been to church again, and I never will. He's a disgusting old guy.' The memory of it made him shudder.

'I'm sorry, Blue.' And then she added, 'It's not right that no one knows. What if he does it to others?'

'He probably did. Jimmy Ewald said he hated him, too. I never asked him why, but I can guess. He was twelve and an altar boy, and his mama loved Father Teddy. Everybody did. She used to bake him cakes. Charlene always gave him money, even though she needed it for her kids. He's really a bad guy.' After what he had just told her, it sounded like a major understatement to her.

Ginny was quiet on the way back to the apartment, thinking about what he'd said. She didn't want to upset him further by asking more, or make him feel embarrassed for telling her. But she was shaken to the core by the thought of him as a nine- or ten-year-old child, being molested by a priest. It was the kind of thing one read about in the newspapers, but it had never occurred to her that it could happen to someone she knew. Blue had been vulnerable, his mother dead, his father in prison, and his aunt completely snowed by the twisted priest. It was no wonder Blue refused to go to church. And she was deeply touched that he had confided in her. She wanted to do something about it, but had no idea where to start or if it was a good idea. And she just hoped that he was telling her the whole story, and that he hadn't been sodomized by the priest. The thought of that possibility made her sick for him. She truly hoped it wasn't the case. What he had told her was bad enough and could affect him psychologically forever. The poor child had been through so much. And his faith in her now seemed like an even bigger gift.

Ginny cooked dinner, and Blue worked on one of his remaining term papers afterward, about the impact of advertising on children watching TV, for his social science class, while Ginny pretended to read a book, but all she could think about was what he had shared with her about 'Father Teddy' that afternoon. She was haunted by the thought of Blue in a church basement, playing the piano, with the priest's hand down his pants, and blaming him for 'tempting' him, and threatening him with jail.

She could hardly sleep that night as thoughts of it came to her again and again. Blue hadn't mentioned it that evening, and she wondered if it haunted him, too, if he had nightmares about it sometimes. He had sounded angry but calm when he talked about it.

The next morning, after he left for school, Ginny stood at the window of her apartment, lost in thought. There was someone she wanted to call, just to talk to him about it. Kevin Callaghan was an old friend from her network news days – they'd known each other for years and been very close. But like everyone, she had severed her ties with him when Mark and Chris died and she moved to New York. She had wanted no link to her past, and they hadn't spoken in more than three years. But she was aching to call him now. He was the best investigative reporter in the business. If anyone would, he would know what to do, how others handled it, and what the procedures were. And he'd know about the possible fallout for Blue. She didn't want to do anything to harm him, but the sheer injustice of it, of exploiting a child that way, made her want to go after the priest on Blue's behalf. She didn't know if it would be the right thing to do. And until she knew more, she didn't want to say anything to Blue.

She waited until noon in New York, when she knew Kevin would be in the office in L.A. at nine a.m., if he wasn't out tracking down a story. Criminal matters were his specialty, and she had a feeling he'd be up to date on this issue, about priests who had molested kids. Talking to him would be emotional for her, since he and Mark had been good friends. And her hand was shaking when he answered his cell phone, and she heard his familiar voice.

'Kev? It's Ginny,' she said in a voice hoarse with emotion, and was met with a long pause.

'Ginny who?' He didn't recognize her voice, and the last thing he expected, after all this time, was to hear from her.

'Ginny Carter. Nice of you to forget,' she teased him, and he let out a shout once he knew who it was.

'Nice of you not to call me for three years, or return my calls or respond to my e-mails and texts!' He had tried to reach her for nearly a year, and finally gave up. He had contacted her sister, to find out how she was, and Becky had told him she was a zombie, spoke to no one, had cut her ties to everyone, and worked for the SOS/HR, in terrifying places all over the world, trying to get herself killed, which was how she saw it. He had been sorry to hear it, although he admired what she was doing. He had written her a number of e-mails, particularly on the first anniversary, and she hadn't responded to anything he sent, so he hadn't written to her again. He figured that if she ever wanted to speak to him, she'd call him. But he had stopped hoping years before. And now suddenly here she was.

'I'm sorry,' Ginny said, sounding apologetic. It touched

her just hearing his voice again – it was a little bit like reaching out to Mark, because they'd been so close. That was why she'd never answered him – it just hurt too much. But in this case, it was different. She was doing it for Blue. 'I've been trying to forget who I am for the last three years. It's been working well for me so far,' she said honestly. She was no longer a wife or mother, and in her own eyes she no longer had an identity without them. She was just a human rights worker being sent from one assignment to the next in the most godforsaken places in the world; she felt like a ghost of who she'd been. 'I missed you, though,' she said quietly. 'Sometimes I think of you from a mountaintop somewhere, and send you good vibes. I've been to some amazing places. I never thought I could do it, but it gives my life meaning.' Nothing else had anymore, until Blue. 'You wouldn't recognize me, I haven't worn makeup or combed my hair in three years,' except for the Senate hearing, when she'd even worn heels. The rest of the time she looked like a hitchhiker and didn't care.

'That's a damn shame,' he said regretfully. 'You were always so cute. I bet you still are.'

'It's not the same, Kev,' she said with strong emotion. 'It's all different, but it is what it is.' She had made the best of it and was helping others. He was one of the few people she thought would understand it, unlike her sister, to whom she was a mystery, and maybe always had been. She was beginning to think so.

'Are you doing okay?' he asked her gently. 'I'd ask you to Skype with me, but I'd probably cry. I've missed you, too. It's not like the old days with the three of us together.' He'd had some hot romances, and lived with a couple of women, but had never married. And she realized that by now he was forty-four years old.

'I'm doing okay,' she answered his question. 'You're not married yet?'

'Nah, I think I missed the boat. I'm too comfortable the way I am. The girls seem to get younger and younger, though. The last one was twenty-two years old, a weather girl on another channel, fresh out of USC. It's a little embarrassing, but I'm having too much fun to give it up.' He was a very handsome man, and women had never been able to resist him. She and Mark used to tease him about it. 'So what made you drop from the skies?' he finally asked her. 'Just saying hi?' He knew her better than that, and suspected there was a reason for her call. Ginny had always been incredibly professional and focused, even when they were having fun.

'I'm in kind of an interesting situation,' she admitted to him. 'I have an unofficially adopted kid – well, not really. Our paths crossed a few months ago, and I guess you could say I'm mentoring him. He's a homeless kid, an orphan. He's thirteen. He's staying with me right now, and he stayed with me a few months ago. My sister thinks I'm nuts, but he's a great kid, a bright boy. I'm trying to get him on the right path here, get him into high school. I'm not in town much, I'm on the road for SOS/HR for three and four months at a time, and I come back to New York for a month till I'm reassigned and head out again. I'm trying to do what I can for him while I'm here. He's a really, really nice kid.'

Kevin waited as she went on, intrigued by what she'd said. On the one hand, he couldn't see her taking on a homeless teenager, but on the other hand, he wondered if having someone to take care of again might save her. She had been such a great wife and mother, and her personal compass had been broken ever since.

'We were talking yesterday and he told me something that stopped me in my tracks. We've all read it before, for the past few years. It's not a new story, but this is a kid I really care about. He was molested by a priest when he was nine. It's just like in the movies, only worse because it's real. Dark basement, the priest luring him to church by letting him use the piano, telling him they had to keep it a secret or the priest would get in trouble. Sitting next to the boy at the piano, kissing him, hand down his pants, then accusing him of "tempting" the priest, so it's supposed to be the boy's fault it happened, and threatening him with jail if he ever told. That meant a lot to the kid since his father was in prison at the time, his mother was already dead. And his aunt thinks this priest is a saint. He tried to tell her, but she wouldn't listen.' It was a typical story they'd all seen on the news, as they both knew.

'God, I hate those guys,' Kevin said in an angry tone. 'It seems even worse to me since I'm Catholic and knew such great priests growing up. Priests who do this are an abscess on the ass of the church. I loathe them, and they give the whole church a bad name. The church ought to throw them out of the priesthood and put them all in jail, not protect them.' But a lot of that had been in the news, too, with their crimes concealed by their superiors and the individual churches. She had known instinctively that Kevin would be the right one to call, and it gave her an excuse to talk to him and connect again. 'Did he rape the boy?' Kevin asked, intrigued by the story, and happy to talk to her.

'I don't think so. Blue says he didn't, but who knows? He might have repressed it. He was very young.'

'You ought to get him to a shrink and see what they say. They might turn something up with hypnosis. If he's lucky, it was no worse than a kiss and a hand in the pants. It's a total violation of trust, not to mention criminal child and sexual abuse.' Kevin was reacting as violently as she had, and it was a relief to talk to him about it. It gave validation to everything she felt herself.

'I don't know what to do, Kev, or where to start. Who do I talk to? Who do I go to? Or do I leave it alone? If we bring charges against the priest, will it make it worse for

Blue, or is it better to punish the molester? I thought about it all night.'

'I take it Blue is the kid?'

'Yes, he has incredible blue eyes.'

'So do you,' he said gently. He had always had a crush on her, but would never have done anything about it – she had been his best friend's wife. Now she no longer was, but he still felt she was off-limits. Hitting on her even over three years later would have still seemed disrespectful to Mark. 'To tell you the truth, I don't know what the procedure is,' he admitted. 'I've heard the stories about it, like everyone else, but don't know much more. Why don't you let me check it out? Besides, it'll give me a reason to talk to you again,' he said with a warm tone in his voice and she smiled.

'I won't disappear on you again,' she said softly. 'I'm better now. Although I'll be back out in the field again in a few weeks. I just got back from Afghanistan.'

'Shit. Nowhere near the human rights guy who got killed by the sniper a few weeks ago, I hope.'

'I was riding in the mountains with him. His horse was cheek to jowl with mine when he got shot. We worked in the same camp.'

'Ginny, that's serious business. Don't risk your life like that.' It sobered him to hear it, and he knew how distraught Mark would have been to think of her in a situation like the one she described.

'What else have I got to do?' she said honestly. 'At least this gives my life purpose and meaning, and I'm useful to someone.'

'It sounds like you're doing a lot for this homeless kid. And you can't help him if you get killed.'

'That's what he says, too. But I love what I do.'

Kevin knew human nature, and he had the ugly feeling that she had been risking her life intentionally, maybe even suicidally, since the death of her husband and child, which he knew was what her sister thought, too. The phenomenon wasn't uncommon, sometimes with tragic results.

'We'll talk about that later,' Kevin said practically. 'I want to check this priest thing out for you. Do you know if he's still at the same parish?'

'I was so stunned by the story, I never thought to ask. I could check it out, or ask Blue. He may not know. He hasn't been back to church since.'

'Just out of curiosity, why don't you find out if the guy's still there, or was moved? Maybe there were complaints about him. That would be good to know.'

'Blue says there's another boy who hates him, and he thinks he did the same thing to him. He was older. The other boy was twelve.'

'Hang on to all this info, and let me find out the procedure for reporting something like this. And then your boy has to be willing, of course. A lot of victims prefer to stay in the shadows forever and don't complain. That's how guys like this get away with it. Everyone's afraid to rock the boat. Or some people are – not "everyone" anymore, thank God. I'll call you when I know something. And check out the whereabouts of the priest.'

'I'll do that,' she promised. 'And Kev, thank you. Really, thank you. It was great talking to you.'

'I'm not letting you disappear again,' he warned her, 'even if you run off to Afghanistan. I wish you wouldn't do that, though. There has to be something equally useful you can do here instead of halfway around the world, in situations where you might get killed.'

'There really isn't. They need us so badly in the places I go.'

'I never figured you for a Mother Teresa type. You were so glamorous on the air.' She and Mark had really been the golden couple of network news, and now she was in Afghanistan riding a mule. He just couldn't see it, but she seemed committed to it, which worried him. He was going to try to talk her out of it, if he could. But he knew how stubborn she was, and he doubted he'd be successful. She sounded like she was on a holy mission, and with the boy, too. He admired what she was doing for him, and he thought she was right to check it out. The boy deserved to be avenged and have the perpetrator punished and put in prison. Kevin hoped Ginny would follow through. 'I'll call you as soon as I know something. Take care, and behave yourself till then.'

'I will. I promise.' She felt better when she hung up. He had been exactly the right person to call.

She didn't say anything to Blue about it that night. She didn't want to until she had concrete information. She wanted Father Teddy's last name, and to know if he was still there, but she thought she could get the information from the parish, if she was clever about it. She wanted to see him for herself.

She was thinking about it that night after she'd gone to bed, when the phone rang. It was Becky. It was rare for her to call so late, which was dinnertime for her in California, when she was always busy with her husband and kids, and cooking dinner for them.

'Something wrong?'

'Dad fell today and broke his arm,' she said, sounding distressed. 'He got lost again. I think the medicine stopped working. We took him to the hospital, and he had no idea who I was. He still doesn't. He might be better in the morning, in daylight, but Ginny, you've got to come out. Dad just isn't going to last forever, and he's getting worse. If you don't come now, and wait till you come home again, I think he'll be gone by then. Or his mind will be. Even if he doesn't recognize you now, at least he's lucid some of the time.' She sounded like she was at her wit's end, and Ginny felt sorry for her.

'I'm sorry, Becky. I'll do what I can. Maybe I can come out this weekend.' She thought about it quickly. She didn't want to pull Blue out of school. She didn't want to do anything to jeopardize his graduating in June. But she hadn't said anything to Becky yet about his staying with her again. And she didn't like the idea of leaving him at Houston Street for the weekend – she would be away for a long time soon enough. 'If I come out,' she said, 'I have to bring someone with me.'

Her sister sounded startled at the other end. 'Are you seeing someone?' Ginny hadn't said a word to her about it.

'Yes, but not the way you think. Blue is staying with me again. I'm trying to get him into a very special high school. In fact, he has an audition and interview there next week, so the weekend would work.'

'Oh my God, not that again. For heaven's sake, what are you thinking? The last thing you need is a homeless teenage boy in your apartment, or your life.'

'He's doing very well.'

'Are you fostering him?' She just couldn't understand what Ginny was doing. It sounded like she'd lost her mind.

'No, I'm mentoring him. But he's staying with me while I'm in town.' The concept was so foreign to Becky that it made no sense to her at all. Nothing Ginny did now made sense to her. But Becky was too tired to think about it.

She had her father to deal with. And at least Ginny had agreed to come to L.A. It was long overdue, and she was glad that she had finally convinced her.

'I don't want to impose on you,' Ginny said respectfully, 'especially since there are two of us. We'll stay at a hotel.'

'We still have a guest room, and the boy can sleep in Charlie's room, if he behaves himself.' She made him sound like a savage. Ginny tried not to react.

'He's very polite. I think you'll like him.' At least she hoped so, but they weren't going to stay long. She was thinking about flying out on Friday afternoon after school, and coming back on the red-eye on Sunday night, to get Blue to school on Monday morning. It was going to be a short trip. 'I'll e-mail you what flight we're on,' she told Becky, and a few minutes later they hung up.

Ginny thought about it afterward, and how upsetting it would be to see her father in that condition. And it would be the first time she had seen Becky and her family in three and a half years. She felt nervous about it. She hoped it would go all right.

She told Blue about it in the morning, and he was excited to go to California. She told him why they were going, because her father was sick and old, but he said he was looking forward to meeting her sister and her kids. He was very upbeat about it, which cheered her up, too. And after he left for school, it occurred to her to call his aunt. Fortunately she was there and answered on the first ring. She told her that she was going to L.A. and was planning to take Blue with her.

'Would you mind signing a letter for me?' Ginny asked her. 'He's a minor, and I don't have custody of him. If someone at the airline asks me for paperwork of some kind, I don't want them to think I'm kidnapping him.'

'It's no problem,' Charlene said willingly, and they agreed to meet at Mt. Sinai hospital again that night, as they had for the school permission. Ginny drew up the letter for her, and they took care of it in two minutes in the cafeteria.

Then Charlene looked at her. She still couldn't understand why Ginny was doing this for Blue, but it was a very nice thing to do. She suspected that Ginny was a very lonely woman, to be so open to taking Blue into her home and life.

'How's he doing?' Charlene asked her as they walked out together.

'He's doing great,' Ginny said with a confident smile. 'He's graduating from eighth grade in June.'

'If he sticks it out,' Charlene added, from experience. She had no faith in his ability to stay in school.

'He will,' Ginny said with a determined look, and they both laughed. She was dying to ask her what Father Teddy's last name was, but she didn't want to arouse her suspicions. Instead, she asked her conversationally what her parish was, and Charlene proudly said it was St. Francis's. To cover her tracks and her interest in it, Ginny told her that she hadn't gotten Blue to church yet, but she was sure she would.

'Don't count on it,' Charlene said knowingly. 'He hates going to church. I finally gave up.' Ginny wondered if she even remembered Blue telling her that the priest had kissed him. It sounded like she had just dismissed it as a childish lie.

Ginny thanked her again for signing the letter, Charlene went back to work, and Ginny took a cab back to the apartment where Blue was getting ready for bed. She had already laid out his travel clothes for the next day. She had bought him another pair of jeans, khaki pants, three collared shirts, a thin windbreaker, a new pair of high-top Converse, and new underwear and socks. She wanted to give him the best chance with her sister that she could. She didn't think new Converse alone would do it – it would take a lot more than that to win Becky over. But Ginny had faith that Blue would behave well and hold his own with her family in L.A. He was thrilled about the trip, though sorry that her father was sick.

'Sleep tight,' she said, stooping to kiss him once he was in bed. She had just checked his suitcase again, and he had everything he needed, including new pajamas.

'I love you, Ginny,' he said softly as she kissed him, and she smiled at him, startled to hear the words. It had been so long since anyone had said that to her, especially a child.

'I love you, too,' she said, smiling, and turned off the light, and went back to her room to pack her own suitcase for the trip. She just hoped it would go all right.

Chapter 9

Ginny picked Blue up at school in a cab on Friday afternoon, and went straight to the airport with him. She had spoken to Becky that morning, and their father was a little better during the day. And Ginny had Charlene's permission letter in her purse. When they got to the airport, she checked their bags, and they went inside. She suggested they go through security early and buy magazines for the flight.

'Can you buy them in the airport?' Blue asked with a surprised look. And she realized then that Blue had never been in an airport or flown anywhere. He had never left New York City, and the only place he'd seen an airport was in movies or on TV.

'You can buy all kinds of things.' Ginny smiled at him as they stood in line at security, and she told him to take the coins out of his pockets, remove his belt, and shoes. And he put his laptop in one of the plastic bins, as Ginny put hers in another one, and got one more bin for her purse and shoes. And then they went through and picked everything up again. Blue was fascinated by the process and watched everything intently. This was a major adventure for him. She was only sorry they wouldn't have more time. She would have liked to show him around L.A. She had some trepidation about going out there, because of the memories it held for her, but she tried to keep her attention on Blue.

They looked around the bookstore, where she bought a paperback for the trip, and magazines for him. They bought gum and candy, and stopped at a souvenir store. He was hungry after school, so they bought a hot dog, and he ate it before they boarded their flight. She had never done as much in an airport on the way to a flight. Usually she just went straight through after security and got on the plane, but he wanted to see everything. He looked jubilant by the time they boarded and took their seats. She gave him the window so he could look out. After they put their hand luggage overhead and sat down, he turned to her nervously.

'It won't crash, will it?' he asked anxiously.

'It shouldn't,' she said, smiling at him. 'Think of all the flights that are taking off and landing right now, and are in the air, all over the world. Thousands and thousands of them. When was the last time you heard of one crashing?' she asked him.

'I can't remember.'

'Exactly. So I think we'll be okay.' He looked reassured. She told him to fasten his seatbelt, and he was excited to hear that there would be a movie and a meal.

'Can I order whatever I want?' he asked her.

'They give you a choice of a couple of things, but you'll have to wait till we get there for a burger and fries.' It touched her to see how new it all was to him, and he looked excited on takeoff, and not scared as the jumbo plane lifted off the ground. He looked out the window for a while, then read a magazine. He took the small video screen when they offered it to him, and selected the movie he wanted to see. Ginny was doing the same, and they both put their headphones on. He was loving the newness of all of it, and he chose what he wanted to eat when they handed him the menu. He ate while watching the movie, and afterward he fell asleep, as she covered him with the blanket. No one had asked for the letter, or questioned why she was traveling with him, or even if they were related.

She woke him before they landed in L.A., so he could see it from the air. He was fascinated when he saw all the lights and swimming pools below, and when the big plane touched the ground, bumped twice, and rolled down the runway to the terminal. Blue had just completed his first flight. She grinned at him. She had almost forgotten why they were there: so she could see her father possibly for the last time. She felt as though she had just come home, even after so much time away. She realized now that L.A. would always be home to her.

'Welcome to L.A.,' she said as they joined the crowd in the aisle waiting to get off the plane, and a minute later they were in the terminal, heading for baggage claim. She had told her sister she would rent a car at the airport so they didn't have to pick her up. And as she stood at the rental desk, she hoped Becky and her family would be nice to Blue. She didn't want him to have a bad time, or feel uncomfortable with her sister's kids. His life experience had been different from theirs in every way. They were the typical suburban family with a mother, a father, a house, a pool, two cars, and three kids. Nothing untoward had ever happened to them. Their kids did well in school, and Charlie, their oldest, had just been accepted at UCLA. Their youngest, Lizzie, and Blue were the same age. She couldn't imagine her sister's children and Blue having anything in common, but she hoped they'd be polite to him at least.

The rental car company at the airport gave her a brand-new SUV, which Blue thought was exciting, and they headed into the traffic on the freeway, toward Pasadena. They had taken a five o'clock flight out of New York, and with the time difference, it was eight o'clock in L.A., as people headed home or out for dinner, on a Friday night, or left work late. The traffic was worse than ever, and it was eighty degrees. Blue loved it and was grinning from ear to ear.

'Thank you for bringing me with you,' he said, looking at her shyly. 'I thought you'd leave me at Houston Street for the weekend.' He was thrilled she hadn't and grateful for everything she did for him.

'I thought you'd have fun here, even if I have to spend time with my dad. But he sleeps a lot, so we can drive around a little, and I'll show you L.A.,' Ginny told him. Except Beverly Hills. She didn't want to go near it, or see the street where they'd lived. She didn't want to be reminded of the life she had once lived here, and had walked away from three years before.

'What did you do when you lived here?' he asked with interest. He had never inquired about her previous life – he knew it was sensitive for her. He never talked about Mark and Chris unless she brought them up first, and she rarely did, except for a passing comment about something she remembered, or something one of them had said.

'I was a TV reporter,' she answered his question, as they crawled along in the traffic.

'Like *on* TV?' He looked stunned as she nodded. 'Wow! You were a star. Were you the one sitting at the desk, or the one standing in the pouring rain with your umbrella inside out when they lose the sound?' She laughed at the description, which seemed apt even to her.

'I was both. Sometimes I filled in at the desk, with Mark. He was the one at the desk every day. And sometimes I covered stories in the pouring rain. Fortunately, it doesn't rain much here.' She smiled at him.

'Was it fun?'

She thought about it, then nodded. 'Yeah, most of the time. It was fun with Mark. People used to get excited when we went places and they recognized him.'

'How come you don't do that anymore?' Blue watched her face as she answered, and glanced at him.

'It wouldn't be fun anymore, without him. I never went back after . . . I stayed at my sister's for a while, and then I left, and went to work for SOS/HR traveling all over the world.'

'Nobody shoots at you when you're on TV. You should go back to it one day.' She didn't answer for a while, then just shook her head. All that was over for her, and she wanted it to be. She could never have gone on doing it without Mark – it would have been too unbearable with everyone feeling sorry for her. Now what she did was new every trip.

They took the Arroyo Seco Parkway exit to Pasadena, an hour after they got on the road. Ginny drove them down tree-lined streets with handsome homes on either side, and then up a small hill and turned into a driveway, outside a large good-looking stone house with a big pool along the side. It had gates, but they had left them open for her. She had forgotten how big their house was, and it suited them perfectly. And a black Lab barked in greeting when they drove up, as Blue took it all in.

'This is like a movie,' he said in awe of the house, the pool, and the dog. And as they got out of the car, Becky came out to greet them, and Ginny was relieved to see she hadn't changed. She was wearing a striped T-shirt, jeans, and flip-flops. Ginny watched her check out Blue carefully and smile coolly at him. She didn't approve of his existence in Ginny's life and it showed. But he didn't seem aware of it, and Ginny was glad he wasn't. He was too busy taking in the scene.

Becky's hair was a darker blond than her younger sister's and it was piled up on her head in a banana clip. She wasn't wearing makeup, and she never did. She looked no different than she had when Ginny last saw her. She had been prettier in college, but after she had Charlie, she had gained fifteen pounds and never bothered to get rid of it. And she wore the same kind of casual clothes and flip-flops every day. She called it her uniform, and she was too busy taking care of her kids, and now their father, to care.

The dog followed them inside. They went in the back way, and walked into the kitchen, where all three kids were having dinner at the kitchen table. They were having pasta and a big salad and chicken wings. Ginny could see that Blue was hungry again, as he walked shyly into the kitchen and hesitated when he saw Becky's children. Margie was the first one to get up and give her aunt a big hug and tell her how glad she was to see her, and then Ginny introduced her to Blue. She wondered what Becky had said to explain him, but Ginny just introduced him as 'Blue Williams,' without saying anything about his relationship to her, or that he was staying with her in New York. And then Charlie came to hug her and shake Blue's hand. Ginny was startled by how tall her nephew had gotten – he was even taller than his father and was over six foot four. And then Lizzie bounded up to them, kissed the air somewhere around her aunt's cheek, and looked straight at Blue. They were exactly the same height and age, and she had long straight blond hair like her aunt.

'Hi, I'm Lizzie,' she said to him with a broad grin, and she still had braces, which made her seem younger than Blue, but she had a woman's figure and was wearing a pink T-shirt and white shorts, and he looked dazzled by her. 'Do you want to sit down with us and eat?' she offered and he looked relieved. He felt awkward standing there and he looked to Ginny for her approval, and she nodded and told him to sit down, while Lizzie got him a plate and offered him a Coke. Margie and Charlie started asking Blue about the trip. They seemed much more grown up at sixteen and eighteen. But Blue looked instantly at home, while Lizzie chattered, and he helped himself to pasta and chicken wings.

'Where's Dad?' Ginny asked her sister in a low voice.

'He's upstairs, sleeping. He usually goes to sleep around eight o'clock.' It was almost nine by then. 'I gave him something for the pain. His arm is hurting him today, and I think the cast bothered him last night. He gets up at the crack of dawn as soon as it gets light. Alan will be home in a few minutes. He played tennis after work.' The strangest thing about being there, for Ginny, was seeing how little anything had changed. They were doing the same things as when she had left, in the same house. Even the dog was the same, and recognized her. The children were bigger, but nothing else was different. In one way it was comforting, but in another it made her feel even more out of step. Her life experience in the past three years had been so far removed from theirs. She felt as though she had just landed from Mars, as Becky poured them both a glass of wine and handed one to her.

They left the kids in the kitchen, wandered into the family room, and sat down. They used their living room only on Christmas and Thanksgiving. They gathered in the kitchen the rest of the time. And they had a huge flat screen TV over the fireplace in the family room, where they watched Monday-night football and sports on weekends, and any kind of play-off game. They were all sports nuts. Becky and Alan were great tennis players, which Ginny never had been, although Mark had played a good game and had played with them sometimes. And all their children were on various sports teams – basketball, soccer, baseball, girls' volleyball – and Charlie was the captain of the swimming team at his high school. He was graduating in June with honors. None of them had ever done anything wrong, or even had bad grades. Becky was smug about it, and she was very proud of Charlie getting into UCLA.

'He's cute,' Becky conceded, referring to Blue, and her sister understood.

'Yes, he is, and smart. He's remarkable considering what he's been through and how little help he's had from anyone. If I can get him into that high school, it would be great for him.' Becky still couldn't understand why Ginny was doing it, but she had to admit he was very polite when they arrived. He had thanked Becky for letting him come when he shook her hand. And when they went back to the kitchen, he and Lizzie were talking about music and seemed to like all the same bands. She was showing him something on YouTube on the computer they kept in the kitchen, and they were both laughing. They seemed to have found common ground. Then Charlie announced he was going out. His mother told him to drive carefully, and as he drove off, Ginny realized that he had his own car now. He really had grown up. Margie drove, too, although she had to borrow her mother's car and didn't have her own.

Lizzie offered to show Blue the downstairs playroom, and she and Margie left with him to play video games. Blue was doing fine. And then Alan walked in and made a big fuss over her. He was pleased to see her, although he told her that she'd gotten too thin. Her face seemed longer and more angular than it had before, and she looked even less like Becky now.

'What are we having for dinner?' Alan asked as he poured himself a glass of wine. 'I'm starving.' He was wearing his tennis clothes and was still a handsome man.

'Salad and scallops,' Becky said efficiently, and put three shells in the microwave that she had gotten at the market that afternoon. With Becky, everything was speedy and well-organized, even if it lacked a certain charm. But the scallops were delicious when she served them, and Alan poured them all more wine.

'I'm glad you finally got out here,' he said to Ginny pointedly. 'The last couple of years have really been hard on your sister. You left at just the right time.' He said it as though she had done it on purpose to shirk her responsibilities, not because her husband and son had died. He said it with just the barest edge of resentment, which Ginny picked up immediately. But she could imagine how stressful and disruptive it must be caring for her father while he was living with them and deteriorating dramatically. She knew it must be upsetting for the children, too.

Ginny helped Becky clean up the kitchen after dinner, and they went back to the family room, as Alan sat down with them. And they could hear music coming from somewhere, and Ginny smiled as she realized what it was.

'Wow, great CD, honey. Did you just get it?' Alan said, and Becky looked puzzled. It was a medley of popular songs.

'No. I don't know what that is. Lizzie must have put it on the stereo downstairs.'

'Come on, I'll show you,' Ginny said, as she beckoned both of them to come with her. They followed her downstairs to the playroom, where Blue was playing the piano they kept there for parties. He was playing all the songs Lizzie asked him to, and in between he played Mozart to tease her and make her laugh, and then he broke into boogie-woogie, with the most skilled hands they had ever seen play their piano.

'Where did he learn that?' Becky said with amazement, as he played a beautiful Beethoven piece, then switched back to one of Lizzie's songs. She was grinning from ear to ear, she loved it.

'He taught himself,' Ginny answered her sister, proud of him. 'He plays the guitar, too, composes, and reads music. He just applied to the high school of music and arts in New York. LaGuardia Arts. I hope he gets in. Music is his passion, and he has an incredible gift.'

'My God, he's like a prodigy. Charlie took lessons for five years and all he can play is scales and "Chopsticks." He never practiced,' Alan commented. Watching Blue play reminded Ginny of the story about Father Teddy in the church basement, but she pushed it from her mind. Blue was having a ball on their piano, and he and Lizzie had hit it off as though they'd grown up together. She was impressed by him, too, but Alan and Becky were even more so. His musical talent was undeniable, and he was clearly a nice boy. He played for an hour, just having fun with it, and then he and Lizzie went upstairs to watch a movie on the big flat screen, while the adults stayed downstairs on the comfortable couch there.

Their whole house was designed for comfort. It had none of the elegance of Ginny's old house in Beverly Hills, but it was perfect for their life in Pasadena, which had always been much more casual than her and Mark's life. Theirs had been more glamorous, and their house had looked it. They had been TV personalities, even if just on network news. Mark had been a very big deal, and made a lot of money. And Ginny had done well, too.

'Becky's been telling me what you've been doing for him,' Alan said, referring to Blue. 'I think it's admirable, Ginny, but you can't forget who he is and where he comes from. You need to be careful.' Alan struck her as pompous, and he annoyed her as he said it. Becky was nodding agreement.

'You mean you're afraid he might steal something?' They both nodded, unashamed of what they had said and what they meant by it.

'I check his pockets every morning before he goes to school,' Ginny said innocently, shocked by their comment and how narrow-minded they were.

'I can't believe you have him staying in your apartment. Why don't you take him to a shelter? He'd probably be happier there.' Her brother-in-law had no idea what he was talking about or the conditions there. He had never even seen a homeless shelter, or who was there.

'People get beaten, mugged, and robbed in shelters every day, and women get raped,' Ginny said calmly. 'I got him into a very good youth shelter where he stays when I'm away.' *If he doesn't run away,* she added silently to herself. She hated how superior they felt, and the assumptions they had made about a boy they didn't know, no matter how bright, decent, and talented he was. They had already judged him, based on their own limited experience in the suburbs in a totally sheltered life. Fortunately, their children were more open-minded than they were, and Lizzie and Margie were having fun with him. He was too young for Charlie to be interested in him, which was why he had gone to visit his girlfriend.

Ginny changed the subject, and they drifted into the topic of her work in human rights, which they disapproved of, too. They thought it was too dangerous for a woman, or for anyone, but she was doing some good in the world, and she loved it. Instead of acknowledging how adventurous and brave she had been to embark on something so different, Becky and Alan both told her she'd never find another husband if she didn't give up running around the globe soon and living in refugee camps. They told her it was time to get over her survivor's guilt.

'I don't want another husband. I still love Mark, and I probably always will,' she said quietly.

'I don't think he'd approve of what you're doing, Ginny,' Alan said seriously, which Ginny thought was totally out of line.

'Maybe not,' she admitted, 'but he'd think it was interesting. And he didn't leave me much choice. I wasn't going to sit in my empty house in Beverly Hills without him and Chris and cry for the rest of my life. This is a lot better.'

'Well, we hope you give it up soon.' He spoke for both of them, and Becky let him. She was having her fourth glass of wine of the evening by then, which surprised Ginny – she didn't used to drink that much. 'Where are you going next?' Alan asked her. 'Do you know?'

'I'm not sure yet. Maybe India or Africa. I'd be happy with whatever assignment I get.' Alan looked shocked, and Becky shook her head.

'Do you have any idea how risky that could be?' he asked her as though she didn't know.

'Yes,' she said smiling at him. 'That's why they send me to places like that, because they have problems and need human rights workers to help them.' And by now, she was a pro. Alan was probably right – Mark might have been shocked by what she was doing. But it was a lot better than committing suicide in the East River, which she had considered not that long ago. And thanks to her work, and Blue coming into her life, she was feeling a lot better now than she had in three years. Neither Becky nor Alan had any idea what that kind of tragedy was like, or what it took to survive it. And she hoped for their sake they'd never know. But they had no concept of what it was like to be in her shoes, and what it took to get out of bed every day.

They sat downstairs for a while, and then Alan went upstairs to watch tennis on TV in their room. Becky took Ginny to the guest room so she could unpack. Blue would be sleeping with Charlie.

'You don't think he'd take anything, do you?' Becky asked her conspiratorially, and for the first time since she was fourteen, Ginny wanted to slap her.

'How can you say something like that, Becky?' She wanted to say 'Who are you?,' but she didn't. How could they have become so narrow-minded and bourgeois to think that, because he was homeless, he was a thief? It was pathetic. 'No, he won't take anything,' she answered. 'He never has with me.' And she hoped he didn't make an exception to that now. They would never let her live it down if he did. But she wasn't worried about him.

They kissed each other goodnight, and Ginny unpacked in the pretty flowered guest bedroom. Blue stuck his head in a while later, on his way to bed. Lizzie had shown him where his room was.

'I had fun tonight,' he said, smiling at her, which was more than she could say. Her sister and brother-in-law had depressed her. 'I really like Lizzie, and Margie's nice, too.'

'They're good girls,' Ginny agreed. 'Maybe we can borrow an old swimsuit tomorrow from Charlie. I forgot to buy one for you.'

'That would be really cool,' he said. He felt like he had died and gone to heaven, in Pasadena. Ginny kissed him goodnight then, and he disappeared down the hall to Charlie's room. She closed her door softly, thinking about her father. She knew it wasn't going to be easy to see him in his diminished state.

But even everything Becky had said to her in recent months hadn't prepared her for how gaunt her father looked and his blank stare when he saw her. The next morning, Ginny sat next to him at the breakfast table and helped feed him, since one arm was in a cast and he had lost interest in feeding himself. She fed him a bowl of oatmeal, and after he'd finished it, he turned to look at Ginny.

'I know you, don't I?' he said weakly.

'Yes, you do, Dad. I'm Ginny.' He nodded, and looked like he was processing the information, and then he smiled at her.

'You look like your mother,' he said in a voice that was suddenly more normal, and she could see recognition in his eyes, and it brought tears to hers. 'Where have you been?' he asked her.

'I've been away for a long time. I live in New York now.' It was easier than explaining Afghanistan to him.

'Your mother and I used to go there on trips,' he said with a wistful look and she nodded. And he was right – she did look like her mother, more so than Becky. 'I'm very tired,' he said to the room in general, and he looked it. Remembering her had taken a superhuman effort, but sometimes he had moments like that, when he remembered things, and then faded away again just as quickly.

'Do you want to go upstairs and lie down, Dad?' Becky asked him. She knew his routine. Ginny didn't. He often napped after breakfast since he woke up so early.

'Yes, I do,' he said, and got up from the table on unsteady legs. Both his daughters helped him up the stairs, and sat him down on his bed. He stretched out then and looked at Ginny. 'Margaret?' he said softly. It was her mother's name. Ginny just nodded, and fought back tears, as she realized she should have come sooner, but he had recognized her for a few minutes. He closed his eyes then, and a moment later he was asleep, snoring softly. Becky gently rolled him onto his side so he wouldn't choke, and then they left him and went back downstairs.

'Will he be okay?' Ginny asked, looking worried, realizing what Becky had to contend with. It was an enormous responsibility, dealing with him. He could choke, die, fall, or get hurt at any moment. And on a good day, he could let himself out of the house and get hit by a car, or get lost and remember neither his name nor his way home. He needed full-time supervision, which Becky had provided for two years.

'He'll be fine for now,' Becky reassured her, 'but not for much longer. I'm glad you came out this weekend.'

'So am I,' Ginny said, and put her arms around her and hugged her. 'Thank you for taking care of him. I couldn't have done it, even if I lived here. It takes a special kind of person to do it.' And Becky had done it faithfully. Ginny was grateful to her for that.

'I couldn't do what you do,' Becky said, crying. 'I'd be scared shitless.' They both laughed and joined the young people at the breakfast table. They were a lively group, and Charlie had just offered to take the others to Magic Mountain for the day.

'Do you like roller coasters?' Ginny asked Blue. And he nodded with excitement in his eyes.

'I love them. I've been on the Cyclone in Coney Island.'

'These are a lot bigger,' she warned him.

'Good,' he said with a grin.

The whole group left a little while later. Charlie lent Blue a swimsuit for the water slide and Ginny gave Blue money. The two sisters cleaned up the kitchen, and then Ginny poured them both a cup of coffee. Ginny hoped she wouldn't say anything unpleasant about Blue again. She didn't. Alan came through carrying his tennis racket a few minutes later. He was wearing shorts and tennis shoes, and he grabbed a banana on the way out, and said he was late for a game.

'He's been a good sport about Dad,' Becky said as they sipped their coffee after he left.

'It must be tough on all of you. I see it more clearly now that I'm here,' Ginny said sympathetically. 'You've been amazing.' Even more than she'd realized.

'I have a woman who comes in to help now in the day-time. If I didn't, I'd be trapped here. It's been so depressing watching him fall apart.' It was a relief being able to say it to her sister. And Ginny was thinking that taking a bullet from a sniper would be a better fate than dying slowly and losing your mind. Her dad had been so intelligent and vital. It was heartbreaking to see him now, at the end.

And you could see looking at him that he didn't have much time left. At least most of the time he wasn't in pain, except for the arm he'd broken recently, but he looked so lost. 'The kids are really sweet to him, and even when he doesn't know who they are, he enjoys them. That's more than I can say sometimes.' She grinned at her sister. 'I know who they are, and they drive me nuts. But they're good kids.' Ginny wanted to say that Blue was, too, but she didn't. He wasn't family. But she didn't have Chris to crow about anymore, and his three-year-old victories. Seeing Becky's children reminded her of just how much she missed that, and nothing would ever replace it.

The woman who helped care for their father came at noon, and Becky asked Ginny if she wanted to go out to lunch, which sounded nice. They went to a small restaurant a few miles away, and chatted easily, and then they came back and sat at the pool. Alan had stayed at the tennis club for lunch. The kids didn't come back until the late afternoon – they had had a ball at Magic Mountain. Blue said he nearly threw up twice, which was testimony to how cool the rides were. And with that, they all jumped into the pool, and Charlie's girlfriend came over to join them.

Alan made a barbecue that night, as he did on most Saturdays, and Becky had a little too much wine again. Ginny went upstairs to sit with their father before dinner, but he was sound asleep the entire time. And Becky decided not to wake him for dinner. She said he would just be confused. He was slipping away slowly, but there was nothing they could do. He had stopped responding to the medication. It made Ginny sad just seeing him that way, and Blue felt sorry for her. He could see how nostalgic it made her.

They all sat in the backyard until midnight, and then everyone went to bed. Ginny lay in the dark, thinking about all of them. It felt warm and poignant being with her family, but she felt like a stranger in their midst. Her life experience now was just too different from theirs, and underneath what they said, there was always a hidden current of disapproval. Even when it was unspoken, she felt it. It was a lonely feeling. It made her feel like an outcast.

She finally fell asleep around two a.m., and got up early to help herself to a cup of coffee. She had just sat down to drink it, when Kevin Callaghan called her. He thought she was in New York, where it was eleven-thirty, and was shocked when she said she was in L.A., and then he apologized for calling her so early.

'What are you doing here?' he asked her.

'I came to see my father for the weekend. He's got Alzheimer's, and I haven't seen him since . . .' Her voice trailed off, and he understood.

'I'm sorry, Ginny. I met him once a long time ago. He was a great guy. He was a handsome man, too.'

'Yes, he was,' she agreed, and then Kevin got down to business.

'I've got some information for you. I called a pal of mine in the police department. A woman, actually – she's a lieutenant in sex crimes. Basically, this is a two-prong issue. First, you have to go to the cops, and they'll investigate it, and then you have to deal with the archdiocese, the church. But if the police are satisfied with the investigation, and believe Blue is telling the truth, they'll handle the church for you. And very frequently, there are several reports about one priest, so they may already have some leads on this guy who molested Blue. Most of these guys have molested many kids over a period of time, not just one. They have great access to young kids, and the sick ones take full advantage of it.

'The first thing you have to do is call the Child Abuse Unit, and they'll get the investigation going. They're part of the Manhattan district attorney's office. The Child Abuse Unit handles these investigations that involve priests. So you and Blue have to go down there and start the ball rolling. But for now anyway, you don't have to confront some angry old priest at the archdiocese. The cops will do it for you. And apparently, the church is taking some very tough positions with the cover-ups, so you may get some real cooperation from the archdiocese. It's certainly worth a shot, and I would report the guy immediately. Screw him, after what he did to the kid, and probably other boys. I'll text you the phone number of the Child Abuse Unit.'

'Wow,' Ginny said, in awe of what he had learned so quickly. 'You're good, Callaghan. I'm impressed.' But she'd always known he was that good, which was why she'd called him. She had great respect for him as a reporter.

'What are you going to do now?'

'I need to talk to Blue. Do we need a lawyer?'

'Yes, but not yet. First you need the police to investigate it. If they think it's a good case, they'll press charges, as in any sex crimes case. If they won't press charges, you can bring a civil action against the archdiocese, but you'd have a much weaker case. What you want is for the Child Abuse Unit to go to the DA and prosecute him. And you can file a civil suit, too.'

'I wonder how traumatic this would be for Blue,' she said cautiously.

'Probably no more than what he went through. And it might make him feel better to have someone go after the guy, and validate what he's saying. It's even worse when people don't believe the victim, or hush it up. And that happened too much in the beginning. Now that this situation has been blown wide open, the Vatican is telling the churches to cooperate, and not protect the perpetrators. They used to just move them around from church to church and hide it.'

'Do you know a lawyer who handles this stuff?'

'No, but I can find that out, too. I'm sure there are some good ones. Give me a couple of days on that.' He had done an amazing job so far at getting information for her. He was as outraged by what had happened to Blue as she was, and it touched her. 'How long are you here for?'

'Till tonight. We're taking the red-eye back to New York. We came out on Friday. I have to get Blue home. He can't miss school, or he won't graduate in June.'

'He's a lucky boy to have you on his team,' Kevin said admiringly.

'I'm lucky to have him, too,' she said softly.

'Do you have time for lunch? Or are you too tied up with your family?'

'I should spend time with my father – that's why we're here. But I could probably go out for coffee. The trouble is, I'm in Pasadena, I'm not in the city.'

'I'll come out there if you want. I know a great place for croissants and cappuccino. What do you think? I'd love to see you.'

'Me, too,' she said sincerely, and she was grateful for the research he'd just done for her, and so quickly.

'It's eight-thirty now. How about if I meet you at ten-thirty?' He told her where the restaurant was – it was only a few blocks away from where Becky lived.

'I'll be there,' she said, and told Becky when she walked into the kitchen half an hour later. 'I won't be out long.

I'd just like to see him for a little while, for old times' sake.'

'Of course,' Becky said good-naturedly. 'Do you want to have him here? You're welcome to.'

'I'd rather meet him at the restaurant. That way he can't overstay, and I'll just leave and come back here. How's Dad today?'

'About the same. He didn't want to get up. I'm going to wait until Lucy comes and see if she can get him moving. She's better at it than I am, and he listens to her. He's too used to me – he just says no if he's tired or not in a good mood.'

Ginny went to see him a little while later, and then she left at ten-fifteen to meet Kevin. She told Blue she was going out to see a friend, but he was busy with Lizzie and didn't mind. He was feeling totally at home with Becky's kids, and they liked him and had welcomed him warmly, which touched Ginny.

She walked into the restaurant at precisely ten-thirty, and Kevin was already there. He was impossible to miss. He was the tallest man in the room by several inches. He put his arms around her and hugged her the minute he saw her.

'It's so good to see you,' he said with a voice full of emotion. He didn't tell her that he still missed Mark every day and wished he could call him. He still couldn't believe he was gone.

They chatted for half an hour about his work, the last woman he had gone out with, her most recent trip for SOS/HR, and her next one, and they talked about Blue.

'I really hope you press charges against this guy,' he said to her, and she could see he meant it.

'I'd like to,' Ginny said honestly, 'but I'm going to leave it up to Blue. I don't want to push him, if he doesn't feel up to it. It'll take a lot of courage for him to face that priest again in a trial.'

'He may regret it all his life if he doesn't. Someone has to stop those guys. They can't just keep moving them around to protect them.' She agreed with him, and they talked of other things again, and he looked genuinely happy to see her. 'I wish you came out here more often,' he said wistfully. He had missed her, too.

'Call me if you come to New York,' she said as he paid for their cappuccinos, and they got up to leave. She had to get back to Becky's. She wanted to spend time with her and their father before she left that night.

Kevin walked her to her car, and promised to call her with the name of a lawyer experienced in cases like Blue's. Then he hugged her for a long moment. 'Take care of yourself, Ginny. He wouldn't want you out there risking your life.' Her eyes filled with tears and she nodded, unable to speak.

'I don't know what else to do, Kev. There was nothing left. At least now there's Blue. Maybe I can make a difference in his life.' It was all she wanted to do now.

'I'm sure you already have,' he reassured her. It was an emotional moment for them both.

'Maybe we can get something out of it for him. That would be great for him to have later on.'

'Talk to a lawyer about it, and start with the Child Abuse Unit. My friend says they're great.' She thanked him again, and a few minutes later she waved at him and drove away. It had been so good to see him, and she was sorry she had waited so long, but she hadn't been ready until now. And Blue had been the catalyst to make her see him again.

They spent the rest of the afternoon at the pool. Her father slept the day away. Even Lucy couldn't get him up. Ginny spent a few minutes with him when he was awake, but he had no idea who she was this time and didn't recognize her, or even mistake her for her mother. It was painful to see him that way, and he was sound asleep when she and Blue left that night after dinner. She kissed him gently on the cheek, and walked quietly out of his room with tears running down her cheeks. She doubted that she'd see him alive again, but she was glad she had finally come to see him. Becky had been right to insist.

Alan and Becky and their children stood outside the house and waved as they drove away. Ginny was quiet on the way to the airport, and Blue was pensive. He had never spent a weekend like it with a normal family, with a father and mother and children, people who liked being together and treated each other well. No one was on drugs, no one had hit anyone, and no one they knew or were related to was in prison. They had everything they wanted, even a pool in their backyard. It was like a dream come true for him. It had been a fairy-tale weekend for Blue and had been a gift to him.

'I like your family, Ginny,' Blue said softly.

'So do I sometimes.' She smiled at him. 'Sometimes they drive me a little crazy, and my sister can be a little tough, but she means well.' They had finally warmed up to him, even Alan, who had played water polo with him in the pool. Their prejudice about his background slowly melted away throughout the weekend as they got to know him. Even Becky said he was a good kid and meant it. And he and Lizzie had promised to text each other every day, on Ginny's phone till she left, and she was thinking of getting him his own, but hadn't gotten around to it yet. Lizzie wanted him to come back soon, or to visit her aunt in New York so she could see him. Ginny had even promised to come to L.A. again, although she still couldn't see living there anymore.

It was dark in the cabin as the plane took off on the late flight, and Blue took Ginny's hand and held it.

'Thank you for the best weekend of my life,' he said to her, and then laid his head back against the seat. He was asleep half an hour later, and she covered him with a blanket and then went to sleep herself as they flew east. She had done what she had come to do. She had seen her father, and whispered goodbye as she tiptoed out of his room.

Chapter 10

Blue and Ginny landed at JFK Airport at six-fifteen on Monday morning, and took a cab into the city. They were at her apartment shortly after seven. She made him breakfast while he showered, and he left for school on time. He had slept for the entire flight. He had a quiz that morning that she'd helped him prepare for, and he had his interview and audition at LaGuardia Arts the next day. They had a busy week ahead of them. She had to go in to the SOS/HR office to discuss her next assignment. And at nine o'clock that morning, she called St. Francis's Church and asked for Father Teddy. She apologized for not knowing his last name, and said she had moved away a few years before, but was back in the area, and wanted to see him again. She said he had been just wonderful when he counseled her. The young priest she spoke to was very pleasant and knew immediately who she meant, and agreed that he was a terrific priest and a great guy.

'I'm sorry to tell you, though, that he transferred to Chicago last year. But any of us would be happy to talk to you, if you like,' he offered helpfully.

'Thank you so much,' Ginny said, feeling slightly guilty for lying to a priest, but it was for a good cause. 'I'll come in sometime soon. Do you know how I could get in touch with him? I'd just like to say hello and let him know how things turned out after I last saw him.'

'Of course,' the priest on the phone said kindly. 'He's at St. Anne's Church in Chicago, and I'm sure he'd like to hear from you. We all still miss him here.'

'Thank you so much,' Ginny said again, and hung up. She wanted to see him for herself. She could fly back and forth to Chicago in a day. She wanted to get a sense of the man who had abused Blue. She believed Blue, but she wanted to see just how treacherous Father Teddy was.

And after that, she left for the SOS/HR office, and spent the rest of the morning discussing her next assignment with Ellen Warberg. It looked like it was going to be India this time, although nothing was definite yet. Ginny was due to go out again in early June, so she had a couple of weeks left before a final decision was made about her assignment. Syria had been a possibility earlier, but it was too dangerous there now. And Ellen said they might send her for only two months this time, which was briefer than usual, but they were trying to rotate workers more frequently in the riskier areas, and keep assignments shorter, which suited her because of Blue. Because her next post wasn't definite yet, she had no advance reports to read, and left the office empty-handed with no homework to do, which gave her more free time for Blue.

That night, they talked about his audition the next day instead. He was going to play Chopin, and had been able to spend a little time practicing on a piano at his school. He also had some other things in mind, if they wanted more current material. He was excited and scared, and he got a text from Lizzie on Ginny's phone saying that she missed him and hoped he got home okay. He was pleased to hear from her and sent her some music to download from iTunes.

Ginny got an e-mail from Kevin with the name of a lawyer, but he asked her to call him so he could tell her about him. She called as soon as she went to her room that night. She didn't want Blue to hear the conversation. She didn't want to distract him before his interview the next day.

'He's your guy,' Kevin said when she called him. 'He's an ex-Jesuit priest. He's an expert on canon law, and spent four years at the Vatican in their legal office. And these cases are his specialty. I spoke to two attorneys today, and they said he's the best, and he's in New York.' His name was Andrew O'Connor, and Kevin had gotten his office number, his e-mail address, and his cell phone. 'Let me know how it works out. Did you call the Child Abuse Unit yet?'

'I'm going to talk to Blue tomorrow after his audition at the music and arts school. We've got a lot going on this week.'

'Keep me posted,' Kevin said. He sounded busy, and a minute later they hung up. She had everything they needed now – a referral to the police, a lawyer – and she was hoping to go to Chicago on Thursday to get a look at Father Teddy. Thanks to Kevin, it was all falling into place.

Blue was tense the next morning at breakfast, and Ginny went with him on the subway to LaGuardia Arts. The high school was in the midst of Lincoln Center, and Blue looked anxious as they walked into the building. It was an impressive place, and hordes of young people were moving through the halls, talking and laughing on their way to classes. It was exciting just being there. And there were notices about auditions for special events posted on bulletin boards around the school.

She and Blue went to the front desk and explained that they were there for an interview and an audition, and the receptionist looked startled at first since there were none at that time of year, then she called someone in the admissions office and smiled warmly at them.

'We'll call you in a few minutes,' she told them, and

they sat down to wait. Blue looked like he was about to bolt out of the building. Ginny tried to distract him, and finally the woman called his name, and sent them to the admissions office, where a young woman chatted with Blue and told him about the school. She said she had gone there herself, and it had been the most fantastic experience of her life. She worked in an orchestra at night now, and in the admissions office three days a week.

She asked him what had drawn him to music, and he told her how he had taught himself to play the piano and learned to read music, and she looked impressed. Ginny thought the interview went well, and they led him away for his audition without her, while she waited for him in the lobby. She had been told that the audition would take two to three hours, and had brought a book to read while she waited. She didn't want to leave the building in case he needed her, and when he finally came back to her, he looked exhausted, with a dazed expression.

'How did it go?' she asked him, trying to seem calm and encouraging, but she had been nervous, worrying about him and hoping it was going well. The audition was a lot of pressure he wasn't used to.

'I don't know. I played the Chopin for them, and then they asked me to play some other stuff that they picked. There was a piece I'd never played before, Rachmaninoff. After that, Debussy, and then I played some Motown. I don't see how I can get in here.' He looked at her hopelessly. 'I'm sure everyone who goes here plays better than I do. There were four teachers in the room, and they made a lot of notes,' he said, still looking anxious.

'Well, you did the best you could. That's all you can do.' They walked out of the building into the May sunshine. They had told him he'd be notified in June. They wanted time to consider their decision, and evaluate if he'd fit in, and if his skills were strong enough to make him eligible, since he had had no formal training. They had also told him there had been nine thousand applicants for 664 places. Blue was convinced he'd never get in, but Ginny tried to be optimistic about it, as they hailed a cab, and she got him a sandwich before she dropped him off at school. He had a math quiz that afternoon. He was under a lot of pressure these days, but in six weeks he'd be finished. She hated to leave New York before he graduated, but there was nothing she could do, unless her assignment got postponed for some reason, but it didn't look that way. If there was a problem in one area, they would just send her somewhere else.

When Blue got home that night, he seemed depressed about the audition, and he looked so tired that she decided not to talk to him about going to the Child Abuse Unit, and wait another day.

She finally brought it up after dinner on Wednesday, and she told him everything she'd learned from

Kevin and said she was going to Chicago the next day to see Father Teddy herself.

'Are you going to say anything about me to him?' Blue looked panicked. 'He told me he'd have me put in jail if I told anyone.'

'He can't put you in jail, Blue,' she said calmly. 'You didn't do anything wrong. He's the one who'll go to prison if we pursue this, but it's entirely up to you. We can do something about it, or we can just keep quiet if going after him is too much for you. You make the decision, Blue. I'll back whatever you want.' She tried to sound neutral about it so he would feel free to decide.

'Why are you doing this?' Blue looked at her intently.

'Because I believe you, and he's a very, very bad man. And I think reporting him to the police and prosecuting him is the right thing to do. Someone like that needs to be stopped. I just want to get a look at him. I won't mention you.' He seemed reassured. He trusted Ginny completely.

'Maybe he doesn't do it anymore,' Blue said cautiously. She could see that he was afraid, and he had good reason to be after the way the priest threatened him if he ever told what he had done. 'What do you think I should do?' He was impressed that she believed him. His own aunt hadn't because she liked the priest so much.

'I think you should do whatever you want to do. You don't have to decide right now. You can think about it for a while.' He nodded and then went to watch TV until he had to go to bed. He borrowed Ginny's cell phone and he and Lizzie texted a few times, but he looked troubled and distracted. Ginny knew he was running all the possibilities around in his head, about Father Teddy.

He didn't say anything about it in the morning, and he was happy and in good spirits when he left for school. Ginny left for the airport shortly afterward and caught a ten-thirty flight to Chicago. And she was at St. Anne's an hour after they landed. She walked into the rectory office and asked to see Father Teddy. The secretary said that he was administering last rites at the hospital, and would be back in half an hour. She agreed to wait, and sat there, thinking about him and what he had done to Blue. She had a knot in her stomach just thinking about it. And while she waited, a tall, good-looking priest walked in. He looked like he was in his early forties, and he exuded warmth and kindness. He was the kind of person you would want to tell your troubles to, and have him as a best friend. He joked with the secretary for a minute, and glanced at his messages, and at a sign from the woman at the desk, he turned and smiled at Ginny.

'You're here to see me?' he asked her warmly. 'I'm sorry I kept you waiting. One of our parishioners' mother is sick. She's ninety-six years old, and she broke her hip last week and wanted last rites. I'm sure she'll outlive me.' He was one of the handsomest men she'd ever met, and everything about him inspired confidence.

'You're Father Teddy?' she asked with a look of amazement. She had forgotten to get a physical description of him from Blue, and had somehow assumed he would be old and creepy-looking. Instead he was this vital, energetic, charming, handsome man, which was even more insidious. Everything about him was so warm and inviting, she could easily imagine why a child would trust him. He looked like a beautiful, happy teddy bear, just like his name.

'I am,' he confirmed his identity to her. 'Shall we go into my office?' It was a pleasant sunny room with a view of the church garden, and he had watercolors on the wall, and a small cross. He was wearing a Roman collar and a simple black suit. There was nothing daunting or dark about him or his surroundings. But she didn't doubt Blue for a minute. She was certain he was telling the truth, no matter how charismatic Father Teddy was. He was a big burly Irishman, and said he had grown up in Boston, when she sat down. 'Did someone refer you to me?' he asked her pleasantly.

'Yes,' Ginny said, looking him over carefully. She wanted to learn everything she could about him. 'A friend in New York. I actually called you at St. Francis's, and they told me you were here. I'm here on business for two days, so I thought I'd come to see you.'

'What good luck for me,' he said, smiling at her. She suddenly understood why Blue's aunt Charlene was so fond of him. He was seamless in his performance of innocence and compassion. 'How can I help you? I'm sorry, I didn't catch your name.'

'Virginia Phillips,' she said, stating her maiden name.

'Are you married, Virginia?'

'Yes, I am.'

'Lucky guy.' He smiled at her again. And then she told him that she thought her husband was having an affair and she didn't know what to do about it. She didn't want to leave him, but she was sure he was in love with the other woman. And Father Teddy told her to pray about it, and be patient and loving, and he was sure he'd come around in time. He said most marriages hit bumps once in a while, but if she was steadfast, they'd recover. And all the while he talked to her, she realized he had cold, angry eyes, and the warmest smile she'd ever seen. Thinking about Blue, she wanted to leap across the desk and choke him. He gave her his card then and told her to call him anytime, and he'd be happy to talk to her.

'Thank you so much,' she said gratefully. 'I haven't known what to do.'

'Just hang in,' he told her warmly. 'I'm sorry not to spend more time with you. I have a meeting in five minutes.' She could see that he was anxious to leave, and after she left his office, she walked into the church to light candles for Mark and Chris. Kneeling in a back pew, she saw him walk into the church, as a young boy came from behind the altar, and they talked for a few minutes. Father Teddy put a hand on his shoulder, and the boy was smiling and looked up at him adoringly. Then before Ginny could react to what she was seeing, Teddy led him through a door, as he bent down to whisper something in the boy's ear, and closed the door behind them. Ginny winced at what she feared might happen next. But there was nothing she could do. As pastor, he had free rein in his parish, just as he had before.

She wanted to run after them and scream and snatch the boy away from him. But she knew she couldn't have done it. The boy looked to be about twelve years old. And all she knew, as she sat staring at the closed door in horror, was that they had to put an end to what Father Teddy was doing, to what he had done to Blue and probably others like him. He was the most seductive man she'd ever seen, and he was preying on children. She felt sick as she left the church, and found a cab a few blocks away, to take her to the airport. She knew what they had to do now. She and Blue had to go to the police. Father Teddy Graham belonged in prison. Only the law could stop him.

Chapter 11

All Ginny could think about on the plane to New York was what she had seen in Chicago. The strikingly handsome man in the Roman collar, the dazzling smile, the eyes that held a thousand secrets and had a frightening harshness to them in contrast to the smile. She couldn't stop thinking of the boy he had led through the door, and that the child's life would be marked forever if something unsavory had happened after that. She had no proof, just her own fear of it. They really had to stop him. For now Father Teddy was doing whatever he wanted to the young boys in his parish, just as he had in New York. She wondered if anyone knew or suspected, and if that was why they had transferred him to Chicago or if, until now, he had been entirely above suspicion or reproach.

Her flights had been on time, and Blue was home from school, watching TV, when she walked into the apartment, tired from a full day of traveling, even though it had gone smoothly and according to plan. Ginny looked serious as she sat down on the couch next to him. He was beginning to know her, and reacted immediately to the expression on her face. He thought he was in trouble, although he had gotten an A-plus on a history test that day, but she didn't know yet. He was excited to tell her.

'Is something wrong?' he asked her nervously.

'Yes, but not with you,' she was quick to clarify when she saw the fear in his eyes. 'I just came back from Chicago. I saw him.' He knew she was going that day, he just hadn't known what time she got back.

'Father Teddy?' His eyes were worried, as she nodded.

'I can see why everyone loves him. He's all bullshit and charm, and he's very good-looking. And he has the meanest eyes I've ever seen.' She didn't tell him how unnerved she'd been by seeing the boy he had led away – she didn't want to remind him of his own experiences with the man, which were upsetting enough. 'I really think he has to be stopped. Either the church knows about him, and they're moving him from place to place to keep him out of trouble, or they have no idea, and they're unleashing him innocently on new communities to damage more kids. Either way, he needs to be exposed, and he belongs in prison.'

'Charlene loves him. She'll never believe anything wrong about him. Maybe no one else will either.' But he liked what Ginny had said about him. It made Blue feel validated.

'We have to find a way to make his victims feel brave enough to come forward.' But she knew many wouldn't, and would stay hidden forever, deeply ashamed and badly scarred. 'I'm not sure where we start,' she admitted to Blue thoughtfully. 'I guess with the police. My friend Kevin says they'll investigate him. But I want to see a lawyer with you, too, to advise us.' She had all the numbers Kevin had given her.

But she looked deep into Blue's eyes with the most important question of all. 'What do you say, Blue? Are you in? Do you want more time to think about it? This probably won't be easy, and if it goes to court, you'll have to take the stand and testify. The judge might let you do it in chambers, because of your age, but more than likely, your identity will come out at some point. How do you feel about that?'

'Scared,' he said honestly, and she smiled. 'But I think I could do it. I think you're right. Someone should. I'm older now, and maybe I'd hit him if he touched me, or maybe I wouldn't even now, since he said he'd put me in jail. But before, I was too afraid to say anything to him, and everyone thinks he's such a great guy. I knew no one would ever believe me . . . except you.' Blue smiled at her with love and gratitude in his eyes.

Ginny wondered if this was why their paths had crossed, so she could help free him from the terrible burden he'd been carrying. She didn't want it to cripple him for the rest of his life, and she knew it could. Damaged relationships, lack of trust, inability to attach, sexual dysfunction, nightmares, panic attacks. There were a host of possibilities, and she wanted none of that for him. She hoped that truth, love, and justice would help heal him.

'I'm in,' Blue said softly then, looking her straight in the eye. He had no doubt, no matter how scared he was. He knew Ginny would help get him through it. 'I want to do it,' Blue confirmed.

'So do I. I'm in with you,' she told him, and stuck out her hand for him to shake. Their eyes met and held as they did. 'I'll call the Child Abuse Unit tomorrow. Let me know if you change your mind,' she said clearly. She didn't want him to do something he didn't feel right about or was too afraid to do. It was entirely his choice.

'I won't,' Blue said, about changing his mind. 'I'm sure.' She got up from the couch then and went to cook dinner, and he opened his laptop and looked at YouTube until it was ready. Then he set the table as he did every night, and they sat down to the simple meal Ginny had put together. She tried to make him healthy meals, which were good for her, too. And both of them were quiet as they thought of what lay ahead. 'When are you going to call them?' Blue asked her, breaking into her thoughts. She was thinking of Father Teddy again, and couldn't get out of her head the vision of the little boy he had led away.

'Tomorrow.' Blue nodded. They both went to bed early.

It had been a long day. And he hugged her when he left in the morning. He had shown her the history test he got an A-plus on, and she had told him how proud of him she was. It still amazed her to realize that she had become the surrogate mother of a teenager overnight, and she felt like she had a lot to learn at times. She just used her heart and common sense, and she reasoned with him like an adult. He was still a kid and acted like it at times. But he was sensible and respectful of her, and grateful for everything she did. He had loved the trip to L.A., and he and Lizzie had become fast friends.

After he left for school, she called the number Kevin Callaghan had given her for the Child Abuse Unit. He didn't have a specific name, just the department number, as his lieutenant friend in L.A. knew none of them in New York. The phone was answered by a woman, and Ginny asked for an appointment to come in and speak with someone.

'What about?' the woman on the phone inquired, sounding bored. They got calls all day, a lot of which wasted their time, but many that didn't. Ginny knew hers would be one that didn't.

'A child molestation incident that was committed repeatedly,' Ginny said clearly. Her years as a reporter helped her go right to the heart of the matter and stay there.

'By whom?' The voice on the phone sounded instantly more serious and was paying rapt attention.

'A parish priest.' There was a pause before the next question.

'Who was molested?' Ginny assumed she was writing it down, possibly on a form of some kind.

'A boy, who was initially nine, and then ten at the time.'

'How long ago was it?' The woman sounded suspicious again. They got plenty of calls like it from forty-five-year-old men, who claimed to have been molested as children. Their claims were valid, too, and so was their sense of violation, but it was more pressing when the cases were more recent. 'How old is the boy now? Is he still a minor?'

'He's thirteen.'

'Please hold,' she said, and disappeared for what felt like forever. And then she was back on the line. 'Can you bring him in with you?'

'Yes, I can.'

'Does four-thirty today work for you? We just had a cancellation.'

'That will be fine,' Ginny said matter-of-factly. It had been a businesslike exchange, and she was glad that Blue wouldn't have time to wait and worry before the appointment. Now that he'd made the decision to report it, she wanted to get it done, so the timing was perfect. 'Thank you very much,' Ginny said gratefully.

'You'll be meeting with Detective Jane Sanders in the

Child Abuse Unit. Please ask for her when you come in.' She gave her the address then and told her how to get there. Ginny thanked her again and they hung up, and she decided to get all her calls over with at once. Next, she called Andrew O'Connor, the canonical lawyer who specialized in child and sexual abuse cases, and got his voice mail. He had a pleasant voice, and she left a message for him. And then she texted Kevin to let him know she had followed up with the name he gave her. And she spent the next two hours reading State Department reports on current hot spots, sent to her by the SOS office. It was useful information for all their workers, and she figured she'd be in one of those locations soon.

She was just taking a break when her phone rang, and it was Andrew O'Connor. She was surprised to hear how young he sounded, particularly for an ex-priest and attorney, who had spent time in the Vatican. She had expected him to be older.

'Sorry I was out when you called,' he said pleasantly. 'I've had a crazy day. I'm between court appearances right now. How can I help you?' It was lunchtime, and he was obviously spending his returning phone calls, so at least she knew he was responsive.

'I just reported a sexual abuse case to the police,' she explained. 'I'm the mentor of a thirteen-year-old boy. He currently lives with me. He was molested by a priest three years ago.' She got straight to the point – he was a busy man, and she didn't want to waste his time, which he appreciated.

'Molested or raped?' he asked her bluntly.

'He says molested, but there's always the possibility that there was more that he's not telling me, or that he doesn't recall himself.' The attorney was well aware of that, too.

'Why has he waited until now to come forward?' He was used to cases where people waited even longer, sometimes twenty years, but he wanted the details.

'He tried to tell his aunt at the time, but she didn't believe him. Since then, I think he was afraid, embarrassed. The priest threatened to have him put in jail if he ever told. And he hasn't had anyone to champion his cause until now. I've only been mentoring him for the last six months, and he told me just recently.' It sounded reasonable to him. There was nothing exceptional there.

'Do you know where the priest is now? Sometimes they move these guys around, to hide them or get them out of sight, particularly if they've had complaints about them.'

'That might be the case here. They transferred him to Chicago last year. I saw him yesterday,' she said. That surprised Andrew O'Connor, who sounded shocked.

'In New York? On the street? By coincidence or appointment?'

'I flew to Chicago to get a look at him. I saw him supposedly for counseling about a fictitious husband.' He was vastly impressed by what she'd done. She was on top of things and proactive, and he liked how intelligent she sounded. There were no frills, no distractions, no tears, just the facts, which saved him time.

'How did he look?' Andrew O'Connor asked, curious about it.

'Like a movie star. Tall, handsome, incredibly charismatic, eyes like a snake, and he could charm the birds off the trees. He's perfect for the part he's playing. "Father Teddy," everyone's favorite teddy bear. Kids probably follow him like the Pied Piper, and the women in the parish must fall in love with him. He couldn't have been nicer. And afterward, I was in the church, and I saw him lead a little boy through a doorway with a hand on his shoulder, and close the door. God knows what happened after that. I felt totally helpless to do anything, but the thought of it makes me sick. What he did to my boy was bad enough. He let him use the piano in the church basement so he could molest him, and then threatened to have him put in jail if he told. And he managed to blame him.'

'Let me guess, for "tempting him," right? That's such an old line for bad priests. The guy sounds like a real winner. I'd like to meet with your boy and talk to him. Could you come in on Monday at three?' Blue would have to leave school early to do it, but she thought it was worth it. 'What's his name, by the way?'

'Blue Williams. And I'm Ginny Carter.'

'This probably sounds crazy, but were you ever on TV? My sister lives in L.A., and there used to be a TV reporter on the news with that name. I used to watch whenever I was out there.'

'That was me,' she said in a small voice.

'Wow . . . that's amazing. You and your husband were such a great team on the news,' he complimented her, and she found herself thinking that she was a different person now. It all seemed so long ago and was part of another life.

'Yes, we were a great team, thank you.' She tried not to sound wistful and just matter-of-fact. He was a lawyer, not a shrink.

'I noticed that you were both off the air the last few times I was in L.A.' He sounded disappointed.

'He died three and a half years ago,' she said simply.

'I'm so sorry. I wouldn't have mentioned it, but you were great.' He seemed embarrassed to have brought it up.

'Thank you.' Now he had even more faith in what she told him. He knew she was used to being accurate and factual, and reporting things as they were, not exaggerating or enhancing them. It made what she said more reliable for him, which made his job easier.

'See you on Monday with Blue,' he said pleasantly, and hung up.

And as soon as Blue came home from school that day,

she told him they had an appointment with the police. He looked frightened for a second, and then nodded. In his previous life, a meeting with police was not a good thing. This time it was.

They took the subway downtown and were on time for the appointment. Ginny asked for Detective Sanders, and a very attractive woman came out to meet them a few minutes later. She was not wearing a uniform, had long red hair, and was wearing a very short tight skirt. Blue looked relieved. She didn't look like a cop to him, or like anyone who would put you in jail, although she had handcuffs at her belt, and Ginny could see the faint outline of her gun in a shoulder holster under her jacket when she moved, and her star was clipped on her belt.

'Hi, Blue,' she said easily, and offered them something to drink when they sat down in her office. She had big green eyes, and a friendly, casual style. Blue asked for a Coke, and Ginny didn't want anything. Detective Sanders spoke directly and kindly to Blue. 'I'm sure it's a little unnerving coming down here. We're here to help you. We won't let anything bad happen to you, and I'm going to tell you what we're going to do all along the way. But people who hurt kids, or abuse them in any way, need to be stopped, for everyone's sake, even theirs, so you did the right thing coming down here.' She glanced at Ginny and included her in what she said, too. 'Is this your mom?' she asked about Ginny.

'No, she's my friend,' he said, and smiled at Ginny.

'He lives with me,' Ginny explained.

'Foster mom?' Detective Sanders asked her, and Ginny shook her head.

'No, he stays with me at times. He has an aunt who's his guardian.'

'That's fine,' Detective Sanders said, seeming unconcerned. She just wanted to know who the players were, and now she did. He didn't need the permission of a parent or guardian to report the incident. 'So, do you want to tell me what happened? First, how old were you?'

'I was nine, I think, or just ten. I was living with my aunt, uptown. And the priest at our church, Father Teddy, said I could play the piano in the basement. He used to listen to me play, and he sat next to me sometimes. That's when he did it.'

'And what did he do?' She asked the question as though it were the most normal thing in the world to be asking him, even having just met him. She was good at what she did.

And she asked specific questions as he told her, about what he touched and how, and exactly where, and whether the priest had hurt him. She asked if he had had Blue expose himself, or if there had been oral sex involved, and Blue said there hadn't been. But the incident had been repeated again and again, and the priest had kissed him and gone a little further each time, and Blue said he'd been scared he'd try to do more, so he stopped going to play the piano. And the priest had tried to get him to come back, but he wouldn't, and the priest had threatened him again then not to tell, or the police would arrest him and send him to jail and never believe him. He had thoroughly convinced Blue that that was true, and as Ginny listened, she realized that the incidents of abuse had happened more frequently than she'd first realized, and Blue hadn't told her, and she wondered now if there was more he had kept from her, or didn't remember. She was even more relieved now that they had come to the police. She had a feeling there was something he might not be saying. Detective Sanders thought that, too, but it was a good beginning.

And then Detective Sanders asked another question: 'Did he ever ask you to touch him?' She acted like it was no big deal if he did. Blue hesitated for a long time before he answered, and then he nodded. Ginny fought hard to follow the detective's example and not react. It was something she hadn't even thought to ask him, and she was horrified by his positive response.

'Sometimes.' His eyes were cast down as he said it, and he didn't look at Ginny.

'Did he threaten to hurt you if you didn't touch him?'

'He said it was my fault he got like that, because I tempted him, and it hurt him, so I had to fix it, and if

I didn't, he wouldn't let me come back, and he'd tell my aunt I'd stolen money from the collection basket, but I didn't.'

'And how did he have you fix it?' There was another long pause, and reluctantly Blue gave an exact description of a blow job, while Ginny tried not to cry as her heart ached for him. 'Did he ever do that to you?' This time Blue shook his head, and he glanced at Ginny from under his lashes to see if she was angry at him. She just smiled and patted his hand. He was being very brave. 'You know, Blue,' the detective went on, 'if we bring charges against Father Teddy, you won't have to see him in court. The judge will read our report, and he'll talk to you in his chambers. But you don't have to be afraid of Father Teddy anymore. He's history for you now, and one day you can put all this behind you and forget about it. It's something that happened to you, but it's not who you are, and none of it was your fault. He's a very sick man who took advantage of a little boy, maybe even a lot of little boys. But you never have to see him again.' Blue looked immensely relieved when she said it. He had been worrying about just that, and she knew it. You could almost see him exhale and relax after she spoke.

'Do you think he did the same thing to any of your friends? Did anyone ever talk about it?'

'Jimmy Ewald said he hated him, too. I was afraid to ask him why, but I thought maybe it was that. No one else ever said anything. They were probably too scared. I never said anything, either, not even to Jimmy. He was in seventh grade then, I was younger.'

She nodded and didn't look surprised at anything he said, not even the blow job. 'Do you remember what Father Teddy looks like? Do you think you'd recognize him if you saw him?'

'Like in a lineup? Like in *Law and Order*?' He looked excited at her question, and both women laughed.

'Yeah, or from a photo?'

'Sure.' Blue looked confident of it, and Ginny spoke up.

'I saw him yesterday, in Chicago, at the parish he transferred to. I just wanted to get a look at him.' Detective Sanders looked startled by that. 'I used to be a reporter.'

'Did he know why you were there?'

'I said I was there for marriage counseling and used my maiden name. But I saw him walk off with a young boy after our meeting. I was in the church, and he didn't see me.' Blue looked surprised at that, and the detective nodded, and Ginny saw a muscle in her cheek tense, but nothing else in her expression gave away how much she hated the perpetrators in these cases. She frequently told her co-workers that the 'perps' should all be castrated. But her anger never showed when she was around the victims.

'You did a great job today,' she said to Blue. 'You really helped me. What's going to happen now is we're going to do some very careful, quiet investigating, to see if anyone has ever complained about him to the church, and if they know about this. That may be why he was moved to Chicago. He could have been doing this for a long time, in other parishes he worked in. I doubt that you're the only one this happened to, Blue. But even if you are, even if he never did it before or after, what he did is still wrong, and I believe you.

'So after we have all the evidence, then we'll bring charges against him and arrest him. And if we do our job right, he'll go to prison. It may take a while to get all the evidence we want to build a strong case, so you have to be a little bit patient. But I'll be in touch with you, and with Ginny, and we'll let you know how it's going. I'm going to have a statement drawn up now, of what you said to me today. And if I made any mistakes, or got some of it wrong, just tell me and I'll change it, and then you can sign it, and we'll open the case and that's it.'

She smiled at him, got up, and said she'd be back in a few minutes. And Ginny could see her through the window, sitting at a computer and typing up a statement for him to sign. The detective had made no notes, so she could focus on Blue, so it would be impressive if she got it all in. She was back in her office five minutes later, with the printed statement for him to read and sign. Ginny had confirmed to her earlier that she hadn't known him then, so she had nothing to add.

The detective handed the sheet of paper to Blue and instructed him to read it carefully, and not to be embarrassed to tell her she had gotten something wrong. She wanted to be totally accurate, since his statement would be the starting point of the investigation. She got his e-mail address, and Ginny's, and her cell phone number.

Blue read the statement carefully and told her it was what he had said. She hadn't left anything out and there were no mistakes. And once he had confirmed that, she asked him to swear that what he had told her was true. He swore to her that it was and signed it, and then she thanked them both for coming, and walked them out of her office. It had been a draining, emotional meeting and Blue looked exhausted and so did Ginny, but she thought it had gone well.

They were in the elevator on their way downstairs when Ginny looked carefully at Blue.

'You okay?'

'Yeah. She was nice,' he said softly, and then he turned sad eyes up to Ginny. 'You're not mad at me?' For the rest he hadn't told her. She knew what he meant. And she admired him for being honest, which couldn't have been easy.

'Of course not. Why would I be mad at you? You're the bravest person I know, and you were right to tell her. The only one I'm mad at is Father Teddy. I hope he goes to prison for a long, long time.' Blue nodded, and she took his hand in hers. As they walked out of the elevator, out of the building, and down the street together to the subway, he started to talk and laugh and come alive again.

When Jane Sanders walked out of her office, with Blue's statement in her hand, she strode into her lieutenant's office with a serious expression, and when he met her eyes, she looked like she wanted to kill someone. This case was no different than the others, but she was so sick of hearing it again and again, and they always assigned these cases to her. After years of psychology and counseling classes, and a master's degree from Columbia, she handled them better than anyone else. And she always got her man. She had never lost a case against a child molester or a priest.

'What you got?' he asked with interest. He had seen that look on her face before. 'A nice serial killer to keep you busy?' he teased her.

'I wish. Another priest. I'm so goddamn sick of these guys and what they do to these kids. Why don't they kick them out of the priesthood? They know about most of them anyway, but they just shuffle them around like peas in the shell game. They give the church a bad name.' And like Ginny, she was sure that Father Teddy had done the same thing, or worse, to other boys in the parish. It was never a one-time thing with sexual abusers like him. And he was probably doing it in Chicago now. She had a team of investigators she used for cases like this, and she was going to put them into action to follow up Blue's case.

'Will it stick?' Bill Sullivan asked her. She was the best detective he had in child sexual abuse cases, she was brilliant at her job.

'Like glue,' she said with certainty. 'The case is solid.' It was like so many others she had had, and it all rang true to her. 'And the kid will make a great witness.'

'Go for it, Jane.' Bill grinned at her.

'Don't worry, I will. I'm on it.' She left a copy of the statement on his desk with a file number on it, and walked back to her office. The hunt for Father Teddy and his victims had begun.

Chapter 12

Their meeting with Andrew O'Connor was very different from the meeting with the police. And to spare Blue the pain and embarrassment of going through the details again, Ginny handed the lawyer Blue's statement to the police and asked him to read it, which he did. And then he looked up at both of them with a serious expression. He was a tall, aristocratic-looking man, and although he was wearing jeans and a blue shirt with his sleeves rolled up, the shirt was well made, and his shoes were impeccably shined. The art on his office walls was expensive, and the diplomas said he had graduated from Harvard. His confidence and demeanor suggested to Ginny that he came from an important family and had money. Kevin hadn't mentioned it, but she could sense it. She could easily envision him as a banker or a lawyer, but not as a priest.

'I know Jane Sanders. She's the right person for this investigation,' he said comfortably. 'I've worked with her before. We've never lost a case together. And I don't think this one will be too difficult to prove. He sounds like he's pretty bold, and my guess is you're just one of a number of victims, Blue, maybe even a lot of them. And if we can prove that the archdiocese moved him knowingly to Chicago to cover up for him, we'll win our case. And I suspect that's exactly what they did. The Vatican has ordered them to stop doing that now, but some of the monsignors and bishops are still trying to protect their own. Canon law makes it very clear that in cases like this, they need to turn an errant priest in to the authorities, but many of them just won't. So a guy like Father Teddy gets away with it again and again. First, we need to stop him and see justice served here for you and all the people he hurt. And then I'd like to see Blue get compensation in the form of damages. Some of these cases have won some very handsome settlements for my clients.'

'What do you mean?' Blue asked him directly, and the ex-Jesuit attorney explained.

'When someone does something bad to you like that, and hurts you or damages you in some way, first you want to send them to prison if possible. That's what the police do. But then you can sue them civilly and get an amount of money to make up for what you went through. That's what I do.' He made it seem very simple.

'You mean I get paid for what he did to me?' Blue looked shocked. 'That doesn't seem right.'

'In some ways it's not,' Andrew agreed with him. 'It doesn't make it right, and in the case of people who are physically injured, it doesn't make them whole again. But it's kind of our system's way of saying that people are sorry, that they have to pay something for what they did. And sometimes that can be a good thing, if the money can help you in some way. And in this case, the Catholic Church is paying the bill, and some of the settlements have been very high. You can't put a price tag on the damage people do, or the trauma you suffered, or the grief they cause. But getting a settlement for some of the victims has been a comfort to them, and made them feel like someone cares. It's how our legal system works.' Blue was still looking ill at ease with the idea as the attorney explained. 'It might be nice for you to have an amount of money in the bank, for your education, to start a business one day, or to help you buy a house when you're older, or even for your kids. It's a way of giving you something back for the innocence you lost and the trust that was abused.' He didn't mention his body, but that was part of it, too. And Blue turned to Ginny with a questioning look.

'Do you think that's okay?' he asked her, unsure, and she nodded.

'Yes, I do, Blue. You went through a lot. It was very traumatic. You're not stealing money from anyone if you get a settlement. You deserve it, and it would be the church's way of telling you they're sorry for how bad Father Teddy was and what he did to you.' It sounded better to him the way she phrased it.

'The state sends him to prison, and the church gives you an apology in the form of a gift. Sometimes a very big gift, which it can afford,' the lawyer said again. Blue was pensive as he mulled it over and didn't respond. He didn't want money he didn't deserve because he had let Father Teddy do something bad. He still felt guilty at times about it, because as he got older, he knew how wrong it was and he hadn't stopped him, but he had been too scared to. And what if Father Teddy was right when he said Blue had tempted him. He hadn't meant to, but what if he had?

'I'd like to work with Jane Sanders on the investigation, and we can hire an additional investigator ourselves, so we tie up all the loose ends, and don't miss something important,' the lawyer told them. 'We want the tightest case possible so we're sure of a conviction. And at the same time I'll prepare a civil suit, and as soon as he's convicted, we should get a settlement from the church.' He was very direct about it, but Ginny knew it wouldn't be as simple as he made it sound. They were complicated cases to bring to trial, and the church wasn't always as cooperative as he suggested. The church protected its own. But his best-case scenario sounded perfect to her, and to Blue.

'And once the state brings charges against him, and the

case is out in the open, I want to send a letter to members of the parish – then, before the incident, and now – and of any other parish where he's been, and see if we can get other victims to come forward. Some people don't want to get involved or have people know what happened to them, but many do, especially once they realize there were other victims. You'll be amazed at how many people come out of the woodwork and admit it happened to them, too. Guys like this don't just do it once or twice, or even a few times. We found ninety-seven victims on one of my cases, but only seventy-six were willing to testify. And they all got settlements from the church, very large ones in fact. It was my most important case so far.'

'How do you charge for this?' Ginny asked him in a quiet tone. She suspected he did it on a contingency basis and took a percentage of the settlement and wouldn't charge them other than that, but she wanted to be sure.

'I think these cases are an important part of our history, as human beings, and as Catholics. We have to make it right. We can't hide it, we have to heal it, whatever it takes. And for those of us who still believe in the church and its integrity, and I do, we have to give something back. I do these cases pro bono. I don't charge for them, no matter how many hours I put in. Even if I litigate. I don't want a percentage of the settlement. In other words,' he said, looking at both of them, 'everything I do on the case is free.' Blue thought that was very nice of him, and

Ginny was stunned, knowing how expensive legal work could be, and how much most attorneys charged, especially when there were settlements involved.

'How does that work?' she asked him, incredibly impressed.

'It just does. I have paying clients on other matters. I think it's vital to demonstrate that there are still good people involved, directly and indirectly, with the church.' He wasn't aware that she knew his history, so he explained, 'I was a priest. I left the priesthood for a variety of reasons, but I am deeply troubled by these crimes of sexual abuse committed on young boys. This is what I can do to help, defending those who need it, and doing it for free. I don't want anyone to think that I'm getting a victim a big settlement so I can take part of it for myself. I'm not the one who got hurt, Blue is. He deserves it all. I've been doing it this way for several years. The archdiocese knows who I am. They don't like me, and I fight hard.' And then he smiled broadly at her. 'And I always win. I haven't lost a single one of these cases yet, and I don't intend to start now. The sword of truth is mighty.' He smiled at Blue. 'We'll use it to cut off Father Teddy's head.' Ginny would have liked to suggest other options, but didn't. She was amazed by the ex-priest who had just offered to represent Blue for free. 'You're his guardian?' he asked Ginny then, and assumed she was. He was surprised when she said she wasn't.

'His aunt is. Do you need her to sign something?'

'Not yet. But eventually when we file the civil lawsuit, his guardian will need to sign it.'

'I'm sure she will,' Ginny said confidently. Charlene loved the boy, and would want what was best for him, and a settlement surely would be. 'I'm sure that won't be a problem.' He nodded, satisfied, and went on, and told them what the game plan was. He was going to speak to the investigator that he used for sexual abuse cases who was great at ferreting out gossip, rumors, and suspicions in the parish, and sometimes a great deal more than that, that might lead them to evidence, and other victims. O'Connor said he was going to keep in close touch with Detective Sanders as her investigation developed. And once charges were brought against Father Teddy Graham by the state, or possibly several states, he would file the civil suit, and at the same time demand a settlement from the church. Once he was convicted, their suit would be indisputable. The only question then would be how much. But there was a long stretch of road to cover before they got there. Andrew O'Connor estimated the whole process would take a year, maybe less, maybe more, in the case of a settlement. An actual trial might take longer, but he doubted it would come to that. And if the archdiocese tried to hide Father Teddy's crimes, and backed him up, it would be even worse for its case. The courts expected the church to show remorse for its priests' crimes, and make restitution.

They chatted for a few minutes then, and Andrew O'Connor tried not to stare at Ginny, but was looking at her intently. She looked different than she had on TV. She was just as beautiful, but in a quieter, more luminous way. He thought she had a face like a madonna. She wasn't wearing makeup, her long blond hair was pulled back, and she had the saddest expression in her eyes he'd ever seen, even when she was laughing. They were two deep pools of sorrow. The only time he saw her look happy was when she talked to Blue.

And as Ginny looked at the attorney as he walked them out, she thought he seemed sophisticated and worldly. He had a very distinguished appearance, and despite gray hair at his temples, he had a young face, and she guessed him to be about forty years old.

She remembered that Jesuits were the intellectual elite of the church. And for him to work in the legal office of the Vatican, he had to be a good lawyer and be extremely bright and Kevin had mentioned something about him having lived four years in Rome. He was a very capable man, and just as she had felt with Jane Sanders, Ginny was confident that, with him, Blue's case was in good hands. On their way back to the apartment, Blue said he liked him, too. He didn't ask how much money he might get in a settlement – the whole idea of it still embarrassed him, which pleased Ginny. Blue was standing up for what was right, and what had been done to him, not for money.

And that night, she called Kevin Callaghan to thank him for the referral.

'He was terrific, and Blue likes him, too. I suspect he's a very good lawyer, and I almost fell out of my chair when he told us he does these cases pro bono.'

'That's amazing.' Kevin was surprised, too.

'It sounds like he still believes in all his Jesuit values – he just wants to get rid of the bad priests,' Ginny told him.

'Interesting guy,' Kevin commented, and Ginny agreed. She had been enormously impressed. It had been a very productive meeting on Blue's behalf, and so had the one with the police.

And after she talked to Kevin, Becky called her. Every time she did, Ginny braced herself for bad news.

'How's Dad?' Ginny asked, holding her breath for the response.

'About the same as when you were here. In and out. And some days he just sleeps now.' He was like a candle slowly flickering as it went out. 'How was your week?' Becky asked her. They hadn't spoken since their trip to L.A.

'Busy, and exhausting.' Ginny was feeling somewhat frazzled, but pleased with all they'd accomplished.

'What did you do?'

'Some very difficult things,' Ginny admitted. 'We dealt with a tough situation for Blue, or started to.' This was just the beginning. Ginny hadn't told her yet, and didn't want to embarrass Blue, but the case would be in the public realm soon, even if his identity was concealed, so she felt comfortable telling Becky.

'Something at school?'

'No,' Ginny said carefully. 'He was molested by a parish priest three years ago, and we've talked about it very seriously, and decided to do something about it. So we met with the Child Abuse Unit last week and today with an attorney who specializes in these cases against the church. It was pretty heavy stuff. But I think it will be a good thing for Blue. It honors and validates what he experienced, and tells him that someone who abuses him can't get away with it, and that decent people care about him.' There was silence at the other end of the phone when she finished speaking.

'Oh my God,' Becky said a minute later, and Ginny assumed she was shocked at what Blue had been through. 'I can't believe you're doing this. You're taking on the church now? And how do you know he's telling you the truth?' Becky didn't believe it for a minute. There had been plenty of false accusations among the real ones that had destroyed good priests' lives. It was the flip side of the coin. But Ginny was certain that that was not the case here. She believed Blue, beyond any doubt. His suffering over it was too real.

'I am absolutely sure that he's telling the truth,' Ginny said calmly.

'You don't know that. Lots of kids have told lies about it. And your getting involved in it is sick. He's not your child, you hardly know him, and now you're attacking the Catholic Church. Don't you even believe in God anymore? What's wrong with you?' Ginny was shocked at what she was hearing, and that her sister had said it to her.

'Of course I believe in God. I don't believe in priests who abuse their position and molest or rape little boys. Let's not get confused here. And who's going to stand up for him if I don't? He has no one, Becky. No parents, no adult who cares about him, and an aunt who doesn't even want to see him, and has three kids of her own in a one-bedroom apartment, and a boyfriend who beats her up. You don't understand what he comes from, and you don't give a damn, but I do.' Ginny was outraged by her sister's reaction. She was always on some kind of warpath against whatever Ginny was doing, whether it was her human rights work, Blue, or now their case against the priest who had molested him.

'You're not Joan of Arc, for God's sake! And going after the church we grew up in is sacrilegious and immoral. I can't believe you'd do a thing like that. Thank God Dad will never know.' Their father had gone to church every Sunday of his life, and their mother had, too, when she was alive. And they had gone to church as children. Becky and Alan went only occasionally on Sundays, and took their children when they did. They were hardly devout Catholics. But Becky felt she had to protect Father Teddy Graham, even though it was he who had violated the sanctity of the church, not Ginny for defending Blue and fighting back. 'You can't be serious about this. You really have to rethink it,' Becky said insistently. Her tone was one of furious disbelief and stern disapproval.

'What? And tell him it was okay that he was molested, that it doesn't matter, and that the priest who did it is a good guy? He belongs in prison. And I'm sure he's done it to lots of other boys. I saw him with one of them myself last week.'

'What were you doing? Following him?' Becky was off on a tangent again. It made Ginny realize once again that all her life her sister had criticized her for something she was doing. But nothing she could say would sway Ginny from supporting Blue with the case.

'No, I went to Chicago to check him out. He's a real piece of work.'

'So are you,' Becky said angrily. 'I never thought I'd see the day when my own sister would attack the church.'

'They need to be attacked on this issue, and these men have to be exposed. They're child abusers in the most perverted possible way. They're pedophiles, and they belong in prison.'

'Blue's not suffering. He looks like a happy, healthy kid. It's happened to others – he'll get over it. You don't need to turn it into a sacred mission and make an ass of yourself.'

'I can't talk to you about this,' Ginny said through clenched teeth. 'What you're saying is too outrageous. What do you think people should do? Uphold the bad priests? Hide them? Forget about it? Because that's what the church has been doing, and it makes the situation even worse.'

'They're sacred men, Ginny,' Becky said in an icy tone. 'God will punish you if you mess with that.'

'He'll punish me a lot more, and so will my own conscience, if I don't help this boy get justice in this world.'

'Why don't you stop worrying about him, and get your own life together, instead of picking up every stray dog you run across, and chasing around the world trying to solve problems that can't be fixed? Stay home, get a decent job, get your hair done once in a while, go on a date, and turn into a normal human being again. And for God's sake, have some respect for the Catholic Church.'

'Thank you for your advice,' Ginny said, and hung up on her, and she was shaking when she did. She couldn't believe the things her sister had said, not just about her but about the priests who had violated every law with total disregard for morality and decency and were raping children. Her sister clearly would have preferred to keep it hidden.

Blue came looking for her in his pajamas a few minutes later with a puzzled look. 'Who was that? I thought I heard you shouting when I got out of the shower.' She was grateful he hadn't heard what she had said.

'It was Becky. We had a stupid argument. Sisters do that. She told me I should get my hair done more often.'

He looked at her long blond hair, and shrugged at the mysteries of women. 'Looks fine to me.'

'Thank you,' she said, and smiled at him. She did not for one instant regret supporting him in this battle. It was actually about respecting the Catholic Church, and defending it, more than the priests who had violated it. And it was about defending the rights of children to be safe and unharmed in what should be a chaste and safe environment for them. She'd had such a good time with Becky when they went to L.A., almost like the old days when they were kids. And now she was on a tirade again, defending what was indefensible in the church. Ginny was furious over it, but it also made her realize that there would be others who would be angry at her and Blue, if they heard about it. They, too, would prefer to keep the sins of a few priests hidden and pretend that the Catholic clergy was infallible. Ginny wasn't willing to do that. She believed in pursuing the truth, exposing evil, seeking justice for innocent victims, and defending the rights of little boys not to be raped or molested by their parish priests. It seemed totally clear to her that these were principles worth defending, no matter what her sister thought. And if Becky didn't approve of her, too bad. Ginny believed a hundred percent in what she was doing, and when Blue hugged her before he went to bed that night, with his faith in her shining in his eyes, she knew that she was right.

Chapter 13

Ginny didn't speak to her sister again after their argument on Monday night. Becky had sent her a text reiterating the same views and opinions, and Ginny didn't answer her. It wasn't even an argument to her. She thought Becky's position was a disgrace.

And on Tuesday she met with Ellen Warberg and after much careful consideration, and consultation with other international human rights agencies, they were assigning Ginny and a handful of others to Syria. The Red Cross was a strong presence there, and SOS/HR had always taken a completely apolitical stance, which protected them, and their workers to some extent. Unquestionably it was a hot spot and there were safer places to go, but Ellen assured her that at the first sign of a change in climate there, or increased tension, Ginny could decide to leave of her own volition, or they would pull her out, if they knew something she didn't, or even heard a whisper about escalating risk. Ginny felt comfortable with what Ellen said to her, and they had never let her down. The problem for her now was Blue. She had undertaken a responsibility to him, taking on their toughest assignments no longer seemed smart to her. She agreed to go to Syria, but wanted to rethink the kind of assignments she would take in future. Her life had changed.

Ellen had no doubt that Ginny could handle it, and the situation was unpleasant, but their presence was direly needed. Boys over the age of fourteen were being imprisoned for no apparent reason, tortured, in some cases, and even raped, and those who survived it often emerged broken and crippled, physically and psychologically, almost beyond repair. And even younger children were being detained in custody; some were being put in prison as well. The Red Cross had two camps set up to minister to them, internationally staffed and run. SOS/HR was supplying two workers for each camp, and Ginny was one of them. It showed their faith in her that she'd been chosen, but it was going to be heartbreaking work. Because it was a hardship post, they had made it a short assignment, and Ellen said they were going to bring her back in eight weeks, at the beginning of August. She was relieved not to be away from Blue for too long, and she told him about it that night.

'I'm leaving in a week,' she told him over dinner, 'which means I'll miss your graduation, which I'm very upset about, but you have to be grown up about this. The good news is I'll be back a month early.' They had expected her to miss the graduation, and she was pleased to be coming back before summer was over. 'I'll get you a cell phone before I leave.' She hadn't done that yet, which was inconvenient at times, when she wanted to track him down, and she wanted him to have a phone before she left. 'You have to be available if Detective Sanders calls you, or Andrew O'Connor, if they need something from you on the case.' For the moment the investigation was getting started, but they might need to confirm something with Blue, or contact him. 'I'll call you when I can, but I don't think I'll have much communication in the camp.' She didn't stress the risks where she was going, and played it down. 'I want you to stay at Houston Street. I know you don't like it, but it's only for eight weeks.' She was matter-of-fact about it, and hoped he would be, too. He had known he was going to have to stay there when she went away.

'Why can't I just stay here?' He looked bitterly disappointed that she was leaving again, even if he'd known she would. The reality of it was hard for both of them, now that the time had come.

'You can't stay alone in an apartment. You're thirteen years old. What if you get sick?' Or if some social worker discovered that he was thirteen years old and living alone.

'No one took care of me when I got sick on the streets,' he reminded her.

'I feel better knowing that you're in a reasonable environment with other kids, with any kind of help you need available.'

'I hate it there.' He crossed his arms and sank into his chair in a slump.

'It's only for eight weeks. I'm coming home early this time, and I'll be here for almost all of August. And they won't reassign me till September,' she said, feeling stressed about it, and sad to leave him. But he had survived without her before they met, and she was leaving him taken care of and provided for. Julio Fernandez had promised to keep a closer eye on him this time, and he could play their piano. But that only compensated a little. 'If you run away, I swear I'm going to have a fit when I get home – tie you to your bed, hide your favorite pair of Converse – something terrible I'll have to think of.' He smiled at her empty threat. She didn't know how to be bad to him, but he still didn't want to stay at Houston Street while she was gone. But he would do it for her, albeit grudgingly and complaining all the way.

Andrew O'Connor called Ginny the day after she got her assignment from SOS/HR. He had thought of something and wanted to talk to her about it, when Blue wasn't around, so he called during school hours, and she was home getting organized for the trip.

'Has Blue ever been to a therapist?' he asked her.

'I don't think so. He would have told me.'

'I think it would be a good idea to have him evaluated by someone. It will strengthen our case if there is some remaining psychological impact from the abuse. And who knows? He may remember something about it he hasn't told us, or even recall himself. It's just a thought. He seems like a surprisingly well-balanced kid given what he's been through, but I'm sure you're an important part of that,' he said, impressed that she had taken all this on. It seemed like a saintly thing to do, to him. And Blue and she obviously cared for each other. She was kind and respectful to him, and very loving.

'I'm only a recent addition,' she said modestly, 'and he did fine without me before. He has a place to stay now, but his mental stability is his own.'

'He's a very lucky young man,' Andrew said, and meant it. But Ginny knew that the ex-Vatican lawyer was part of that good fortune, taking on his civil case for free.

'I'm leaving in less than a week, but I'll try to get him to someone before I go. Any idea who?' He gave her the name of a psychologist he had worked with before, very successfully, particularly with boys in cases like this one, and Ginny jotted her name down.

'Where are you going?' he asked, curious about her. Even though she was no longer a TV reporter, she seemed like an interesting person. He thought she had a fascinating job as an international human rights worker, but he didn't know much more.

'Syria, actually,' she said, as though it were a normal place to go.

'Syria? Why there?'

'I work for SOS/HR, as a field-worker. I usually go on three- or four-month missions three times a year, mostly to refugee camps. I just got back from Afghanistan.'

'How long have you been doing that?' He was even more intrigued by what she said. She obviously went to dangerous places, was a gutsy woman, and had suffered in her own life.

'I've been doing it since . . .' She caught herself. 'For three and a half years, since I gave up TV news.' She didn't want to sound pathetic by talking about Mark and Chris.

'Where will Blue be while you're gone?'

'I'm only going for eight weeks this time. I made a deal with him, and he's not happy about it. He stays at the Houston Street Shelter, which is a very decent place. He ran away when I was in Afghanistan. He promised he wouldn't do that again. I'm giving him your number, too.' Andrew was smiling as he listened to her. She was a real person, and a pretty terrific one in his opinion, given what she was doing for Blue.

'By the way, I think you'll probably need a release from his aunt for the psychologist. She might not see him without it. Therapists can be sticklers about that.'

'I'll call his aunt and get her to sign one,' Ginny said easily.

'It must be frustrating having her be the guardian when you have physical custody of him.'

'Not really. She's been very nice about signing whatever I've needed so far. I'll give her a call.' They chatted for a few more minutes about her trip to Syria before they hung up. And knowing that Charlene was home in the daytime, since she worked at night, Ginny called her. She was very pleasant when Ginny told her how Blue was doing and that he'd be graduating in a few weeks, although sadly, she wouldn't be there to see it. Charlene didn't offer to go, and then Ginny explained that she needed her to sign another release.

'What's it for this time?' his aunt chuckled. 'You taking him to Europe for his summer vacation?' She had been impressed when Ginny took him to L.A. He was a lucky kid in her opinion.

'No,' Ginny said seriously, 'I'd like to take him to a therapist.'

'What kind of therapist?' Charlene asked. 'Did he get hurt? That boy is always jumping on or off something. I'm not surprised.'

'No, he's fine,' Ginny said calmly. 'I mean like a psychologist, that kind of therapist.'

'Why would you want to do that?' Charlene sounded

shocked, and Ginny wondered if she was nervous because her boyfriend had taken a swing at Blue, and didn't want it known. Ginny hadn't intended to explain it to her on the phone, but she felt like she had no choice, since Charlene had asked, and she didn't want to lie to her and say it was for something else.

'I think Blue tried to tell you about it a long time ago. He was very young, and he probably didn't express himself convincingly at the time.' She was trying to give Charlene a gracious out for having failed to listen to him about something so important. 'It seems that Blue was the victim of sexual abuse by a priest in your parish church when he was nine or ten. And we're doing something about it now. We filed a police report last week against the perpetrator, and we're going to file a civil suit against the archdiocese once he's been charged with the crime.' There was dead silence at the other end.

'What perpetrator?' Charlene said in a shocked voice.

'Father Teddy Graham,' Ginny answered, as Blue's aunt let out a piercing scream.

'You can't do that! Blue is lying to you! That priest is the finest man on Earth. Blue will burn in hell forever if he tells lies about that man!' She was frantic in the priest's defense, much to Ginny's dismay.

'I've seen him, and I understand why you feel that way. He's a very personable man. But the fact is, he sexually molested your nephew, and possibly other boys in the parish. He's out there ruining young lives, and he has to be stopped. The police are investigating him now. And Blue isn't going to hell for that or anything else. He was the victim of a sexual crime.' Ginny tried to stay as reasonable as possible and not lose her temper at Charlene.

'He's a liar and always was! He tried telling me that. I can tell you there's no truth in it. You're the one committing a crime if you try to put that man in jail. Father Teddy is a saint!' Listening to her made Ginny want to scream. But she forced herself to stay calm and rational, and she needed the release for him to see the shrink.

'I know this is very upsetting. And I'm sure it's hard to believe, since you like the man. But I think he duped everyone, and the truth is going to come out. Other boys will speak up. But in the meantime, I need that release for Blue.'

'I'm not giving you a release or anything to help you persecute that man. And I don't mean prosecute, I mean persecute! I'm not signing anything to help you do this ungodly thing, and you can tell Blue to forget I'm related to him if he doesn't drop the charges against Father Teddy right now.' She made herself very clear, and a minute later Charlene said goodbye and put down the phone.

Ginny called Andrew O'Connor back immediately and told him what had happened. He wasn't surprised.

'It happens all the time. It's very threatening to people

when you force them to face something like that, and she probably feels guilty for not listening to Blue earlier.'

'It doesn't sound like it. The man is so convincing and seductive, I saw it myself. In any case, she won't give me a release, so I can't take him to the shrink.' Ginny sounded discouraged. It had been a terrible conversation with Blue's aunt.

'Don't worry,' he reassured her, 'we don't need the release now. It's not pressing. You can try again when you get back.'

She said that she would, but it didn't sound likely that Charlene would sign it. And her own sister had taken the same extreme position to preserve the silence around the church, no matter what this very sick priest had done. Andrew wished Ginny good luck on her trip again, and they hung up.

She didn't tell Blue about her conversation with Charlene – there was no point.

She got Blue the promised cell phone that week as a graduation present; it comforted her to know that she could reach him if she could get to a phone herself.

She also called her attorney and added an amendment to her will, and had it notarized. She still had money from Mark's life insurance, the house sale, and her own savings, and she added a sizable bequest to Blue. Becky and her family didn't need it, and if something happened to her, she wanted Blue to have it. It felt like the right thing to do. And on Saturday she helped him move to Houston Street. He looked bereft when she helped him unpack. She had promised to take him out to lunch the next day, and she was leaving on Monday.

She checked the mail when she got home, and there was a letter for Blue from LaGuardia Arts high school. Ginny's heart pounded as she carried it upstairs. She was itching to open it herself, but she didn't. She would save it for lunch the next day, so he could open it himself. She hoped it was good news.

When she picked him up at Houston Street on Sunday morning, Blue was waiting for her at the door. They had lunch at an outdoor café in the Village, and then she remembered the envelope in her purse. They both knew what it was. She was as nervous as he was while he opened it, and she was worried about what would happen if they'd turned him down. She knew he'd be bitterly disappointed, and she didn't want to leave him for two months on a sour note. She watched his face intently as he read the letter, and for an instant nothing showed. And then, halfway through it, his big almost-electric blue eyes opened wide and stared at her.

'OhmyGod, ohmyGod, they accepted me!' he shouted. Several heads on the terrace turned, and he didn't care. *'They accepted me!'* He stood up and jumped and threw his arms around her. 'I go to LaGuardia Arts high school now!'

'I guess you do.' She sat beaming at him with tears in her eyes. It was a huge accomplishment for him that she hoped would change his life, which had been her intent when she got the application for him and made him apply. He could hardly speak for the rest of lunch. They walked around the Village for a while, then hopped into a cab and went to Central Park. They both ate ice cream, took a long walk, and lay on the grass. He looked happier than she'd ever seen him, and justifiably proud of himself. And she was very, very proud of him. He had texted Lizzie in L.A. on his new phone right after lunch, and she was thrilled for him. She had gotten into her first-choice high school, too, in Pasadena. And they wanted to see each other again. He kept hounding Ginny to invite Lizzie to New York.

This time when she left him at Houston Street, he didn't look upset. He was too excited about being accepted at LaGuardia Arts. He told Julio Fernandez about it as soon as he walked in the front door.

'I guess we'd better enjoy your company before you get too famous to hang out with us anymore,' Julio teased him, with a grin at Ginny. 'I hope you're intending to play our piano while you're here. We could use some decent music,' he said to Blue, who was ecstatic.

Blue was still smiling when he hugged Ginny, and she kissed him goodbye. 'Be good. If you run away this time, I'll kill you,' she warned him, but she was smiling, and he knew she didn't mean it. 'I'll call you whenever I can.' But she had told him again that it wouldn't be often, because of where the camp was situated. As usual, she'd be out of touch most of the time.

'Take care of yourself,' he said with a tender look. 'I love you, Ginny.'

'I love you, too, Blue. Remember that. I'll be back,' she said, to remind him that he was no longer alone, that she loved him and cared about him. Blue was on his way to the amazing life she had promised. It made her aware, more than ever, that she wanted to come home safely from her next trip. She had to be there for Blue.

Chapter 14

Ginny didn't call Becky before she left New York the next day, and didn't want to talk to her, after everything she'd said about Blue, and their sexual abuse case against the priest. She had sent her a text that she was leaving, with her contact numbers for the next eight weeks so Becky would have them, in case something happened with their father. Becky didn't respond, but she had all the information she needed.

It was another endless journey to get to the camp near Homs, and when she arrived, conditions were even worse than she'd been told. Children in heartbreaking condition lay glassy-eyed on cots, barely clinging to life. There were young boys who had been raped, others with severed limbs, a beautiful young girl with her eyes gouged out by her father, whose family had abandoned her on the road rather than take care of her. Torture was being committed on children. It made Blue's experience with Father Teddy look minor in comparison. She spent her time with injured young people in shocking situations, with inadequate provisions, under relentless tension. And each day more children were brought in. The Red Cross and medical volunteers did a heroic job and Ginny and the others did whatever they could to help. And because of the volatile political climate, all the workers were exceptionally careful, stayed in the camp, and went everywhere in pairs, or larger groups, whenever possible. Ginny concentrated on the injured children, and not the risks. The assignment broke everyone's heart. And the rare times she was somewhere that she could get Internet access, she checked for e-mails from Andrew O'Connor and Blue. There were none from her sister on this trip. But at least it meant that their father was still alive. Ginny had never felt so physically and emotionally drained in her life. She was relieved it was only for eight weeks.

Blue sounded all right in his e-mails to her. He complained about Houston Street, but less acutely than before. He seemed to have made his peace with it, and said he was composing music on their piano, which made her smile. If he was involved in music, she knew he'd be okay. His graduation had gone well, after she left, and he was doing odd jobs at the shelter to help out. He said it was hot in New York, and she was startled and pleased to read that Andrew O'Connor had come to visit him and Blue thought he was a great guy.

Andrew's e-mails to her were particularly interesting and hopeful. He told her that the police investigators had turned up several other instances of abuse committed by Father Teddy at St. Francis's. Five other boys had come forward, and two at St. Anne's in Chicago, and Andrew was sure there would be more. They had opened a Pandora's box that had been tightly closed and sealed for years about the wayward priest, and the police suspected now that the archdiocese had been aware of some of the cases, and had moved him to Chicago so he could start with a clean slate. And once there, he had done it again. She could hardly wait to get home and learn more about what was going on, and be back with Blue again. For the first time on one of her assignments, she was anxious to get home. Andrew and the police had not shared any of the reports with him in her absence, and didn't intend to until she got back. Andrew thought it best to wait until she returned, and so did she. There was nothing she could do from where she was.

He mentioned seeing Blue, too; he had thought that Blue might be lonely without her, so he dropped by as a friend. He asked her permission to take him to a baseball game. She was touched that Andrew had asked her and e-mailed him back immediately to thank him and said Blue would be thrilled to go to a game with him, since he was a passionate Yankees fan. Andrew responded that he happened to know the owner of the team, and might be able to introduce Blue to some of the players. And the next time she heard from Blue, he raved about the fun he'd had and the players he'd met. He'd gotten two signed balls, a bat, and a glove, and he had Julio lock them up so they didn't disappear. And he'd written a piece of music for Andrew to thank him. He wrote that Andrew played the piano, too, and had liked his composition. She was grateful for the time that Andrew was spending with him in her absence. It made her feel less out of touch halfway around the world, and she thought it was good for Blue to have a positive male influence in his life.

She thanked Andrew herself by e-mail, and he responded and inquired about her work in Syria. It was hard to describe in an e-mail the daily tragedies she was encountering, which were routine there, and the injustices that were commonplace, mostly against women and children. He responded thoughtfully, with compassion, and he sent her a joke and a *New Yorker* cartoon at the end of it, which made her laugh before she went back to work. It made civilization seem a little less remote. He sounded like a nice person, deeply committed to his work and clients, which she had suspected when they met.

Conditions in the camp remained tense while she was there, and everyone was busy. The Red Cross had sent additional workers, as had other international groups. It would be hard to relate to ordinary life after an experience like this. New York seemed like another planet, compared to what she was doing and seeing every day. The sheer human misery of such severely injured children who had no hope of a better life was overwhelming. It made her want to take them all home with her.

Her living situation in the camp was the worst she'd been in. The time in Syria seemed longer and harder to her than her previous assignments, and the eight weeks she spent there felt like an eternity, and she was relieved when her replacement arrived, only two days before she was due to leave. Several of the workers were starting to get seriously sick, and were being sent home. Ginny had had dysentery for weeks, and had lost ten pounds since she'd arrived. It had been one of her toughest assignments yet, many of the less experienced workers were severely disheartened, and the more seasoned ones were exhausted. There was still so much left to do when she left, but she was ready to go home, and excited to see Blue again. She slept without stirring on the first leg of the trip, from Homs to Damascus.

It felt surreal to see civilization again when she got to Damascus, and she walked around the airport literally feeling dazed, not sure what to do, overwhelmed by people, crowds, and airport shops, after what she'd seen and lived for two months. And on the second flight from Amman, Jordan, she slowly returned to the land of the living as she ate a light meal and watched a movie. She wondered if her stomach would ever be the same again.

And all she wanted to do was forget what she'd seen in the camp.

It had been a depressing trip, she had never cared for so many people, all of them children and young people, for whom she could do so little to help. She knew the memory of it would be with her forever. Everything had been ten times, sometimes a hundred times, worse than they'd said it would be. But she was still glad she'd gone, even to do the little she had. She felt as though she'd been gone for a year, not a mere eight weeks. It was the first week in August and she was hoping to go away with Blue for a few days somewhere before he started school, and she had to leave again.

When the plane landed in New York, she wanted to kiss the ground. As she walked through the airport, she looked like a refugee from some terrible place. She couldn't wait to get home and sit in the bathtub and soak, but she had promised Blue she would pick him up on her way in from the airport. She had been traveling by ground and air for more than twenty hours by then. She gave the cabdriver the address of Houston Street, and told him there would be a second stop after she picked someone up.

Blue knew what time she was due in, and she texted him when she left the airport. He was waiting with packed bags when she arrived at the shelter. She looked exhausted as she came through the door and beamed when she saw him. Blue was shocked, but happy to see her, too. She was deathly pale, rail thin, and had dark circles under her eyes. Her two months at the camp had taken a heavy toll, more than she realized.

'Holy shit! You look awful. Didn't you eat while you were there?' He was visibly thrilled to see her, but it looked like she had starved.

'Not much.' She smiled through the grime of the trip, her hair loose down her back, and gave him a fierce, tight hug. She was so happy that he was healthy, whole, and uninjured, and would never know the hardships of the young lives she had just seen. Whatever happened to him, it could never be as bad as that. The young people she'd worked to help had no way out, but he had a whole life ahead of him, with great opportunities, particularly now going to a high school where his talent would be nurtured and he'd learn new things every day.

Blue carried his bags downstairs after they thanked Julio Fernandez, who grinned at Blue. He was carrying the autographed bat and glove he'd gotten when Andrew took him to the Yankees game. He had shown Ginny immediately and said he wanted to put them on a shelf in his room.

'Something tells me we won't be seeing you again, champ.' Julio glanced at Ginny as he said it. She was his way off the streets, and although she wasn't his legal guardian, he wasn't really homeless anymore. He had her.

They looked like a family as they left the shelter. 'Don't be a stranger, come to visit. I'll miss you,' Julio said to Blue sincerely. Blue hugged him, then raced down the stairs to the cab and followed Ginny in. She had come back, just as she had said. That had registered strongly with him. He knew he could trust her, as long as nothing happened to her. And she had e-mailed him from Syria as often as she could, to reassure him.

She gave the driver her address, and they headed home. It was a steaming-hot day in early August, as she peeled off the layers she'd been wearing on the trip, and they chatted in the cab. She wanted to throw away everything she was wearing when she got home. She felt even dirtier than she looked, but they were smiling at each other, and Blue was talking a mile a minute.

'So what have you been up to that you didn't tell me in your e-mails?' she asked as they rode uptown.

'Andrew invited us to a Yankees game on my birthday.' Blue looked excited about it – he was turning fourteen, and she was thrilled to have made it home in time. 'Can we go?' She had no plans except to be with him for the next four to six weeks. She'd had an e-mail from Ellen, saying they might send her to India. But all she could think of now was Blue, spending time with him, and getting him into school after Labor Day.

'Of course we can go.' She grinned at him.

'Andrew is a cool guy – he knows all the big Yankees

players. It's hard to believe he used to be a priest.' It was high praise from him, as he chattered on about the two Yankees games he'd been to with him. Andrew had taken him to a Mets game, too. And Jane Sanders, in charge of the police investigation, had dropped by to see him at the shelter. He said he'd played the piano for her. But Blue made no mention of the investigation, and Ginny didn't ask. She was going to call Jane Sanders herself to catch up on the news.

Her apartment looked like heaven to both of them when they got home. She sent Blue out to buy groceries while she headed for the bathroom. She could hardly wait to take a real bath. And when she emerged, clean and scrubbed in a pink terry cloth robe, she ate a sandwich with him, told him she loved him, and went to bed. She could barely stay awake. Blue settled in to play video games and watch movies, ecstatic to be home with her, and sleep in his own room again, and his own bed.

She slept until the next day and woke up feeling full of energy and ready to get busy with Blue. She called Jane Sanders for news about the case, and Andrew O'Connor to thank him for his kindness to Blue and to accept his birthday invitation to the Yankees game.

'Your e-mails described a rugged life,' Andrew commented when she called him. He sounded impressed.

'It was pretty bad,' she admitted. 'It feels good to get

home. Blue looks great. Thanks for taking him out and visiting him.' She had a life to come home to now. It made a huge difference to her, as well as Blue.

'He's a fantastic kid,' Andrew said easily, 'and unbelievably talented. He played for me a couple of times when I visited him.'

'He says you're pretty good, too,' Ginny said pleasantly, enjoying the exchange.

'I'm a pathetic amateur compared to him. He composed a piece of original music for me.'

'LaGuardia is going to be great for him,' Ginny said happily.

'*You're* great for him. He couldn't wait for you to get home,' Andrew said honestly.

'Me, too. It was a rough trip, shorter than usual, but a lot harder.' It had been eight weeks in hell, which he had guessed, even from the little she said.

'Where to next? Do you know yet?' he asked her with interest.

'I'm not sure. Maybe India, in September. I hate leaving Blue again so soon.'

Andrew didn't want to tell her how much Blue had missed her. He had talked about her constantly and had been worried about her. She was the hub of his existence and the only adult he'd ever known whom he could trust and rely on and who had never let him down.

'Maybe they'll let you spend a little more time at home

between trips,' Andrew said hopefully. She had been thinking about that, too, although she didn't know how Ellen would react to it. The nature of her job was to be gone at least nine months of the year, which was her agreement with SOS. And she had told them she had no attachments, and was unencumbered and free.

'We'll see,' Ginny said vaguely, and Andrew said he'd call her in a few days to check in.

She and Blue made lunch after that. He looked as if he'd grown two inches in two months. She was sure it wasn't that much, but he looked taller to her. And healthy. They had fed him well at Houston Street, and the portions had been generous, since most of the residents were teenage boys.

She was happy to be home. She had worried about him, but this time he had stuck it out at the shelter. She was proud of him for that and said so, as they finished lunch and put their dishes in the dishwasher, before going to a concert in the park.

'You said you'd kill me if I ran away, so I stayed,' he said, teasing her. And then he showed her his diploma. He had found it in the mail while she was sleeping that morning. She promised to frame it and hang it on the wall in his room, along with his autographed Yankees memorabilia.

She had sent Becky a text the night before, and hadn't heard from her, so she called her after lunch. They hadn't spoken to each other or communicated at all, in more than two months. Their last conversation, if you could call it that and not a fight, had left a bad impression on both of them. Neither was anxious to talk to the other. Becky thought she had gone off the deep end again, as she seemed to do all the time now, with one crazy thing after another, and Ginny thought she had a heart of stone and her head on backward, if she was willing to protect sexually abusive priests out of respect for the Catholic Church, with total indifference to the children who'd gotten hurt, like Blue. But Ginny wanted news of their father and had had none since June. She assumed nothing had changed.

Becky sounded surprised to hear from her when she answered.

'You're back?'

'Yes. Still alive. How's Dad?' Blue listened with quiet interest as he sat at his computer. Lizzie had told him in texts that her grandfather seemed about the same.

'Fading away slowly. He just wakes up a few times a day now and goes back to sleep,' Becky answered. 'He doesn't recognize any of us anymore.' Ginny's heart went out to her – she knew it must be hard to watch day to day. It made her less angry at her sister, for her diatribe about their case against the priest.

'And how are you?' Ginny asked her, sounding gentler.

'I'm okay. What about you? Ready to give up your witch-hunt?' Becky was hoping that her mission in Syria had swayed her from her outrageous plan to help Blue bring a lawsuit against the archdiocese, and criminal charges against a priest. Becky still got upset about it every time it came to mind, and Ginny's heart sank as she said it. She was still Becky, with all the same limitations and prejudices and narrow point of view. It was disappointing to hear.

'It's not a witch-hunt,' Ginny said coolly. 'It's real. Real kids have gotten hurt by those priests, who committed real crimes. Think how you'd feel if it was Charlie.' Becky ignored what her sister said.

'For heaven's sake, Ginny. Give it up,' she said in exasperation. And Alan didn't approve of the plan, either. They had discussed it at length and were both shocked at what Ginny was going to do. He was even more incensed than Becky. He thought the case was sinful, and would bring disgrace on them all. He was just praying that no one he knew would find out. And they had told their kids how wrong it was, too. Lizzie had reported her parents' position to Blue, and told him she didn't agree and thought he was really brave. He thanked her and was pleased, and she didn't ask him any questions about it. She was a polite girl and liked him a lot and didn't want him to feel awkward with her, now that they were friends.

The conversation with Becky was strained, as there had

been no mellowing of their positions, on either side. Ginny got off the phone as quickly as she could. She had wanted information about her father, Becky had given it to her, and there was nothing else to say. Ginny tried to put it out of her mind, and half an hour later she and Blue left for the concert in Central Park.

It felt strange to Ginny at first, listening to Mozart in the peaceful setting, surrounded by happy, healthy-looking people, after two months in the rigors of Syria. Being back still felt unreal to her, but she and Blue loved the concert.

And Andrew called her when they got home. He had heard from the archdiocese that afternoon and the timing was perfect, since she was in New York.

'They want to see us,' he said, sounding pleased. 'We have a meeting next week with the monsignor in charge of these cases, at the archdiocese. He's a stubborn old guy, also a Jesuit. I worked with him for two years in Rome. He'll be tough. But he's also smart. Eventually he'll cave. They don't have a case,' Andrew told her. 'I spoke to Jane today. More and more victims are coming forward – some of them are men now. The oldest one I saw on the list is thirty-seven. He was fourteen when Father Teddy molested him, fresh out of the seminary, in Washington, D.C. None of this looks good for him. He's obviously had a problem for years, and they know it. It makes Blue's case even stronger.'

'What about Blue's friend Jimmy Ewald?' she asked him, satisfied with what he said.

'The police investigator talked to him. He denied everything. He says Father Teddy is the greatest guy he ever met. I don't believe him, but I think he's too scared to tell the truth. Father Teddy must have threatened him, too.' As things stood now, even before the end of the investigation, the evidence was building, and Andrew said that fifteen more boys had come forward, with stories almost identical to Blue's, about sexual abuses committed on them by the charismatic priest. The monsignor wanted to meet with her and Andrew, but not Blue. It was going to be a very interesting meeting, and Andrew reassured her that it would go well. She was worried that all the archdiocese's energy would go into defending Father Teddy, and the church, instead of making up to Blue for what had been done to him. Andrew had warned her that they still might do all they could to debunk and undermine Blue, and probably would at the first meeting.

'Don't worry, we'll get there,' Andrew said, 'even if they play hardball in the beginning. They don't scare me. Don't forget, I used to be one of them. It's a distinct advantage, and I know a lot of the players, particularly the ones with any power. I know this monsignor very well. He's a hard man, but he's honest and fair.' Listening to him made her curious again about his history, and why he had left the church, but she would never ask, just as he wouldn't ask what terrible crimes she was atoning for with the life she led in refugee camps around the world.

They agreed to meet half an hour before the meeting at the archdiocese on Monday, at a coffee shop nearby. She told Blue about it when she hung up.

'Is that good or bad?' he asked, looking worried about the meeting.

'Just standard procedure,' she said calmly. 'The monsignor wants to meet us to talk about it. You don't have to go. Just me and Andrew.' He looked relieved at that, and they went to a movie that night, and to Coney Island the next day, so Blue could ride the Cyclone, which he said was less good than the roller coaster at Magic Mountain, and he texted Lizzie about it. Then he and Ginny lay on the beach for a while. They were happy together, and Ginny was thrilled to be home.

They were on their way back to the city, when Becky called Ginny on her cell phone. She could hear the sorrow in her sister's voice when she answered and knew immediately what had happened before Becky said a word.

'Dad?' was all Ginny said, and Becky confirmed it.

'Yes. About an hour ago. I checked on him after lunch, and he was sleeping peacefully. And when I went back half an hour later, he was gone. I never got to say goodbye.' She started to cry then, and so did Ginny.

'You've been saying goodbye to him every day for over

two years, with everything you did for him, the way you took care of him, letting him live in your home. He was ready to go. It wasn't a good life for him anymore. This is better for him,' Ginny said quietly.

'I know. It's just sad. I'll miss him. It was nice being able to do things for him. He was always so good to us,' Becky said, crying. He had been a wonderful father, all their lives. They'd been blessed to have him, and their mother had been a kind, loving woman, too. They'd had good parents, unlike Blue, who had no one after his mother died. Stories like his always made Ginny want to give back to others less fortunate.

'He's with Mom now,' Ginny said peacefully through her tears. 'He'd rather be with her.' They both knew it was true – they'd had a love affair for their entire marriage.

'When are you coming out?' Becky asked her.

'I don't know. Let me figure it out when I get home. I guess tomorrow. Do you know when you want to do the funeral?' Ginny asked her. The recent friction between them had been instantly set aside, faced with their shared grief. This was more important and drew them together. In spite of the battle they'd had recently, both of them put their weapons down. For now at least, there was a truce.

'In a few days, I guess. I haven't called the funeral home yet. They just took him away.' It had been painful watching him leave the house on a gurney, wrapped in a blanket that covered his face. She'd been relieved that all the kids were out. She hadn't told them yet. She'd wanted to tell Ginny first, although she'd called Alan immediately at his office and he was on his way home to be with her. They'd been expecting it for months, but it was still sad when it happened. And it made Ginny feel even more adult, thinking that both her parents were gone now. And all she had left was her sister and her family, and now Blue. She no longer had parents or a family of her own.

'I'll let you know our flight when I book it,' Ginny said softly. 'I'll text you,' she promised. Ginny went online as soon as they got back to the apartment, and she booked two seats for her and Blue on the first morning flight the next day.

And then she called Andrew O'Connor and told him that she couldn't make the meeting at the archdiocese because her father had just died in L.A., and she wouldn't be back in time.

'I'm so sorry. Of course I'll rearrange it. When do you think you'll come back?' He sounded sympathetic and practical, and he could hear how sad she was.

'Maybe in four or five days, a week at most,' she answered. After the arrangements and the funeral, she and Becky would have to dispose of their father's things, although he didn't have much left. They had sold his house when he moved in with Becky.

'Was this very sudden?' Andrew sounded kind and

compassionate, and listening to him, she could suddenly imagine him as a priest. He had a gentle way about him, cared about people, and listened well.

'No, he'd been sick for a long time. He's been fading away. I went to see him before I left for Syria – I had a sense it would be the last time. This is better for him, but it's strange for us. He had Alzheimer's, and he had no quality of life anymore.'

'Don't worry about the meeting. We have time. I think they just want to feel us out and see how serious we are.'

'Very,' she said in a firm voice, and he laughed. She was sad about her father but still able to focus on Blue's case.

'So am I,' he assured her. 'It's the ultimate abuse of trust, of the worst kind. I hope Blue will make a full recovery from it, but he may not. It could impact him forever. He deserves serious compensation for that.' And Andrew intended to get it for him.

'I believe he can recover from it,' Ginny said thoughtfully, and she was determined to make that happen, with the other good things happening in his life. 'I want him to. I don't want that bastard stealing his life, or his future. Blue has every right to put this behind him. I want to do everything I can to help him do that.' The strength in her voice took Andrew by surprise. She was an iron woman at times.

'We all have our demons,' he said quietly. 'Some are just worse than others.' And as he said it, she suspected he had his own. He had left the priesthood, after all.

'He's too young to have that on his back for the rest of time. That's not fair.' She was anxious to do all she could to help Blue recover fully from what had happened.

'That's exactly why these cases are so important. Because they're not fair.' Andrew agreed with her on that. 'Maybe what you're doing for Blue will show him how much he matters to you. It's very touching that you believe in him as much as you do. That's a tremendous gift to give anyone.' Blue's own aunt hadn't believed him, but Blue knew Ginny did. That had touched the ex-Jesuit lawyer, and impressed him about her.

'I want him to come out of this unscathed.'

Andrew thought it was a loving wish, but not very realistic. He had seen too many adult clients unable to lead normal lives after the abuses committed on them as children. Sometimes love wasn't enough to heal them, and the money they won in settlements was consolation but it never gave them back the innocence, trust, and balance they had lost. A number of his adult clients who'd been abused as children had been unable to have normal relationships. All he could do was hope that Blue wouldn't be one of them, no matter how committed Ginny was.

'We'll do our best,' Andrew promised her, moved by her strength and dedication to the boy. 'I'll let you know about the appointment. I'll send you an e-mail when you get to L.A.'

'Thanks so much.' She hung up, thinking about the lawyer for a moment. There was something very warm about him, yet slightly removed as well, as though he were protecting wounds of his own. It was an odd combination, and she wondered if it was because he'd been a priest. She was still intrigued by why he'd left the church, and fantasized that he'd fallen in love with a nun. People who left the church always seemed mysterious to her.

Ginny sent Becky a text message with their arrival time the next day, and then went to help Blue pack.

'We'll have to get you a suit when we get to L.A. We don't have time now.' He had no grown-up clothes to wear to her father's funeral. Shopping for a suit for him would give them both something more to do than sitting around the funeral home.

They had a quiet dinner, and Blue went to bed early. Ginny sat alone that night, thinking about her father. It had been a turbulent homecoming, with her father dying, but at least she was back in the States. It was an odd, poignant feeling knowing that he was gone. She was more than ever grateful for Blue, who filled the empty spaces in her life. And now there was one more.

Chapter 15

The flight to L.A. seemed to take forever this time. It was always longer heading west, but there was nothing festive about it. Even Blue seemed somber on the plane. But he had had his own losses, too, with both his parents gone. And he didn't like funerals any more than Ginny did.

'Are you okay?' he asked her gently as they were about to land. He had seen tears in her eyes, and she smiled at him wistfully.

'It just seems weird that he won't be there.' Blue nodded in response and held her hand.

She rented a car again, as she had the last time they came, and when they got to Becky's house, the whole family was sitting in the kitchen eating breakfast and looking glum. Lizzie jumped up the moment they walked in, threw her arms around Blue's neck, and hugged him, and he seemed just as happy to see her. It lightened the moment for all of them, and everyone started talking at once as Ginny and Blue sat down.

After breakfast, the two sisters slipped away and drove to the funeral home. They picked out everything they needed to, the casket, the mass cards, the program, the leather guest book for the rosary, and then they went to the church and met with the priest, and made the rest of their decisions with him, about the music, the prayers, and who would speak. Their father hadn't seen his friends in several years. Many of them were still alive and doing well, since he hadn't been very old. But his mind had been gone for several years, and he hadn't wanted to see anyone as his Alzheimer's took control.

Becky was quiet as they left the church, and looked at her sister, when Ginny drove them home.

'I'm surprised you're not embarrassed to talk to the priest, given what you're about to do in New York,' she said, with an edge to her voice.

'As far as I know, Father Donovan isn't raping little boys,' Ginny responded as she drove.

'How can you be so sure that priest in New York did? You know, a lot of kids who've accused their parish priests of that turned out to be lying. Are you that sure Blue is telling you the truth?' She sounded skeptical as she asked.

'Yes, I am. And fifteen others have come forward during the investigation. Becky, this isn't a small thing. It ruins people's lives.' Ginny tried to reason with her, but Becky was on the opposing side, and firmly believed she was right.

'And what about the priest? What about his life if he winds up in prison for a crime he didn't commit? That happens all the time, too.' She didn't even know him, but she was convinced of Ted Graham's innocence, just because he was a priest.

'What if all these kids are telling the truth? Doesn't that scare you to leave a guy out there who's molesting little boys, especially if he's a priest?' Becky was silent, thinking about it, but to her it seemed like just one of Ginny's crusades. There was always something with her now – human rights, a homeless boy, and now a vendetta against the church. She had nothing left in her life except causes. Ever since Mark and Chris had died, she had filled her life with other people's battles to fight, and victims to save. Everything about her had changed, and it was hard for Becky to relate to her now. She had become some kind of freedom fighter, fighting everyone else's wars, because she had no life of her own.

'I just think you're very, very wrong. You don't go against the church,' Becky said with an angry look. 'It violates everything we were taught.'

'You do when someone in it is doing something wrong,' Ginny said quietly. She had no doubts at all about Blue's honesty or the case.

They rode the rest of the way in silence with a chasm between them a mile wide. And after that Ginny took Blue downtown to buy him a suit. They got a simple dark blue one that Ginny thought he could use again, maybe for a recital at his school. He was very proud of it, and the white shirt and dark tie they picked to go with it. And when he wore it to the rosary that night, he looked like a man.

He and Lizzie sat in a back pew chatting softly to each other, while Margie and Charlie stood with their parents, and both sisters greeted the guests. It made Ginny realize how long she'd been gone. She hardly recognized anyone, since most of the mourners were friends of Becky and Alan. And everything about it reminded her of Mark's funeral. As soon as the rosary was over, she couldn't wait to get back to the house and pour herself a glass of wine. Her computer was sitting on the table, and she saw an e-mail come up from Andrew O'Connor. She sipped her wine as she opened it and read it. He had moved the appointment at the archdiocese to a week later. It was nice having news from the outside world. The funeral atmosphere was oppressive.

The kids all went down to the playroom then, and a few minutes later the adults heard Blue playing the piano, and they went down to join them. He gave them all a little impromptu concert and had everyone sing along. It turned their mourning into dancing, as it said in the Bible, and at the end, he sang a gospel song in a clear, strong voice that touched them all and brought tears to Ginny's eyes.

'My mama used to sing that song,' he said softly to Ginny. He had a powerful voice, and they all sat around and talked afterward. Blue's playing the piano for them had cheered them all.

The following day was the funeral, and Blue came downstairs in his suit again. Lizzie came down a few minutes later in a short black dress her mother had picked out for her. The two of them looked very grown-up. An hour later the whole family had gathered and left for the service in the two black limousines they had hired at the funeral home the day before.

The church was more crowded than Ginny had expected – it was a very respectable turnout for her father. Blue stood beside her, looking proud to be there, as Becky and her family filled the rest of the pew.

After the service, they stood outside greeting people, and then went to the cemetery briefly to leave her father's casket there. And suddenly as she stood there, Ginny saw Mark and Chris's graves, and the feeling of loss was so overwhelming that it almost took her breath away. Blue saw the look on her face, and leaned closer to Lizzie.

'Is that them?' he whispered, nodding toward the two graves, and she nodded back. There was a space left for Ginny next to them – she had bought all three plots on the same day. Chris's headstone was slightly smaller. After the brief graveside service, Ginny walked over to them, when the others walked away. She leaned down and touched her son's headstone, as tears rolled down her cheeks, and when she turned, she saw Blue standing next to her, with two long-stemmed white roses in his hand. He dropped one on each of the graves as Ginny reached out to hug him, and they stood there embracing as she cried. Then he gently led her away. He got in the limousine with her, and held Ginny's hand all the way back to the house.

There were people already waiting for them, and a buffet full of food. The guests stayed until the early afternoon, and then finally they were alone again. Charlie put on jeans, and his girlfriend came over, and the younger ones decided to get into the pool. Ginny smiled at them from the kitchen window and turned to her sister. It had been a beautiful, traditional service that was exactly what they thought was appropriate for their father. They had agreed on all the details.

'That's what Dad would have wanted, to see them out there playing like that.' He had always been a happy person and loved having his grandchildren around him. And Ginny had the feeling that, despite the unusual circumstances, he would have liked getting to know Blue.

'What are you going to do with him now?' Becky

asked her as she saw her sister watching Blue in the pool.

'What do you mean?'

'You can't keep him forever. He's almost an adult, and you're gone most of the time. You're not going to adopt him, are you?'

'I don't know. I haven't thought about it. You make him sound like a fish that I'm supposed to throw back.' But the truth was that he had nowhere to go, and they loved each other. He had become an important part of her life. Becky didn't seem to understand that. 'It doesn't make much sense to adopt him. He'll be eighteen in four years.' But his aunt Charlene didn't want him with her, and Ginny didn't want to put him in foster care. 'Maybe he'll just stay with me till he's old enough to live on his own. He's starting high school next month.'

'But he's not yours, Ginny. He's not part of our family. He doesn't belong with you. And your life's not set up for children anymore, not with the life you lead, flying all over the world.'

'And if I don't take care of him, who will?' Ginny turned to look at her sister, who seemed to have no room in her life for anything unusual or different, only what fit in. And everything about Ginny's life was unusual and different now. They seemed to have nothing in common anymore, except their father, and he was gone. And whether she meant to or not, Becky was always stepping on her toes.

'He's not your problem. You're not your "brother's keeper," nor that of someone else's son,' Becky said stubbornly.

'If that were true, none of the adopted children in the world would have a home,' Ginny said quietly. 'I don't know why Blue and I found each other, but we did. Maybe that's good enough for now.' They walked out to the pool then and watched the kids play Marco Polo with Alan, and they were all having fun. It was a perfect end to a bittersweet day. There was something peaceful about it. It wasn't like the shocking agony of Mark and Chris's funerals, where everything had been so out of order and so wrong. This was the way it was meant to be, when parents slipped gently away, and the next generations moved on.

The kids stayed in the pool until dark, and then they ate leftovers from the buffet that the caterer had provided, and everyone went to bed early that night. Alone in her room, Ginny thought about what her sister had said. It amazed her that she had so little understanding that other people's lives could be different from her own. Her world was limited by Pasadena and had room in it only for 'normal' people, whose lives mirrored hers with Alan. There was no room for a boy like Blue in it, or anything out of the ordinary. And then Ginny remembered Becky's question that afternoon about whether she was going to adopt Blue. She hadn't really thought about it till then, but she was suddenly wondering if she should. He needed a family and a home. It was something to think about.

They spent another day in Pasadena, and then she and Blue went back to New York. They had lives to get on with, and a battle to wage against the archdiocese. She called Andrew O'Connor the day they got home. Their appointment with the monsignor was in two days.

'I just wanted to let you know I'm back,' she said, sounding tired.

'How was it?' he asked, and seemed concerned.

'About the way you'd expect, sad but appropriate in the order of things. It was a little awkward with my sister. She's furious about our challenging the church. She thinks it's a sacrilege and that priests can do no wrong. She and her husband are very traditional people. I keep trying to stay off the subject, but she insists on wanting to discuss it with me and show me the error of my ways. She really doesn't understand.'

'A lot of people don't. They don't want to believe that these things happen, or see the damage that they cause. It takes a lot of guts to go against the currents, but it's the right thing to do. I got death threats when I started taking these cases. I always find it interesting when people threaten your life in the name of religion when they don't like what you do. It's a fascinating contradiction.' She had never thought about the risk taking cases against the church could pose for him.

'Then I guess you have to be pretty brave, too,' she said with admiration.

'No, just convinced of the rightness of what I'm doing. That's always gotten me in trouble, but it's how I want to live.' He sounded determined as he said it.

'My life was different when my husband and son were alive. I was busy with them. Now I'm engaged in battling the injustices in the world, and trying to turn the tide for people who can't help themselves. But I guess speaking up and taking risks like that is very threatening to people. They don't like unpopular positions that force them to look at what they believe, and question its merits.'

'That's true,' he agreed. 'My family thought I'd gone off the deep end when I joined the church. They were fiercely opposed to it and thought it very odd. Then they were even more horrified when I left the church. I guess I'm always shocking them about something they don't approve of.' He didn't sound bothered about it, and Ginny laughed.

'That's how my sister feels about me.'

'It's good to keep them on their toes,' he quipped, and they both laughed. But he sounded more serious when he went on. 'I was never in the church for the right reasons. It took me a long time to figure that out. I thought I had a vocation, but I didn't.' It was more than he had ever said to any client, but she was a compassionate woman, with an open heart and open mind, and he liked talking to her.

And he admired her deeply for what she was doing for Blue.

'That's a big mistake to make,' she said honestly, 'and a major change of direction when you left the church. It can't have been an easy decision.'

'It wasn't. But after I went to Rome, I realized how political the church is, in its upper stratosphere. It's full of intrigue and a power game of sorts. The church was never about politics for me, although it was certainly interesting being in Rome, with all the cardinals around, and it was magical working in the Vatican. It's very heady stuff. But it's not what I joined the church for. I'm more useful now, doing what I'm doing, than I was when I was a priest. I was really just a lawyer in a Roman collar, and I didn't have the vocation to work in a parish, especially not after Rome. And once I understood that, it was time for me to get out. I wasn't helping anyone. And I really wanted to be a lawyer, not a priest.' He seemed perfectly at peace about the choice he'd made, and it seemed to be the right one for him.

'I'm actually disappointed to hear it,' she said, laughing softly. He liked the sound of her voice. He could tell by how she dealt with people that she was no stranger to human suffering, including her own.

'Why is that?' he asked, puzzled by her comment.

'I was kind of hoping that you fell in love with a nun, ran away together, and lived happily ever after. I always love those stories. I guess I'm a romantic at heart. An impossible love that finally works out.'

'I like those stories, too,' he admitted. 'They don't happen very often. And let's face it, most nuns today don't look like Audrey Hepburn in *The Nun's Story.* They're a little portly, have funny haircuts, look like they forget to comb their hair, and wear sweatshirts and jeans, and only wear their habits when they go to Rome, and then they never seem to have their coifs on straight.' She could tell he was speaking from experience, and she laughed at what he said, although her sister would have been shocked by his irreverence. But he said it in a kind, humorous way, and it was true. 'The only thing I fell in love with was studying canon law when I worked at the Vatican. It was fascinating, but I never saw a nun there who made my heart skip a beat.' She wondered if someone else had since. He was such an interesting, intelligent man.

And then he answered her question without her having to ask it, as though he'd read her mind. 'I never fully made it back into secular life. Maybe I left the church when I was too old and waited too long. I was fully released from my vows five years ago, when I was forty-three, kind of like an honorable discharge.' She was surprised – he was older than he looked. She had guessed him to be about thirty-nine or forty, not forty-eight. 'But most of the time, I still feel like a priest, with all the typical Catholic guilt. Possibly being a Jesuit is forever. It had a powerful hold on me. I was very young when I went in. Too young. People don't join the church as early today, which is better. They know what they're doing when they make the decision. I had a lot of high ideals that never really made sense. But it took me a very long time to figure that out. I was in the order for twenty-five years. It'll probably take me twice that long to really get out, if I ever do. So for now, I'm satisfied to be a troublemaker going after the bad ones like Father Teddy Graham.' He spoke of him with utter contempt. 'That's what I really wanted to do in the beginning. I was something of a crusader then. I wanted to be a good priest instead of a bad one. Now I'm just happy putting the bad ones behind bars, and shaking the tree for settlements for their victims. It's not an entirely noble pursuit, since it involves money, but it works, as long as the money isn't for me.' He was a purist at heart, and she wondered again if he was from a wealthy family, so he could take cases like Blue's for free. There was something very aristocratic about him, but in a very unpretentious, modest way.

'I suppose we're both crusaders for human rights,' she said thoughtfully. 'My sister accused me of that recently. Of being a crusader, with a Joan of Arc complex. She thinks it's ridiculous. But it makes sense to me. I don't have a husband and children. I have time to try to heal the ills of the world.'

'We all find the paths that work for us sooner or later,

some earlier than others. It sounds like you made the best of a bad situation and put it to good use. That's an art,' he said, and he respected her for it, and a lucky boy named Blue had benefited from it. She could have spent the rest of her life crying over what she'd lost, but instead she was serving others.

'My sister asked me if I was planning to adopt Blue. I never really thought about it seriously until she said it. Maybe we should talk about it one of these days.'

'It would be wonderful for him, if that's what you really want to do. You should think about it for a while and be sure.'

'I will. That's good advice.'

'Well, I'll see you at the archdiocese on Monday. I'll meet you at the coffee shop around the corner, just to brief you on some of the details and the cast of characters. It never hurts to have the inside scoop.'

'That will be great. Thank you again,' she said warmly.

'And my condolences again,' he said, and they hung up, she went to see what Blue was doing, and he surprised her by saying he felt sick.

'What kind of sick?' she asked him, and put the back of her hand on his forehead to see if he had a fever, but he didn't. 'You're probably just tired from the trip.' They'd had a hectic few days with the funeral and the rosary and the flights back and forth to California. But she noticed that he looked pale, and just before he went to bed that night, he threw up. She thought he had a touch of stomach flu. She sat up with him for a while, and when he dozed off finally, she went to bed herself.

What seemed like minutes later, someone was shaking her awake, and she woke up with a start. She looked up, confused about where she was for a minute, and Blue was standing next to her bed, crying, which he had never done before.

'What's wrong?' she asked him as she hopped out of bed.

'My stomach hurts. I mean really, really hurts . . . a lot.' She told him to lie down on her bed, and thought about calling a doctor, and then he threw up again and doubled over in pain, and when he showed her where it hurt, she could see that it was the lower right quadrant of his abdomen. She'd had enough advanced first aid training to know what that was. She got dressed immediately, and told him gently that they were going to the emergency room. He said he felt too sick to get dressed, so she helped him put on a robe over his pajamas, and he slipped his feet into his high-top Converse, and they were on the street five minutes later, hailing a cab. She told the driver to take them to Mount Sinai Hospital, which was the closest medical facility to her apartment.

They were in the emergency room five minutes later, and Blue described his symptoms to the nurse, while

Ginny took care of the paperwork at the admissions desk in the ER. She filled out everything she needed to, then realized she didn't have an insurance card for him. She ran back to talk to him at the nurses' station, where he was sitting in a wheelchair, looking green and holding a bowl under his chin in case he threw up again.

'Blue, do you have insurance?' she asked him gently, and he shook his head, and she ran back to the admissions desk, and told them he didn't have any. The admissions clerk did not look happy about it.

'You can just bill it directly to me,' Ginny said quickly, and added her address to the form. She'd stumbled for a minute over the part that said next of kin, and thought of putting her own name down, but she listed his aunt instead, which was the truth. She had put herself on the form as the person who brought him in.

'We're not allowed to do that. We can't bill you,' the clerk said as she looked over the form. 'It would be better if he had an insurance card.' She wrote 'No insurance' on the form.

'Are you his mother?' she asked suspiciously.

'No, I'm not,' Ginny said honestly, wondering if it was a mistake.

'Then you can't sign the admitting form. He's a minor. It has to be signed by his next of kin or a parent or guardian.'

'It's four-thirty in the morning, and I don't want to

waste time finding her,' Ginny said, distracted and frantic.

'We can treat him in an emergency, but should notify her,' the clerk said sternly, as Ginny wondered if Charlene was on duty at the hospital that night. It would simplify everything if she was.

By then, Blue was with the doctor, who was examining him, and Ginny walked in to join them. Blue looked terrified, and she patted his hand. The doctor walked out of the exam room with her to talk to her in the hall.

'He's got a hot appendix,' he explained to her. 'We have to take it out tonight. I don't want to wait.' She nodded – she had suspected as much.

'That's fine, but we have a problem. I'm not his guardian, his parents are deceased, he has an aunt who is his guardian but whom he never sees, and he lives with me. Can I just sign the form?' The doctor shook his head.

'No, but you don't need to. You can try to locate her while we're in surgery. We can take him to the OR now, but his guardian should be notified.' Ginny agreed and decided to wait to call Charlene until after Blue was wheeled away. She went back into the room to see him then. He was throwing up again while a nurse held the bowl for him. He looked miserable, and his eyes were bigger than ever in his suddenly very pale face. They were anxious to get him to surgery and he had an IV in his arm. A male nurse came in a minute later and explained the procedure to Blue. He was crying and Ginny kissed his forehead as they wheeled his bed into the hall, and minutes later, they rolled him into the elevator and took him away, as Ginny stood alone in the hallway, crying, too.

She called Charlene's cell phone then, hoping she was at work, but a sleepy voice answered. It was Charlene. She was startled to hear Ginny crying at the other end. Ginny explained the situation to her, and she could hear a male voice next to Charlene, complaining about the call waking them at 5 a.m. She assumed it was Harold, Charlene's boyfriend.

'He'll be all right,' Charlene told her, sounding less worried than Ginny. 'I'll sign the admitting forms tomorrow when I come to work.' She sounded casual about it, which upset Ginny. They hung up a minute later, and Ginny went to sit in a waiting room, to wait for Blue to come back from surgery. And he'd have to go to the recovery room first. It gave her time to think of their situation again. Legally, she and Blue were in limbo, and his getting sick made her think that becoming his guardian made sense. Charlene didn't want responsibility for him, and Ginny did.

Blue came back from the recovery room at eight in the morning. They put him in a semi-private room with an empty bed. He was groggy and slept until noon, and

Ginny took advantage of it to go home and shower and change clothes. When she got back, she sat on a chair next to his bed, and she dozed while he slept all afternoon. And at five o'clock, she went to the cafeteria, to meet Charlene. Ginny had the admitting forms with her, and Charlene signed them and handed them back to her. And then she startled Ginny with what she said.

'I don't want to be his guardian anymore. I never see him. He's not my son. And he lives with you,' Charlene said sensibly.

What she said made perfect sense and made Ginny realize that she did want to be his guardian, but Blue had a voice in it and she wanted to ask him.

She spent the night at the hospital with him, and two days after his surgery, she took him home and pampered him. They sat on the couch watching TV together, and she asked him about her becoming his guardian. He broke into a broad smile when she did.

'You'd do that for me?' he asked her with tears in his eyes.

'If you want me to. I can ask Andrew about it,' and when she did, he said it was a simple procedure, especially at Blue's age. At fourteen, he had a say in it, and with Blue wanting her to, Ginny wanting to become his guardian, and Charlene asking to relinquish guardianship, the hearing would only be a formality. Ginny was a responsible person, and Andrew said no court would object to her.

And she made reliable arrangements for him when she traveled.

'I can handle it for you, if you like,' Andrew volunteered, and Ginny asked him to get the process started. He was going to request an early hearing, in Blue's circumstances, and with the investigation ongoing, Andrew felt sure they would agree to the change of guardianship quickly.

Just talking about it made Ginny and Blue happy. She knew it was the right decision, and Blue blossomed, knowing that she wanted him in her life long-term, and was willing to take responsibility for him. Nothing else mattered to either of them. And as he recovered from the surgery, they celebrated their plan. They talked about what they were going to do as soon as he could go out. She made him his favorite foods, and they watched his favorite movies. Knowing she was going to be his guardian strengthened the bond between them. His bout of appendicitis had turned out to be a blessing for both of them. They could hardly wait for the hearing to confirm it.

Chapter 16

Andrew came to visit Blue at the apartment while he was convalescing. He brought him sports magazines and a video game. Blue was feeling better by then, and was happy to see him. He thought it was nice that Andrew had come, and he liked the game. Andrew told them both that he had set the wheels in motion for the change in guardianship, and requested the hearing. He had also gotten the meeting at the archdiocese moved from Monday to Friday, while Ginny was taking care of Blue after the surgery.

'He's a nice guy,' Blue said, lying on the couch, after Andrew's visit.

'Yes, he is,' Ginny agreed, thinking of the upcoming meeting at the archdiocese, which was two days away.

'You should be with someone like him,' Blue volunteered. She thought it was an odd thing to say.

'Why would I want to be? I don't want to be with

anyone,' she said. She still felt married to Mark, and was convinced she always would. She had never taken off her wedding ring. 'Besides, I have you now.'

'That's not enough,' he said wisely.

'Yes, it is,' she said, smiling at him. And now that she was going to be his legal guardian, it was more than enough.

The morning of the meeting with the archdiocese, she left him in bed with his laptop and a stack of video games, then took a cab to meet Andrew at the coffee shop. She was ten minutes late and apologized profusely.

'I had to get Blue organized before I left. Sorry,' she said, and ordered coffee. He was wearing khaki slacks, a navy linen blazer, and a blue shirt with an open collar. He warned her that the monsignor and whoever he had with him would probably be stern with her in order to scare them off, and might even accuse Blue of lying. No matter what the monsignors thought privately, initially they would defend Father Teddy, and deny everything Blue had said. Andrew knew their game.

'Monsignor Cavaretti's theory was always that the best defense is a good offense. Don't let him impress you. He's no fool, he knows we've got them on this one, which will make him try to scare you off, if he can. He doesn't want the bad publicity, and if the archdiocese knows what Ted Graham was up to, it's in for a heavy dose of it for covering it up and moving him someplace else. None of this looks good for them.' And ultimately, he thought Blue would be an excellent witness, he was such a straightforward, ingenuous kid. 'I've got it covered,' Andrew said reassuringly as he paid for their coffee, and they walked around the corner for the meeting.

Just arriving at the archdiocese was impressive, as Andrew and Ginny were led into a waiting room with high ceilings, beautiful serious antique furniture, carved wood panels, and a crucifix on the wall. The building was pleasantly air conditioned in the New York summer heat. Ginny felt momentarily overwhelmed.

'Are you okay?' Andrew whispered to her, and she nodded, though it was daunting. And a moment later, a young priest came in to lead them upstairs to Monsignor Cavaretti's office, and Ginny saw that there were three monsignors waiting for them in the handsomely appointed room. There was a beautiful portrait of the Holy Father above the desk, and photographs of a number of bishops and cardinals around the room. And as soon as they walked in, a small round man in monsignor's robes came toward Andrew with a warm smile. Monsignor Cavaretti had been a priest for nearly fifty years, and had the bright lively eyes of a much younger man.

'It's good to see you, Andrew,' he said, patting him on the shoulder affectionately, with a genuinely pleased look in his eyes. 'So when are you coming back to us?' he teased him. 'You should be working with us on this,' he said more seriously. They had worked together on many projects in Rome, for two of Andrew's four years there, and the older monsignor had great respect for Andrew's abilities. He had always said he was one of the best lawyers at the Vatican, and would be a cardinal one day. It had been a great disappointment to him when he heard that Andrew had asked to be released from his vows, although he hadn't been entirely surprised. Andrew had always been very independent, freethinking, at times more dedicated to the ideals of the law than to the church, and he had a deeply questioning, sometimes cynical mind. He never accepted things at face value, nor did what he was told to do. He had to believe something was right, and that it conformed to his principles as well, before he did it. It made him a formidable opponent at times, as he suspected he would be now. He didn't underestimate Andrew, just as Andrew didn't underestimate him.

In Rome the monsignor had treated him like a son, and had taught him the inner workings of Vatican politics, and they had spent a number of late nights drinking many glasses of wine at the chancellery in Rome. It was at the time when Andrew had started having doubts about his vocation and the path he was on. And his reasons for leaving made him even more dangerous now, as the monsignor was well aware. Andrew was an idealist, and these cases were a holy crusade for him, while for the monsignor, they were just part of the work he did for the church. Andrew had expected every priest to be perfect, including himself. Monsignor Cavaretti knew the weaknesses of the priests, as well as men. 'You'll be back one of these days,' he said to Andrew with such certainty that Ginny was surprised and wondered if it was true.

'Not just yet,' Andrew joked with him. 'And in the meantime, we have work to do.' He introduced Ginny then, and the monsignor shook her hand.

Monsignor Cavaretti introduced the other two monsignors standing in the room with him then, and Andrew explained that Ginny was becoming Blue's legal guardian, and he lived with her and then the short round monsignor waved them toward a couch with a low table and several comfortable chairs. He wanted to set an informal tone for their first conversation to see if they could dissuade Ginny and Andrew from taking the matter further. The police had brought no official charges against Ted Graham yet, so this was the time to try to change their minds, particularly before it caught the attention of the press. So far, there was no harm done, which would not be the case in a few weeks, once the matter was scheduled to go to the grand jury.

Monsignor Cavaretti glanced carefully at Ginny, taking her measure. She was wearing a serious black linen pant-suit, and no jewelry except her wedding band. He was surprised to note that she was married – the information he'd been given was that the previously homeless boy lived alone with her. He wondered why she'd gotten involved with him. He also knew that she'd been a television reporter, which the monsignor thought was a dangerous combination with Andrew, if she had an investigative style, coupled with his burning passion for a cause. They could turn out to be a lethal team. Cavaretti was taking that into account, and proceeding with caution.

'So, here we are,' Monsignor Cavaretti said, smiling at both of them after the young priest who was his assistant offered them all coffee, tea, or cold drinks, which they had declined. 'What are we going to do about this unfortunate matter?' he said pleasantly. He had taken control of the meeting as soon as they walked in, with his friendly reminiscences of Rome with Andrew, his jocular comments, and his high praise for him. 'We have the future of a young priest at stake here, not only in the church, but in the eyes of the world. There's no question, this case will destroy him, his career, and his faith in himself if it goes to court, or worse if he goes to prison.'

Ginny couldn't believe what she was hearing, but neither she nor Andrew said a word.

'We also have to consider, on our side, what accusations like this do to the church, how they undermine us. Yet we must also respect the law. This case is about people, not just a church, but it's about our concern for our parishioners as well.' He looked calm and benevolent as he said it.

'Father Ted Graham is much loved, both at his last church and at his current one.'

'Is that why you moved him to Chicago, instead of dealing with it here?' Andrew asked quietly. He had fired his first shot across their bow, and he could see in the old priest's eyes that he had scored. But Cavaretti was much too smart to be surprised by Andrew's comment and knew him too well. He was prepared.

'It was time for him to move to another parish. You know that, Andrew. We don't want anyone getting too attached to one place and losing his objectivity and perspective. There was an opening in Chicago at the right time, and he was badly needed there. He has been extremely well liked and an exemplary pastor everywhere he's been.'

'Was it the "right time" because someone complained – an altar boy's parents who actually believed their son?' They both knew that was rare. Parents were more likely to put their faith in their priest than in their sons, out of habit and respect for the church, no matter how unfounded. Andrew knew better and believed the child every time. He had never yet had a case where the child was lying, but always the erring priest, and Cavaretti knew that, too. 'Or did one of the other priests see something that worried you? Apparently all his parishioners in New York were crazy about him – he was a beloved parish priest. So why move him to Chicago?'

'The pastor at St. Anne's had died suddenly a month before, and we had no one else at the time.' The shrewd old priest met Andrew's eyes fearlessly. The church had covered all its bases with where it had moved him. 'The transfer was justified.'

'I wish I could say that I believed that,' Andrew said cynically, as he challenged him. 'There is always someone else, particularly if you have a parish priest who is doing well where he is and is so well liked. You almost never move him in that case. And it's interesting that we now have fifteen cases, in addition to Blue's, at both St. Francis's and St. Anne's. Monsignor, I think you have a serious problem, and you know it.' Andrew was respectful, but tough. And Cavaretti's face gave away nothing. The other two monsignors hadn't spoken since they were introduced, and Andrew was sure they had been told not to. He expected Cavaretti would do all the talking. He was the senior man in the room and knew Andrew well, which was an advantage.

Ginny was fascinated by what she was hearing and the style of the two men, Andrew and the monsignor, as they fenced elegantly with each other. It was almost like a dance, and hard to say at this point which one would win. She was betting on Andrew, for Blue's sake. But the monsignor was highly skilled at what he did, too.

'I think we all need to think of the damage that will be caused here, if the case proceeds,' Monsignor Cavaretti said seriously. 'The lives that will be destroyed, not only Father Graham's, but the boy's. Would it really serve him well to expose this, even if his story is true, which I don't believe? I think he's a frightened boy, who perhaps tried to seduce a priest, then thought better of it and tried to turn it around to his advantage. We're not going to pay him a cent for lying,' Cavaretti said, his eyes boring into Andrew's and then taking in Ginny, who looked shocked at what he'd said.

'This isn't about money,' Andrew said clearly, as Ginny almost jumped out of her chair but controlled herself, 'nor the alleged seduction of a man in his forties by a nine-year-old boy. That's a clever theory, Monsignor, but it won't work here. My client is the innocent victim, not Father Graham. And the church will pay whatever the courts decide, for impacting his life forever. You know the toll these incidents take, and so do I. We're talking about a crime, Monsignor. A serious crime, committed on a child. Ted Graham belongs in prison, not moved to a different parish, to do it again.

'If this goes to court, and it will, the world will be looking at you and asking why you moved him and didn't stop him from doing it to someone else. This is a grave crime, committed against my client. You all bear responsibility for it, for not stopping the perpetrator, and for transferring him to another city. You know me well enough to know that I will be relentless in my pursuit of justice here, both moral and material, as a demonstration of your remorse and good will.'

And with that, the lawyer and the priest exchanged a long silent look, and Andrew stood up and signaled to Ginny to do the same. She watched Cavaretti in amazement, and saw him purse his lips. He didn't like the position Andrew was taking or his unwillingness to drop the case or to be intimidated by the older man. He had hoped the meeting with Andrew would go better than it had. But for now at least, Andrew wasn't budging an inch.

The old monsignor looked at Ginny then. 'I urge you to talk to the boy, and think of the lives he will destroy here, most especially his own. This case will get ugly and hurt everyone involved, even Blue himself. We leave no stone unturned.' It was a direct threat, but Andrew cut him off before she could respond. She didn't know what to say, other than that she believed Blue, who was the victim here, and that their priest was a liar and a pervert, and that the police were gathering testimony and evidence to prove it, from his other victims as well. This was not going to be a small matter for Father Teddy Graham or the church, especially once it hit the news.

'Thank you, gentlemen, for your time,' Andrew said politely, then turned to Cavaretti again. 'Good to see you, Monsignor. Have a nice day.' And with that he propelled Ginny out of the room by her elbow, signaled to her not to speak, and found their own way downstairs and back out to the street. His eyes were icy, and there was a look of steel on his face when he spoke to her as they walked away. 'He's a cunning old devil. I knew he'd try to scare you off by threatening Blue. And there's no question, it will be a tough case – they always are when you go up against a mammoth institution like the Catholic Church. But goodness and truth are on our side, not theirs, and they know it. And when we start rolling out teenage witnesses with stories similar to Blue's, they're going to be begging for mercy. This won't be a pretty case, for them. And it will be costly for everyone. So if they can scare you off, they will. Are you still in?' Andrew looked at Ginny with concern, but she was much tougher than he knew, and furious at what she'd heard.

'What a slimy thing to do, and it's so wrong!' she said, with a look of outrage in her eyes. 'They should be crawling on their knees over what happened!'

'This is just posturing in the beginning. They can't just give in to us immediately – they have to play the game. But they will pay in the end. Sometimes a lot. They pay huge damages and settlements in these cases. It won't change what happened, but it could give Blue a better life than he might have otherwise, and some security for his future. That could be very important for him.' All Andrew could do now to help him was convince the church to pay a handsome settlement. And he wasn't going to rest until that was achieved.

'What was that meeting about? I thought we were going to have a serious conversation about what to do. All they wanted to do was terrorize us.' Ginny was angry, but Andrew knew the dance had only just begun.

'They don't scare me,' Andrew said calmly. 'And I hope they don't scare you. They wanted to see if we'd dump the case before it goes to the grand jury and turns into a much bigger headache for them. Blue will be protected by anonymity because he's a minor. Now it's Father Teddy's turn to pay the price for his crimes. This was just a saber-rattling contest. After this, it will get serious, and they'll get tougher before they cave.'

'Do you think they will cave?' she asked, looking worried, and relieved they hadn't wanted to see Blue at the meeting. She wouldn't have brought him, even if they did. If Blue had been there, Cavaretti would have tried to pressure Blue and make him recant and confuse him about what had actually happened.

'They really have no choice here, if Blue sticks to his story.'

'It's not a story, it's the truth,' Ginny said hotly.

'That's why I'm here,' Andrew said quietly. 'Try not to let them get to you this early. We have a long road ahead of us. Which reminds me – once you have guardianship, I want you to take him to the psychologist whose name I gave you. I want some kind of assessment of his mental state, and the extent of the psychological damage, in a doctor's opinion.' He had requested temporary guardianship for her, pending the hearing, and saw no reason why she wouldn't get it.

'Will she use hypnosis, or just talk to him?' Ginny asked, concerned.

'It depends on what she thinks. She might use hypnosis if she thinks he was sodomized and doesn't remember it, but testimony based on hypnosis can be sketchy and unreliable, and some judges won't accept it. I'd rather rely on her assessment, and what Blue says himself.'

Ginny nodded in agreement – she just wanted to warn Blue of what would happen when he saw the therapist. She had already told him he would probably have to see one for an evaluation, and he had no objection. He was like an open book.

'Well, try to do something more pleasant for the rest of the day,' Andrew suggested as he left her at the corner. Nothing that had happened in the meeting had surprised him, but Ginny was upset and shaken.

Andrew had a busy afternoon ahead of him. He was meeting a new client in a similar case, although in that case the boy had been sodomized and had shown signs of psychosis ever since, and had just been released from a psychiatric hospital after attempting suicide. He saw many worse cases than Blue's, but his was important as well, and Andrew took it very seriously, as he did all of them. There were fragile young lives at stake that would be impacted forever, in obvious and subtle ways. He wanted to achieve retribution for them by putting all the perpetrators in prison.

He smiled at Ginny, wishing he could make this easier for her and Blue.

'If you don't mind, sign a release for the therapist so I can discuss the case with her, and I'll be in touch. I'm waiting to hear from Jane Sanders about when this will go to the grand jury. From what she said yesterday, I think they're almost ready to submit it, and we'll be off and running after that,' Andrew said, and Ginny nodded. He was efficient and on top of all the details, as well as extremely competent at sparring with old priests. She had been very impressed by his performance in the meeting. He was the classic iron hand in the velvet glove, and much tougher than she'd thought. And somehow it helped that he had been a priest. He was like a secret agent who had defected from the other side, and he knew all the private ins and outs of the church. Andrew O'Connor was no slouch. She was intrigued, too, by the old monsignor being so convinced Andrew would go back, particularly since he knew him so well. 'I'll call you,' he promised. 'Say hi to Blue for me.' He waved and got into a cab, and she took the subway back uptown.

Blue asked about the meeting as soon as she walked into the apartment, but she didn't want to worry him.

'What did they say?' He looked concerned, and had been lying on the couch, watching TV. He was still pale after his surgery.

'Not much,' she said honestly. It had been basically bluster and veiled threats when you got right down to it, and a few elegant flourishes and jabs from Andrew's side. She liked his style. 'Mostly, they wanted to know if we were serious about the case. Andrew said we are, in so many words. He threatened them a little, and then we left.' She had summarized it succinctly, without the twists and turns and blackmail of the monsignor's words. 'Andrew knew the monsignor, which doesn't hurt. I think the archdiocese will get more serious after this. I think they were hoping we'd drop it before it goes to the grand jury, but we won't.' She changed into jeans, a T-shirt, and sandals then, and felt more relaxed, and then she called the therapist Andrew had referred her to. She made an appointment for the following week and told Blue about it.

Andrew called to check on Blue that night. Ginny thought he sounded tired, and he admitted he'd had a long day.

'How's the patient doing?' he asked in a friendly tone.

'Getting restless, I think. He wants to go to the beach tomorrow. I think we should wait a few days.'

'What if I bring dinner tomorrow night?' Andrew suggested, and Ginny was touched.

'He's desperate for a Big Mac,' she said, laughing.

'I think we can do better than that. My apartment is near Zabar's. I'll bring a picnic over tomorrow after work,' he offered generously. 'And don't forget our Yankees game.' It was going to be on Blue's birthday. Ginny wondered if he was this attentive to all his clients. He seemed to have a soft spot for Blue. 'See you tomorrow night,' Andrew said, after chatting with her for a few minutes, and she reported to Blue that Andrew was coming to dinner the following night.

'He likes you,' Blue said with a goofy grin.

'He likes *you,*' she corrected him, and the following night Andrew showed up at their apartment with flowers for her and a sumptuous meal. There were several kinds of pasta, roast chicken, salads, a number of good French cheeses, a bottle of excellent French wine for him and Ginny, and a mountain of desserts. The three of them spread it out on their dining table and shared a delicious meal. He and Blue talked baseball and music, and after Blue went to bed, he and Ginny talked about her travels, and he reminisced about how much he had loved Rome.

'It's the most romantic city in the world,' he said nostalgically, and it seemed like an odd comment from an ex-priest, and he grinned, aware of that himself. 'I only figured that out after I left the church. I'd love to go back one day. It was very exciting being at the Vatican, although I worked fifteen hours a day. I used to go for long walks at night when I finished. It's an exquisite city. You should go there with Blue one day.' He treated her as a friend more than a woman, and it was nice being able to share her concerns about Blue with him, and her hopes.

'There are a lot of places I'd like to travel with him, although not the countries where I work. Maybe I can take some time off and go to Europe with him next year.'

'It sounds like you've earned it.'

'I was thinking about taking him away for a few days before he starts school.'

'You should go to Maine. I spent my summers there as a kid.' And then his face lit up as he thought of something. 'Do you like to sail?'

'I haven't in years. I used to love it.'

'I keep a ridiculously small sailboat at Chelsea Piers. It's my pride and joy. I take it out on weekends, when I'm not buried in work. We should take Blue out on it some weekend.' Like Ginny, he wanted to introduce him to some of the joys in life, and it sounded like fun to her.

They chatted for a while, about his summers in Maine, and hers in California, while they finished the wine. It was a nice, relaxing, family-style evening, and she thanked him for the delicious meal. And before he left, he promised to call her about going out on his boat.

Ginny heard from Ellen Warberg at SOS/HR the next day, and she said they had an assignment in India that they were considering her for. It was at a shelter for young girls who had been used as sex slaves, and the human rights workers were rescuing or buying them back one by one. There were more than a hundred girls in the camp, and it sounded interesting to Ginny, but she had so much going on at home now.

'When do you need me to leave?' she asked, sounding worried.

'Our main worker who's running it now has to be back in the States on September tenth, so I think the latest we can send you is around September fifth, so she can brief you before she leaves. At least it's not a hardship post, and you won't get shot at for a change.'

But the date she had mentioned was the day Blue started school at LaGuardia Arts, and it was only three weeks away. She didn't want him staying at the shelter on his first day at such an exciting new school. She wanted to be there to support him, but didn't know if her superior at SOS would understand. Ellen had no kids and had never been married, and her concern for children was more political and on a much broader scale than one teenage boy on the first day of school. Ginny thought about it quickly before she spoke.

'I've never done this before, but I honestly can't get there on that date. I've got a lot going on here right now,' she said, thinking of the grand jury hearing, possibly Father Teddy's arraignment immediately afterward, Blue starting at a new school, and the ongoing investigation to unearth additional victims. She didn't see how she could be in India in early September, and not be around to support Blue with a new school and an impending criminal case.

'When do you think you could go?' Ellen asked her, sounding tense. She had to fill the post rapidly, but she was also well aware that Ginny had accepted every assignment, no matter how terrible, without complaint, for more than three years. She had a right to pass one up now.

'Ideally, I'd like to be here for the month of September, if you can work that out. I'll go anywhere you want as of October first or thereabouts.' It would give her a month and a half at home, which seemed like enough time to get everything off and running, and Blue settled in. Then she could leave in good conscience to do her work for them.

'I think that'll work. We'll send someone else to India, I have someone in mind. She's not as experienced as you are, but she's willing, and I think she'll do a good job. We'll send you somewhere else in October, Ginny. I can't promise where, and if you go out on October first, we'll bring you back around Christmas, or just after, which will give you three months in the field.' She was organizing it in her head and talking out loud, and Ginny's heart sank as she said it. She was going to be Blue's guardian now, and had a responsibility to him, and bringing her back 'just after Christmas' was going to be a terrible blow to him. She didn't want to leave him to spend Christmas at an adolescent shelter, while she spent it in a refugee camp halfway around the world, not even able to communicate with him. Her life was getting more complicated by the day, especially with their case against the church about to heat up dramatically. 'That'll work,' Ellen said again cheerfully. 'Enjoy your time at home.' She imagined that Ginny was relaxing and going to movies and museums. She had no idea that she had taken a homeless teenage boy under her wing nearly eight months before.

Ginny was still thinking about it when Andrew called her and told her a date the next week had been chosen for the case to go to the grand jury, and that she might be called on to be interviewed by them. And another victim in Chicago had come forward, another altar boy. Andrew could just imagine Cavaretti's reaction to that. Things weren't going well for their side. And he noticed that Ginny sounded distracted – she had hardly reacted to the news that they had found another victim of Father Teddy's at St. Anne's. 'Is something wrong?' he asked her, she usually sounded much more engaged when he gave her news of new developments in the case. Ginny seemed like she had a lot on her mind.

'I was just negotiating with my office. They wanted to send me to India in a couple of weeks, and it's a bad time to leave Blue, so they agreed to give me September at home, as long as I leave by the first of October. But I probably won't make it back for Christmas. It's a trade-off, but there's always a hitch in there somewhere.'

He didn't say it, but he didn't see how she was going to juggle a job like hers and Blue, especially if she was gone for months at a time, and away three-quarters of the year.

She was realizing that, too, and it put a lot of strain on her. The work she did was important to her, but so was Blue, and he needed her. 'It all was pretty easy when I had no one in my life.'

'That's why I stay single,' he said, laughing, trying to ease the tension for her, 'so I can leave for India or Afghanistan at the drop of a hat.' He had no idea how she managed what she did, and tolerated it for long periods of time, with or without Blue. It seemed admirable to the point of saintly to him, as well as foolhardy at times, but she didn't seem to mind the dangers or discomforts, at least until now.

'Put Syria on that list, too. Anyway, I'll see how it all shakes out, and where they want to send me then. At least I'll be home for a while right now.'

'I think that's a good idea, at least until after the arraignment and we lay the groundwork for the civil suit.' He wasn't going to file it yet, but there was work to do. 'And you don't know what's going to hit the press, or how hard the church will fight back. They might lob a couple of bombs over the fence.' He had promised Blue anonymity, which he was guaranteed because he was a minor, but there was no telling what they'd say about Ginny or why she was involved.

And as the case heated up, Andrew was worried the archdiocese wasn't going to play 'nice.' He thought it best if she were home for that to support Blue, but he could well imagine the pressure it was putting on her, in a job where she was essentially gone most of the time, and rarely even able to be in communication. Her life had not been set up to accommodate a teenage boy, or an attachment of any kind, which had suited her perfectly till now. 'What do you think you'll do about it long term?' he asked. She was wondering about that herself. If Blue stayed with her, she might have some difficult choices to make.

'I can't even get there yet in my head,' she said carefully. 'I'm just trying to get through September here, and my next assignment, and then I'll figure it out. Till now, for the past few years, all I had to do was hold a bowl of bloody rags in a surgical unit without fainting, climb a mountain now and then, and try not to get shot by a sniper. No one was counting on me at home, or cared where I was most of the time, except occasionally my sister, but she has her own life and family to think about. Now, suddenly, I have all this going on at home. I wasn't expecting that.' She had never thought of even the vague possibility of it when she had let Blue sleep on her couch for a few days over Christmas nearly eight months before.

'I think that's how life works. Just when you think you have it all set up and perfectly arranged, someone sneezes, or God blows on it, and all the building blocks come tumbling down.' That had certainly happened to her nearly four years before, when she and Mark and Chris had left the party on the night before Christmas Eve, and now she had built a life that finally worked for her, and here she was again, with bits and pieces all over the place and a life to rearrange. But as far as she was concerned, Blue was a good problem to have. She just had to figure it out. She didn't want to give anything up yet, neither her work, which she loved, nor him. And she was even more committed to Blue as his guardian now. It was a lot more than just paperwork to her. 'Let me know if there's anything I can do to help. I can keep an eye on him for you when you're gone if you like, and visit him at the shelter again.' But they both knew he needed more than that. He needed the home life he'd never had till her, and she knew parenting wasn't a part-time job.

'I guess I just have to work it out as I go along.' He thought toning down the risks she took on a regular basis would be a good idea, but she seemed to be committed to her work. Yet, however much time she dedicated to Blue, the boy would benefit from it, and already had.

'By the way, I don't have to work this weekend,' he said as an afterthought. 'I could take you both out for a sail on Sunday.' It sounded great to her. She wondered suddenly if Blue got seasick, and she realized he had probably never had the opportunity to find out.

She told him about Andrew's invitation that night at dinner, and Blue was excited about it. They were going to the Yankees game on Saturday, and possibly sailing on Sunday. They talked about it for a while, and then she told him that the grand jury hearing had been scheduled, and that she had talked to SOS and was staying home for another six weeks. He looked even happier about that, and the relief in his eyes tugged at her heart.

'I was scared you wouldn't be here when I started school,' he said softly.

'So was I. I couldn't leave before that,' she said quietly, feeling the weight of her responsibility to him now.

'I wish they didn't send you away for so long,' Blue said wistfully. 'I missed you while you were gone,' he admitted, and she nodded.

'I missed you, too. Maybe they can give me shorter assignments.' But she knew that wasn't the nature of her job, and one of the advantages she offered SOS was that, until now, she had been completely unattached. And she suddenly felt guilty leaving him at the shelter for months. The landscape of her life was changing fast.

* * *

The night that she and Blue spent at the Yankees game with Andrew on Blue's birthday was one of the high points of his life. Andrew picked them up in the Range Rover he drove on weekends, and Blue chatted excitedly on the way to the game, wearing his Yankees hat. And Andrew had planned a series of surprises for him. He took him onto the field before the game started and introduced him to several more star players in the dugout, who wished Blue a happy birthday and signed two more balls for him, which he told Ginny to put in her purse and guard with her life when they went back to join her in their seats. Andrew bought them all hot dogs, and right before the game started, the scoreboard lit up with 'Happy Birthday, Blue.' Ginny nearly cried when she saw it, as Blue let out a shout of delight. He couldn't stop grinning, as Ginny and Andrew exchanged a look over his head, and she thanked him when they sat down, and so did Blue.

The game itself was exciting. It was tied until the Yankees won in the twelfth inning, with all the bases loaded, and Blue was jumping up and down as they scored the winning run. And his name was on the board again when they left. It was every boy's dream birthday, and Ginny had had fun, too. Andrew came back to the apartment with them to share the birthday cake Ginny had kept hidden.

'I've never had a birthday like this,' Blue said solemnly after he blew out his candles and looked at them both.

'You're my best friends.' Then he remembered the two autographed balls in Ginny's purse, took them out, and put them proudly on the shelf in his room with the others he'd gotten with Andrew the last time.

'You gave him an incredible birthday,' Ginny said to Andrew as she handed him a piece of cake, and they sat down at the kitchen table, which was barely big enough for the three of them.

'It's nice to be able to make him happy,' Andrew said with a quiet smile. 'It's not hard to do.' Blue came back to the kitchen then and sat down to eat his cake. It had been a perfect night.

'I've never had a birthday cake before,' Blue said looking thoughtful as he finished his second piece, and both of the adults were stunned. It put into perspective for them the life he had led before. It was so different from Andrew and Ginny's own life experiences in stable families, growing up in traditional homes.

Andrew volunteered that he had two older brothers who had given him a hard time. One was an attorney at a law firm in Boston, and the other was a college professor in Vermont. They had both thought he was crazy when he became a priest.

'I have a nephew your age,' he said, smiling at Blue. 'He wants to play football in high school, and his mother is having a fit.' He smiled at Ginny, and she realized as he did that both of them had nieces and nephews but no children of their own. And after they finished the cake and sat down in the living room, Andrew looked at the photographs of Mark and Chris.

'He was a beautiful little boy,' he said gently to Ginny, and she nodded and couldn't speak for a moment. It still hit her hard sometimes. Andrew could see it, so he talked to Blue about the game. They both agreed that the Yankees had played masterfully, and Andrew promised to take him to the World Series if they played. As he said it, Ginny realized that she would be away by then. It suddenly seemed hard knowing she was going to miss things that were important to Blue. But she had a job that she felt she had to do.

When Andrew left, he wished Blue a happy birthday again and told them he'd see them in the morning at Chelsea Piers.

It was another memorable day for Blue as Andrew taught him to sail on his small, beautiful sailboat. It was an old wooden boat that he had restored himself. Ginny helped him handle the lines as they left the dock on a gorgeous sunny August day with a perfect breeze. And then she helped him with the sails, as he showed Blue what to do. He got the hang of it quickly, and they flew along for a while, and then tucked into a small harbor, where Andrew dropped the anchor. They had lunch, and then they lay on the deck in the sun. It was an ideal boat for the three of them.

'I usually take it out alone,' Andrew said to Ginny as they watched Blue at the bow. And as Ginny looked at Andrew, she had a sense that he was a solitary man, as sailors often were. 'It's nice having people on board,' he said, smiling at her. 'I sailed her to Maine last summer. My family still has a place there. I try to get there for a week or two every year to spend time with my brothers' kids. I'm the weird uncle who used to be a priest.' He smiled as he said it. He didn't seem to mind being different, or alone, in much the same way Ginny was now, or had been until Blue.

'I think I'm getting to like being weird,' she said with a grin. 'My sister thinks I am, too. I'm not sure what normal is anymore.' Once it was being married and having a child, and now it was wandering around the world like a lost soul, living in refugee camps. And for him it was helping boys who had been molested by priests. Normal had become the lives they lived, entirely different from the lives they had expected and planned. It was enjoying the good times as they came, like the day they spent together on the boat. And Andrew had made a sailor of Blue by the end of the day. Andrew managed to sail the boat almost up to Chelsea Piers, and then turned the motor on to come into the dock, and Ginny and Blue helped secure the lines and tie her up. Blue helped wash the boat, and they all agreed it had been a terrific day. They had relaxed and talked, and when Andrew drove them home, Ginny and Blue thanked him for a wonderful time. Ginny invited him to come up for something to eat, but Andrew said he had work to do, and she didn't know why, but she sensed that he used his work as a way to keep just enough distance between himself and the rest of the world. It was a place where he could hide, just as he had done when he was a priest.

'I wish we had a boat,' Blue said with stars in his eyes as they rode up in the elevator, and Ginny laughed.

'Don't go getting fancy on me, Blue Williams,' she teased him, and he grinned.

'One day I'm going to make a lot of money being a famous composer, and I'll buy you a boat,' he said as he followed her into the apartment, and she turned to look at him and thought he just might. The possibilities were limitless. Nothing was impossible for him now.

Chapter 17

Blue wasn't enthused about going to a therapist, but had agreed because he knew it was important to the case, and both of them were pleasantly surprised when they met with her the Monday after they'd been on Andrew's boat. Her name was Sasha Halovich, she was a small wizened woman who looked old enough to be Ginny's grandmother, but she was very wise and met with Blue alone in her office for two hours, and then came out to talk to Ginny with Blue's permission. She said that she felt confident that nothing more had happened than what he said, which was certainly bad enough and very traumatic for him, but she thought he was handling it well, in great part thanks to Ginny. Halovich found him to be a stable, healthy boy who had had a hard life but weathered it remarkably. She saw no need for hypnosis, and she said she would write a report, and was willing to testify in court. And she thought it a good idea to see him occasionally to help him through the months ahead, and Ginny agreed.

Andrew called to discuss it with Ginny the next day, since she had signed the release for the therapist to speak to him, and she had. 'It sounds like he's in pretty good shape, thanks to you.' He gave her the full credit for it, which she humbly declined.

'Thanks to himself, and a little help from his friends,' she corrected. 'He's a wonderful kid. I have total confidence in him, and I believe in him a thousand percent.'

'That's what it takes. If more parents felt like you, there would be better people in the world.'

'All I want is for Blue to have an amazing life,' she said firmly. 'And I think he will.' What she had done to get him into LaGuardia Arts was nothing short of miraculous in Andrew's opinion. She was the kind of person who changed people's lives, not just in Syria and Afghanistan, working for human rights, but in her own life at home every day. The court case he was spearheading for them was proof of it, and the psychologist had been very impressed, too. She had told Andrew that Blue was adjusting very well to his new life, in spite of the stress of the court case coming up. Dr. Halovich had told Andrew that Ginny was just what the boy needed, and it had been a miracle in his life that they had found each other. And from what he knew, Andrew agreed, and after they talked about the therapist, Ginny thanked him again for the fabulous day sailing and the Yankees game.

The next big step in the case was when the police presented all the evidence they had to the grand jury, and there was reams of it: interviews with other victims and their families, and witnesses who had surfaced who had seen suspicious occurrences once their memories were jogged. There were statements from irate parents and traumatized children. 'Father Teddy' had sodomized the older ones, who were his altar boys, and had had oral sex with the younger ones, as he had done with Blue, and fondled a number of children, always accusing them of tempting him, and threatening them with jail, or even hurting them physically if they told anyone, so they had the burden of secrecy as well as guilt to carry, too. It was heartbreaking to read the report. By the time it went to the grand jury, they knew of eleven victims in New York and six in Chicago. NYPD had notified their counterparts in Chicago, who were investigating, too. Andrew and Jane Sanders were sure there were more who would come forward eventually.

And in sharp contrast to the trauma of the victims was the outrage of the parishioners who continued to believe in their favorite priest, and insisted that the boys were lying. Andrew could never understand how people could cling to their loyalty to someone in spite of undeniable evidence to the contrary. But their love for Father Teddy was unconditional, and their belief in the purity of the church so strong. They forgot that, like any organization, it was made up of individuals, and that there were sick people everywhere, in every walk of life. Ted Graham was one of them. And the second worst crime that had been committed was the cover-up by the archdiocese. There was no question of it now, although it still had to be proved. But two young priests had spoken up at St. Francis's in New York, and said that they knew, and had seen things they didn't like and had reported Ted Graham to a monsignor in the archdiocese, and nothing had been done to remove him. And when they reported it a second time, they had been reprimanded.

But six weeks later, Graham had been moved to Chicago, to do whatever he wanted there. One of the young reporting priests had already left the church because of it, and the other was contemplating leaving but hadn't decided yet. But he had told Jane Sanders when she interviewed him that he was totally disillusioned about the church, and was almost certain he would leave. He had wanted to be a priest all his life growing up, and he no longer did. He said his grandmother was heartbroken over it and so disappointed. She was from the old country, and two of her own sons had become priests.

Reading Detective Sanders's report to the grand jury, it was amazing how many lives had been touched by the perfidies of Ted Graham. He had injured children, possibly irreparably, physically damaged the ones he'd sodomized at such a young age, devastated parents, torn apart families, disillusioned his peers and shaken their faith, and put his superiors in danger when they tried to protect him and would now answer for it. A young monsignor had spoken to him before he was transferred to Chicago, and asked him if the allegations and suspicions were true, and Father Teddy had denied it and given a lengthy but credible explanation about why people were jealous of him, and he had portrayed himself as the victim, when the reverse was true. The monsignor he had lied to was now in serious trouble over the transfer to Chicago. He had been naïve. But his superiors had known what they were doing when they hushed up the problem and tried to solve it geographically, and foisted him off on other innocents. It was a tragedy for all concerned, even Ted Graham himself, although he denied that, too, and said he was a martyr for the church.

The grand jury deliberated on the case and voted to indict Father Teddy. There was no doubt in anyone's mind that he was guilty, as much as the church was for concealing what it knew of his crimes.

Days after the grand jury voted to indict, Father Ted Graham was extradited to New York to be arraigned. The Chicago courts were going to arraign him later. He flew in from Chicago with two deputy sheriffs, and walked into the NY Supreme Court with his attorney and two priests accompanying him, and entered a plea of not guilty on eleven counts of sexual abuse of minors, including sodomy, oral sex, and abuse of trust. He was smiling as he entered the courtroom, and respectful as he addressed the judge. He was remanded into custody, with bail set at one million dollars, and then he was led away in handcuffs by two sheriff's deputies, while speaking pleasantly to them. He looked completely unconcerned and neither guilty nor frightened. Ginny hadn't gone to the arraignment, but Andrew did, and watched the proceedings carefully to report them to her later. She was disgusted when she heard of Ted's performance in the courtroom. He was playing the role of great guy and Christian martyr to the end.

'What happens now?' she asked Andrew when he called her. 'He sits in jail until the trial?'

'Not likely,' Andrew answered cynically. 'The church will post bail quietly in a day or two, when it won't attract too much attention. His attorney asked for him to be released on his own recognizance, saying he's not a flight risk, but the judge denied it. They'll have to pay a hundred thousand dollars to spring him, and post bond for the rest. The church is good for it, so they'll get him out. And eventually, they'll have to do it all over again in Chicago, when he's charged there.' It had been an extraordinary series of events: Blue had had the courage to speak up, she had believed him, they had gone to the proper authorities, and Andrew had taken their case. And it was by no means over yet. In the months ahead, there would be further investigation, careful preparation of the case, and the trial in about a year, unless Graham pled guilty before that and spared the state the expense of trying him. And after that, he'd have to face trial in Illinois on the charges there. But there was no doubt he would go to prison, where Blue, Ginny, and Andrew knew he belonged.

With everything going on related to the case, Ginny never managed to organize a vacation for herself and Blue, but they went to the beach for the day on Long Island, and went to another concert in the park. And Andrew took them to Blue's first Broadway musical. They saw *Phantom of the Opera,* and he loved it. And they went sailing again on Labor Day weekend.

As things began to calm down slowly, Blue started school the week after Labor Day, at LaGuardia Arts. Ginny took him to the first day, as she'd promised, and walked him to the entrance on Amsterdam Avenue, but she didn't go in with him. He was on his own now, a high school freshman, hopefully to start a career in music. It reminded her of Chris's first day at nursery school, and she cried all the way home on the subway. She thought about calling Andrew, but didn't want to be maudlin, and she knew he was busy. But Blue had become a strong bond between them.

It was a strange feeling going back to the apartment

after she dropped Blue off. Becky called her that morning for the first time in weeks, and Ginny told her that Blue had just started school that day.

'I can't believe you did that for him,' Becky said, sounding admiring this time, and less critical than usual. Her own kids had returned to school the week before, and she said it was nice to have time to herself again. It had been a long summer, with the kids home for three months and her father dying. Ginny mentioned the arraignment to her, too, and the fact that there were now seventeen known victims of the errant priest, including Blue. Becky listened in shock. 'It's hard to believe a priest would do something like that, although I've read about it. Do you suppose he'll plead guilty?' She suddenly sounded more interested in the case, although she hadn't believed Blue or her sister before. But because others had accused him, too, it now seemed credible to her. Not even she could believe seventeen boys, including some grown men who had been his early victims, were lying. They talked for a few minutes, and then they both had things to do.

Kevin Callaghan called Ginny that week, too. He had read about the priest being charged with sexual crimes in New York and suspected it was Ginny's case that she had called him for advice about months before.

'Is that the guy?' He was curious about it, and he hadn't talked to her for a while.

'Yes, it is. There are sixteen more victims, and there will probably be more before it's over.'

'How's your boy doing?' He admired her for championing Blue's cause and for believing him when no one else had.

'Amazingly well,' she said proudly about Blue. He was a source of constant joy to her. She told Kevin about his starting a special high school for musical arts. He was going to have his first recital in December. She was glad that he would have a year of peace before Father Teddy went to trial. He needed the time for healing.

'And what about you? When are you going on the road again?' Kevin asked her.

'October,' she answered, feeling guilty. 'I'm waiting for my next assignment.' He thought she was remarkable for that, too, and he was sorry that she didn't have more time in her life for old friends, relationships, or romance, but he didn't see how she could with everything she was doing, and now Blue and the trial. Her plate was very full. She promised she'd call him before she left again.

The rest of September sped by peacefully, while Blue settled into school, and Ginny took care of their errands, kept up with State Department reports, and waited to hear about her next assignment, which she was expecting any day. And they managed to have Andrew for dinner again, and Blue told him all about school and showed him his assignments, which impressed Andrew. Blue was composing music, and was thrilled with his new school. It was easy to see that he was thriving.

Andrew and Ginny sat and talked after dinner, when Blue went to his room to watch TV there. They had hardly had time to talk recently. Andrew said he was swamped with new cases. And he told her that there was going to be an important meeting at the archdiocese in October, to discuss a possible settlement for Blue that would avoid a civil suit. And if there was a settlement in the civil suit, Ted Graham would plead guilty to criminal charges. The monsignors, bishops, and archbishops were beginning to understand that there was no way out in the Ted Graham case, and they wanted to get a sense from Andrew about how much he had in mind. They hadn't agreed to anything yet, but it was the first sign of movement from the church, and they wanted to put it behind them. And they had all the other victims to negotiate with now, too.

'I think you should be there,' Andrew said quietly as Ginny looked at him with panic in her eyes.

'I can't . . . I'm leaving before that. I don't know where yet, but I agreed to go on October first. How can I be at the meeting?'

'I don't know. And if you can't, you can't.' He looked disappointed but understanding. 'It would be much more effective if you could speak on his behalf. And your testimony will carry more weight than a parent's would, because you came into his life recently and can still be somewhat objective. If you can't be there, I'll handle it, but if there's any chance you can, I think you should.' He had never pressed her before, and what he said was important to her, but she couldn't delay her departure date again. She had an obligation to SOS, too.

That night she lay in bed feeling sick, thinking about the hearing that Andrew wanted her to attend in October. She just didn't see how she could do it.

Two days later, Ellen called and told her that SOS/HR had her assignment. They were sending her to a different part of India than they had suggested to her before. It would be a little bit more rugged. She'd be working in a large refugee camp in Tamil Nadu, in southeast India. And they wanted her to leave in ten days, at the beginning of October, just as she had promised in September.

She thought about it incessantly for three days, torturing herself about it, and she finally went to the office to talk to Ellen in person. There was always something now, and all of it associated with Blue, but she loved having him in her life. She didn't know what to do, but she didn't feel she could leave before the meeting at the archdiocese in October. She didn't want to hurt Blue's case against Father Teddy, and Andrew thought it would if she was away. She had called to discuss it with him again, and he'd been candid with her. He said he needed her there, if she could do it.

She sat down across from Ellen with a sigh.

'You look harried,' Ellen said to her, handing her the packet of information she needed to read before her assignment.

'It's incredible how stressful it can be to be at home. It's a lot simpler just worrying about dysentery and snipers.'

Ellen laughed at what she said. Sometimes she felt that way, too. She had been a field-worker for years like Ginny and still missed it. But she'd had some health issues, from years of getting diseases on her assignments and poor medical care, and had finally decided it was time to work in the office, not the field. She felt that Ginny was still years away from making that decision.

'Excited to be leaving again?' she asked her with a warm smile, and Ginny almost burst into tears. She wasn't excited, she was wracked with indecision. But in her heart of hearts, she knew she had no choice. She needed to stay with Blue. He would never have said it to her, but she knew how much it would mean to him, and maybe it was a sacrifice she had to make.

'I don't even know how to say this to you, Ellen, but I think I have to stay home till the end of the year. I don't want to screw up my job, and I love what I do, but I've become the guardian of a fourteen-year-old boy. We're involved in a lawsuit, and there are criminal proceedings where he's a victim. He just started a new school. And I think I need to stick around.' She looked unhappy as she said it.

Ellen looked shocked. She could see how torn Ginny was, and she was one of their best workers – they didn't want to lose her from the field. It would be an enormous loss to them. 'I'm so sorry, Ginny. Is there anything I can do?' She was a compassionate woman, and would like to help if she could.

'Yes, baby-sit him while I go.' She hadn't been home for this long for three and a half years, and at times it felt strange. But leaving Blue for three months and coming back after Christmas would have been infinitely worse.

'Do you think you'll give up fieldwork?' Ellen asked her, looking worried.

'I hope not. I honestly don't know. I have to see how it goes – everything is still so new. And I'm trying to get adjusted to having a teenage boy.'

'Are you planning to adopt him?' It was a reasonable question, given what she'd said.

'I don't know,' Ginny said thoughtfully. 'I'm already becoming his legal guardian, and I'm not sure we need more. But the one thing he doesn't need, and that I don't want to do to him right now, is me leaving for three months when so much is happening in our lives.' And getting herself killed on an assignment would be disastrous for him. She had thought of that, too, although she didn't say it to Ellen. She wasn't ready to quit SOS/HR, she just wanted time off while she tried to figure it all out, and she was sure that by the end of the year she would. 'Can you put me on leave until the end of the year?' Ginny asked her, looking anxious.

'I can,' Ellen said fairly, 'if you really think that's what you have to do.' Ellen gazed at her with unhappy eyes, afraid that she'd never go back. Ginny was afraid of that, too. She thanked her for her understanding, signed a form for the leave of absence, and left the information packet for India on Ellen's desk. Then she went home to wait for Blue to come home from school. She sat in her living room feeling like someone had died. She didn't feel liberated or relieved to be staying home. All she felt was that she had done the right thing, for Blue. She wasn't at all sure if it was right for her, and she knew she'd miss the work she'd been doing until now.

The phone rang while she was sitting there thinking about it. It was Andrew, and he picked up on the tone of her voice immediately. 'You don't sound like a happy camper,' Andrew said to her. 'Is something wrong?'

'I'm not sure,' she said honestly. She didn't feel great about it, even if it was the correct thing to do. 'I just extended my leave of absence until the end of the year. I didn't feel right leaving Blue. But I'm not ready to give up human rights work, either. I already miss it. All I do is go to the grocery store, and play cards with Blue. I need more in my life than that,' she said miserably. 'And I also didn't want to be gone for your meeting with the archdiocese next month.' She wanted to be in two places at once and knew she couldn't.

'Why don't you go easy on yourself for a while? Maybe it'll do you good to stay home for a few months. All the sorrows of the world and broken people will still be out there in January, and then you can go back. Maybe you can do shorter assignments or troubleshoot for them, instead of going for three months at a time.' It wasn't a bad idea, and she hadn't thought of troubleshooting before. It cheered her up as he went on. 'I know Blue will be happy, and so am I,' he said, sounding elated. 'How about having dinner with me next week to celebrate your being here?' It was sweet of him to ask, although it seemed a little strange to her. She liked and admired him, but he was Blue's lawyer, not her friend. And she was sure he felt that way, too.

'To talk about the case?' she asked him.

'No,' he said calmly and clearly, with a smile she couldn't see. 'Because I like you. I think you're a fantastic person, and I just remembered I'm not a priest anymore. Is that okay with you?'

She thought about it for a long moment, and then nodded, smiling, too. 'Yes, it is.'

'I have good news for you, too. They had an opening in the family court calendar next week. They're doing the guardianship hearing. I'll need you and Blue for that, and Charlene if she's willing.' It was fantastic news.

'Why don't we schedule our dinner after that, so we'll have something to celebrate?'

'With Blue?'

'No, just the two of us,' he said firmly.

And when she told Blue that night that she was staying till January, and would be home for Christmas, he gave a scream you could have heard all the way to Central Park. Her decision to stay with him and not go to India for three months had now been met with warm approval by her fans, and she was pleased. Suddenly her decision to stay home made sense, which felt good to her. She knew it was what she was meant to do.

The guardianship hearing was as easy as Andrew had said it would be. The judge was sympathetic to Blue and knew about the impending criminal case. He was deeply respectful of Ginny's human rights work, and everything she had done for Blue. And Charlene showed up. It was the first time she and Blue had seen each other in a year, and it was bittersweet when she saw him. But she hadn't been there for him, and Ginny was, despite her traveling for work. She had already changed his life immeasurably, and the judge had no problem awarding her guardianship. Andrew and Ginny took Blue to lunch afterward, but Charlene said she had things to do and scurried away as soon as they left the courtroom.

So Ginny was officially Blue's legal guardian. It was a big step for both of them, and a commitment to each other. If she had gone to India, she wouldn't have been there for the hearing, so her instinct to stay had been the right one. There was a kind of magic to it, the things that had happened, the people who had come into her life, the school he was going to, Ted Graham being brought to trial. The hand of destiny had touched them all, and all because of Blue.

Chapter 18

The meeting at the archdiocese in October was frustrating and confusing. She went with Andrew, and he lost his temper several times. He and Monsignor Cavaretti locked horns repeatedly, veiled threats were tossed around like tennis balls, and some of them were not so veiled. There were six monsignors in the room this time, and a bishop at one point, and Andrew was alternately diplomatic and returned their threats in kind. The monsignors present flip-flopped between hinting at a settlement, and saying it was out of the question – mostly to check Andrew's reaction, Ginny suspected. Andrew knew they were testing the waters, to see what he wanted for his client, but they were impossible to deal with. And in spite of the fact that seventeen men and boys had given the police statements about Father Teddy's sexual abuse when they were minors in vivid terms, the priests were still implying that he was innocent and the boys were lying.

'Seventeen little boys and respectable men are *lying*?' Andrew asked them with a look of outrage. 'How do you figure that? Your man is a sociopath. He's a pedophile who's making a mockery of everything the priesthood represents. I'm not even a priest anymore, and I'm indignant at the idea that he claims to be. How can you defend him? And knowing what you did, how could you cover up for him and send him to another city so he could do it again? The destruction of those children's lives is blood on your hands. You are just as responsible as he is, and I don't know why you're not forcing him to enter a guilty plea. He's going to be convicted at trial and go to prison. You're wasting everybody's time,' Andrew accused them. The meeting grew increasingly heated for three hours, and finally, admitting it was going nowhere, Monsignor Cavaretti adjourned it. He said they would have to discuss the matter further and meet again.

Andrew's eyes were ablaze with fury when they left, while Ginny walked along beside him and agreed with everything he had said.

'What's the point of defending a man we all know is guilty? All they wanted to know today was if we're weakening. But Cavaretti knows me better. I'll go to my grave making sure Father Teddy is stopped and convicted, and I will fight for the best settlement for Blue I can get.' Andrew felt they owed it to Blue, and so did Ginny, and they had no intention of giving up. Cavaretti and the other monsignors knew that now. And they had all the other victims to contend with, too. It was going to be a costly case for the church, particularly because they had hidden Ted Graham's transgressions and done nothing about them, or to stop him; they had just closed their eyes and moved him on. It was one of the worst elements of the case. They had had the power to protect all those children, and they hadn't, and now lives had been ruined because of it, if the boys didn't recover from the trauma. And some of those who were grown men now hadn't.

Things seemed to calm down again for a while after the futile meeting, and for the next two weeks, Andrew was busy with other cases, and she didn't hear from him. They managed to have one very nice dinner at an Italian restaurant, and they enjoyed talking to each other and relaxing and not discussing the case for a change. They had agreed not to, and stuck to it. They were just two adults who liked each other, having dinner. And they had a good time, but she didn't hear from him afterward. And she helped Blue with homework every night. He was a whiz at everything that involved music and was composing concert pieces of his own, but he needed help with the academic subjects. She worked on English and history with him, but chemistry wasn't her strong suit, so she really had to concentrate and jog her memory to explain it to him.

She was on the way home from the gym one afternoon,

where she had started exercising, when she stopped to buy magazines and saw a photograph of herself on the *New York Post* and another one on the *National Enquirer*. They had both used old photographs from her TV news days, and they were about five years old. She hadn't seen the paper yet that day, bought them both immediately, and read them the minute she got home. The *New York Post* story was closer to the truth but had strong implications she didn't like. It said that she was a party to a sexual abuse case, which involved a priest who had molested seventeen young boys in both New York state and Illinois. He was out on a million dollars bail, all of which was true and a matter of public record, and the article listed all the charges accurately. Then it went on to say that her involvement was due to a homeless boy she had taken in and housed who was one of the victims. It did not state his name, since the names of the victims were protected and would not be released.

The article went on to say that Virginia Carter had virtually disappeared from public life and TV news when she and her husband had had too much to drink at a Christmas party four years before, as a result of which her husband had been killed drunk driving, and so had their three-year-old son, and she had been in seclusion ever since. The article didn't say it but heavily implied that she had psychiatric problems as a result of her husband and child's death, and she herself had also been under the influence the night they were killed, and no one had seen her since the accident. It made it sound like she'd been drunk for the last four years.

Then the article questioned what she was doing with a homeless boy, and how she had gotten tangled up in the latest scandal in the Catholic Church. It described similar stories of pedophile priests who had been convicted. In conclusion, it said that the defendant in the case, in which Ms. Carter was mysteriously involved, would be tried sometime in the next year. Church officials were unavailable for comment, the attorney of record for Ms. Carter's ward was Andrew O'Connor, a former Jesuit priest, and Ms. Carter herself remained MIA. And the last words of the piece were 'To be continued . . . stay tuned for breaking news,' which had been the closing line on her broadcast when she did the news.

She sat there staring at the piece. It had gotten the facts right, but it had implied that she and her husband were drunks and that he had killed their child while drunk at the wheel, and that she had disappeared immediately afterward, implying subtly that her psyche had been shattered. She hadn't been in the news since Mark had died. Someone had talked to them, and she had no idea who but she didn't like it. The reporter could get the list of charges from the court's public records, but the list of details had come from a person. She hated to be in the spotlight again, or to drag Blue into it with her, even unnamed, because she'd once been better known than she was now. She hated the tabloid feeling to the article, and being in the news at all.

And the *Enquirer* went straight for the throat as it always did. It ran an old photograph of her on the front page next to a giant question mark where it said, 'Back from the grave with a fourteen-year-old homeless boyfriend?' And it managed to make the court case sound as though she were somehow involved in it in a seamy way. She hated everything about it, and called Andrew as soon as she finished reading.

'Did you see the *Post* and the *Enquirer* today?' she asked in a tense voice as soon as he came on the line, and he laughed.

'No, they're not usually top of my must-read list. I read *The New York Times, The Wall Street Journal,* and the London *Financial Times* when I have time. Why, what do the other two say?'

'I'm on the cover, and the *Enquirer* wins the prize. They're asking if I'm back from the grave with a fourteen-year-old homeless boyfriend. And the *Post* seems to know a lot about the case. It talks about my husband driving drunk the night he and my son died in the accident. It makes it sound like I've been in a psychiatric hospital ever since, which I never was, and it's questioning what I'm doing now with a homeless kid, involved in a sex scandal in the church. So who do you think is talking?'

'Interesting question,' he said thoughtfully. 'You know more about that stuff than I do. I don't think Cavaretti would ever plant a piece like that. He's giving us a hard time, but he's a responsible man. Maybe Blue's aunt said something to someone, and they found her, and they probably looked the rest of it up once they had your name. It's probably somewhere on the Internet, from the time of your husband's death.' Then he lowered his voice and spoke softly. 'I'm sorry, Ginny. I'm sure this must be painful for you. But it's just tabloid garbage – no one reads it.'

'Yes, they do. You don't, but lots of people do. Imagine calling Blue my fourteen-year-old homeless boyfriend. For God's sake, what's wrong with these people? It makes me feel embarrassed that I was ever a member of the press.'

'That's how I feel about Ted Graham, having been a priest,' he said quietly.

'What if Blue sees this, or if they start hounding us? They can make our life miserable. I don't want them naming Blue as part of Ted Graham's case. He has a right to privacy, he's just a child.'

'You'd better tell him,' Andrew said seriously, 'because someone will if you don't. You should defuse it.'

'I hate to show him crap like this,' she said, sounding acutely unhappy. But she did what Andrew said and told Blue about it when he got home. She told him that it was just junk. And they talked about the night Mark died, and she admitted that he'd been drinking more than she'd realized at the time, but he hadn't been obviously drunk, or she wouldn't have let him drive. But there was no denying that his blood alcohol level had been well above the limit.

'You must have felt terrible about that,' Blue said sympathetically, and in order to be honest with him, she said that she had felt guilty ever since for letting him drive that night. She cried when she said that maybe if she hadn't, they'd still be alive, and Blue felt awful for her. She was more upset than he'd ever seen her. He didn't know what to say, so he tried to lighten the mood. 'They think I'm your boyfriend?' His voice cracked when he said it, and they both laughed.

'I hate this kind of stuff,' Ginny said as they sat side by side on the couch, looking at the papers on the trunk she used as a coffee table. 'I don't know who talked, but I don't like it. I never did. They hounded me for months after Mark died to see what I was doing. All I was doing then was crying. Do you suppose your aunt had something to do with this?' Ginny looked pensive as she said it, although it seemed unlikely.

'She could have. She wouldn't go to the newspaper. But maybe she shot her mouth off and someone else did. She likes to talk a lot and gossip. Maybe she wanted to get even with you for going after Father Teddy. She'll never forgive you for that. She still thinks he's a saint. I don't know who else would do it. I never knew you were that famous, Ginny,' he said, a little in awe of her.

'I used to be. Mark was, too. No one cares what I'm doing now.' And she liked it that way. And she knew from experience that you never found out who talked. The tabloids just picked up bits and pieces and wove them into a story, whether true or not, but they had a lot of the facts right this time.

'I'm sorry. If you hadn't tried to help me, they wouldn't be writing this junk about you. It's all my fault,' Blue said unhappily.

'Don't be stupid, Blue. It's Mark's fault for being drunk that night and driving, and killing himself and Chris. And mine for disappearing for four years. And yours for having the courage to speak up about Father Teddy, which was *entirely* the right thing to do and still is. It's all our faults for being alive and breathing. Everything is someone's fault, and so what? None of this bullshit matters. It's Father Teddy's fault for molesting a bunch of innocent kids, and the church for protecting him. Every day, good stuff and bad stuff happens to us. It's what you do about it and how you handle it that matters. You just can't let it break you. You have to keep fighting. And guilt and regrets never get us anywhere.' She smiled at him, got up, and put the two papers in the garbage, but he looked deeply sorry that because of him she had been embarrassed.

'That garbage will be in someone's hamster cage tomorrow.' He nodded but didn't look as though he believed her.

The topper on the day was when Becky called her after dinner.

'For chrissake, Ginny, none of us needs the headache of you in the tabloids again! It was bad enough after the accident, when they made you sound like a couple of drunks. Everyone kept asking me if you and Mark were alcoholics.' Her words smarted far more than what was in the tabloids, and Ginny winced as she listened. 'You don't know how hard it is for me and my kids and Alan to see you on the cover of the *Enquirer* while they talk about your fourteen-year-old boyfriend.'

'I don't have a fourteen-year-old boyfriend,' Ginny corrected her, but Becky was so quick to blame and attack her about everything she did. 'Are you under the impression that I gave them an interview?' Ginny snapped at her.

'You don't have to. Your life is a soap opera. You were always in the tabloids when you and Mark were on the news. Then he got drunk and killed Chris, and you were with him. Now you have a homeless kid move in with you, and go after a parish priest on some kind of crusade that's none of your business, and suddenly there you are on the front page of the *Enquirer* with a "fourteen-year-old boyfriend." You have no idea how embarrassing that is for the rest of us. Do you know how many people I'm going to have to explain it to? And poor Alan at work. We lead quiet, respectable lives, and somehow you're always slipping on a banana peel and falling ass-backward into the news. I wish to hell you wouldn't do that.'

'So do I,' Ginny said, suddenly furious with her sister, who was uncharitable and mean-spirited at best. And Blue listened to her on the phone with a look of pain. But Ginny didn't see it. 'You know, I wish you'd grow up one of these days and notice that there's a world out there bigger than the matchbox you live in. While I'm working my ass off to save kids in Afghanistan, you're driving to the grocery store and the dry cleaner in Pasadena, and you think that's all there is in life. Your house and your swimming pool, your kids and your husband. I may make an ass out of myself sometimes, but at least I'm living. I had a husband and a kid, too, but I wasn't as lucky as you are, so now I'm trying to make a difference in other people's lives, instead of sitting home and crying about them. And all you do is bitch about what I do and tell me it's not "normal."

'And to be honest, I don't give a damn what you think about my taking on the Catholic Church with Blue. You're always looking down your nose at me. And let me tell you, that boy has more balls than either of us. Do you know what it took for him to come forward? And go against a priest, for chrissake? While you tell me how immoral it is to go after a priest who sexually molested seventeen little boys! And where do you get off always disapproving of me? Well, let me tell you, I'm goddamn sick of it. Who died and made you queen?'

Blue was staring at her when she finally finished, and Becky was nearly choking. But Ginny's speech had been a long time coming and was overdue. She was tired of her sister criticizing her for everything she did. 'I'm done,' Ginny said, feeling better after she'd said it.

'So am I,' Becky said, in a voice shaking with fury. 'I'm through being embarrassed by you, or explaining you to people, or making excuses for you because they think you're weird. And don't drag me into this mess with you. You may not mind being in the tabloids, but I do. Just leave me alone!' she said, and slammed down the phone.

'Is she really pissed at you?' Blue asked, with eyes filled with remorse, convinced it was all his fault, no matter what Ginny said.

'She's always pissed at me about something,' Ginny said, smiling at him. 'She'll get over it.'

'It's all my fault,' he said miserably, and when he went to bed, Ginny reassured him again and kissed him goodnight. 'If it weren't for me, you wouldn't be in the newspapers, and they wouldn't have said that stuff about Chris and Mark,' Blue said as he looked up at her from his bed.

'It doesn't matter. Whatever anyone says, they're still gone. You didn't do anything wrong. In fact, you've done everything right since you came into my life. Now stop worrying about it and go to sleep.' She smiled at him and kissed him again.

She tried not to think about it herself that night, or the fight with her sister. Some of it had needed to be said. And finally, after playing it over in her head several times, she fell asleep.

The next morning when she got up, she made herself a cup of coffee and read *The New York Times* online. There was nothing in it about her, although there was a very good op-ed piece about priests who molested kids and how they all needed to be brought to justice and not hidden by the church. She would have liked to send it to her sister, but she didn't want to start the fight all over again. They had said enough.

She waited for Blue to get up so she could cook him breakfast, and suddenly she realized he was going to be late, and she hadn't heard his alarm go off, so she went to his room and pulled up the shade. She turned to smile at him, and saw that he was burrowed under the covers. She gently poked his shoulder with her finger and told him it was time to get up. But what she poked was not his shoulder. It was a pillow. She gently pulled the covers back and saw that he had stuffed the bed. And on top of the pillow he had left a note for her. She read it, and it nearly broke her heart.

'Dear Ginny: All I ever do is cause you trouble. I'm

sorry about the newspapers and what they said, it was all because of me and Father Ted. And I'm sorry about your fight with Becky, and that she's mad at you because of me, too. You don't have to be my guardian anymore if you don't want to. Thank you for everything you did for me. I'll never forget it. I love you, Blue.' Tears rolled down her cheeks as she read it, and then she looked around the room and in his closet. He had taken his rolling overnight bag, a couple of jackets, some shirts, socks, and underwear, and his Converse and running shoes. His toothbrush and toothpaste were gone, and his comb and brush. All his schoolbooks were piled up on his desk, and then she saw that his laptop was gone and his cell phone, so she could at least communicate with him. She called him immediately, and he didn't answer. She left him a message and sent him a text. 'Where are you? None of it's your fault. Come back. I love you, Ginny.' But he didn't answer that, either. She sent him an e-mail that said the same thing, and then, with a trembling hand, she called Andrew. She didn't know what else to do.

'He ran away,' she said, sounding upset and frantic.

'Who did?' He was busy and distracted.

'Blue.'

'When?'

'Sometime last night. I just found his bed stuffed with pillows, and he's left me a note.'

'What does it say?'

'He apologizes. He feels terrible about the stuff in the newspapers yesterday. And Becky and I had a fight about it last night, and he overheard it. She said I'm an embarrassment to her. Blue blames himself for everything.' She was on the verge of tears again.

'Did you try calling him?' Andrew sounded worried, too. Blue and Ginny had been under a lot of strain for months with the court case and everything else.

'I called, texted, and e-mailed. He hasn't answered yet.'

Andrew thought about it for a minute. He was a fourteen-year-old kid, and he knew life on the streets better than they did. And New York was a big city. 'Why don't you wait and see what he does today? He may just calm down and come home this afternoon.'

'He won't. He thinks he's ruining my life. He isn't. He's the best thing that's happened to me in the last four years.'

'Don't panic,' Andrew said gently. 'Even if he stays away for a day or two, he'll be back. He loves you, Ginny.'

'That's what he said in his note,' she said, with tears in her eyes and a lump in her throat.

'Just try to relax, he'll come home. Boys do this stuff. And he has a lot going on in his head.' Even though Andrew had no answers for her, his voice was soothing.

'I don't know where to start looking for him.'

'You don't need to right now. It's daytime. I'll come over after work, and we can look for him together,' he said. 'Call me if he turns up.'

She spent the day waiting to hear from Blue, calling his cell phone regularly, and she sent him a few more texts, and an e-mail. But he didn't answer anything. She felt like she'd been going around in circles all day by the time Andrew came at six o'clock. She hadn't eaten but had had about four cups of coffee, and she looked jangled beyond belief.

'What if he never comes back? He's all I have,' she said, as tears rolled down her cheeks. Instinctively Andrew put his arms around her and held her. He could feel her heart pound against his chest.

'Let's have something to eat, and then we'll go out and take a look,' he said calmly. He texted Blue from his cell phone, too, but Blue didn't respond to him, either. And when he called his cell, it went straight to voice mail.

Andrew made them each a sandwich with what was in the fridge. He had gone home to change into jeans, and was wearing a hooded jacket and a dark blue sweater and running shoes. He had a feeling they were going to do a lot of walking that night, to all the places Ginny could think of where he might be.

They started at McDonald's, where they had had dinner the night they met. His favorite pizza restaurant. A couple of other burger places. The bowling alley downtown. They stood outside a movie complex for a while, and didn't see him, and at eleven p.m. they went to Penn Station, and crossed over the tracks to the tunnel where he'd been living when he ran away from Houston Street. There were half a dozen kids, and only one of them said he knew him, but he said Blue hadn't been around in months. She called Houston Street, but they hadn't seen him either, and they said they'd tell their street outreach team to keep an eye out for him. But he was nowhere. She didn't bother to call his aunt, because she knew there was no way he would go to her. At midnight, they sat on a bench in Penn Station and Ginny put her face in her hands and Andrew put an arm around her shoulders.

'What am I going to do?' she said, looking at him miserably.

'All you can do is wait. He'll come home.' And then she thought of Lizzie, her niece in California. It was still early enough to call there. When she did, Lizzie picked up, but said she hadn't heard from him all day. She figured he was busy at school.

'Is something wrong?' she asked her aunt, and Ginny didn't want to explain it to her.

'If you hear from him, just tell him I'm looking for him, and to come home.'

'Okay.' Lizzie hung up, sounding unconcerned, as Ginny looked up at Andrew.

'Thank you for doing this with me.'

'Don't worry about it. I haven't been much help.'

'It's nice to have company,' she said, looking exhausted. All she wanted to do was find Blue and bring him home. 'I guess we might as well go home,' she said as they wandered slowly through Penn Station, walked up the stairs, and Andrew hailed a cab. She leaned against him on the way home, and it was comforting to have him there next to her. And when they got to her address, she suggested they walk along the river, to see if he was sleeping on a bench there. It was October, and the nights were chilly, but the days were warm. Walking along, looking down at the river, reminded her of when she'd seen Blue for the first time. They sat down on a bench, and Andrew pulled her closer. He could see the sadness and defeat in her eyes.

'The poor kid feels like everything is his fault,' Ginny said sadly. 'All that crap in the tabloids yesterday, and my sister getting mad at me and calling me a weirdo and an embarrassment to her.' She smiled up at Andrew. 'I guess I have been kind of a weirdo for the last few years, running around the world, trying to get myself killed. I felt so guilty for letting Mark drive that night, and for not realizing how much he'd had to drink. My sister's life is about the size of a teacup, and she doesn't get it. Nothing like that has ever happened to her.'

'You and Blue have a lot in common,' he said gently. 'You feel guilty about your husband and son. Blue still has

Father Teddy's voice in his head telling him that he "tempted" him, that it was his fault. He knows better now, but it's going to take a long time for that voice in his head to go away. The best thing you've done for him is prove to him, not just with words but with actions, that he's worth everything you've done for him, that you stand behind him, and that he's not guilty of anything. You told me when I met you that you wanted him to have an "amazing" life, not just a good life. Well, he does, thanks to you. And one day, because of you, that accusing voice in his head will go away, because your voice telling him what a good kid he is, in spite of everything, will be louder than Father Teddy's.'

What Andrew said to her touched her deeply, and she looked up at him with questioning eyes. 'How do you know all that?'

He hesitated for a minute before he answered, and he looked off into space while he told her, remembering. 'The same thing happened to me when I was a kid. I was eleven. Father John – he was a big, fat, funny, jolly guy. He had a fantastic collection of comic books he promised to let me read, and baseball cards to show me. So I went to his house, and he did pretty much the same thing that Father Teddy's been doing to all these kids. And he told me it was my fault because I tempted him, and that the devil would kill me on the spot if I told anyone. It took me months, but I finally told my parents.

'They didn't believe me. Everyone in the parish loved Father John, and I was always kind of a mischievous kid. We never talked about it again. I knew what a bad person he was, and I felt guilty for what he did to me, so I decided that one day I would become a priest, but a really, really good priest, so I could make it up to God for what I thought I had "tempted" him to do. I went right into the seminary straight from high school. And I became a very, very, very good priest, just as I promised God I would.

'But I was miserable. I didn't have the vocation I thought I did. I wanted to go out with women, and have a family.' He smiled at Ginny as he said it. 'But I felt guilty again, about leaving the priesthood. And then these incidents started to surface in the church. People started talking about priests like Father John and Father Teddy. Nothing ever happened to Father John, he must have molested hundreds of kids over the years, and he lived out his days in peace. But when people started talking about it openly, all I wanted to do was get out of my vows, and work as a lawyer defending these kids that no one ever used to believe, just like me. I knew that if I tried to do it from within the church, they would pressure me into defending the perpetrators or even covering for them.

'So I finally left and stopped feeling guilty. I miss being a priest sometimes – there were some things I liked about it. But I'm much happier helping kids like Blue put the bad priests behind bars. And I don't even have to be a priest to do it. The strange thing is,' he went on, 'I think I still had some kind of residual guilt from my childhood, and when I saw how you believed in Blue, how you stuck by him, and defended him, I think it healed something in me, too. You're a very healing woman, Ginny, and a very loving one. Maybe that's enough to undo the damage done to people like Blue and me, or at least start the process. It's a little late for me, but I hope so.

'And you don't need to feel guilty about anything. Your husband did whatever he did that night. You couldn't have stopped him. You didn't know. And Blue couldn't have stopped Father Teddy any more than I could have stopped Father John. Whatever they did is their responsibility, not ours. What we have to do is what you've been telling Blue. We owe it to ourselves to allow the healing to happen and move on. And even my life is going to be better now because of you. Everybody has something they can beat themselves up for. It's just not worth the energy to do it.' They sat there quietly for a long time, and he pulled her closer to him, and she looked at him and smiled.

'I'm sorry that happened to you,' she said.

'So am I, but I'm fine now. And Blue will be, too. We're among the lucky ones. You taught me that. I've learned a lot from watching you with Blue.' She nodded, thinking about Blue, and hoped he'd come home soon. And then as she looked at Andrew, he leaned toward her, put his arms around her, and kissed her. He had been wanting to do that since the day they met. He remembered how beautiful she was when he saw her on TV, and she was even more so now. He had never dreamed that he'd meet her one day and fall in love with her. She kissed him back, and they sat together for a long time on the bench next to the East River. They got up after a while, and started to walk slowly back to her apartment, and then she thought of something and turned around.

'Wait a minute,' she said softly to Andrew, and walked to the shed where she had first seen Blue, a short distance away. She stood looking at it for a minute and saw that the padlock was off. She could hear something stirring inside, and as Andrew walked up to her, she slowly opened the door and saw Blue sitting inside, with his bag next to him, and he was concentrating on his laptop. He looked up at her in surprise, and said the only thing that came to mind.

'Don't you knock?'

'You don't live here anymore,' she said, smiling at him. 'Come on, let's go home.' He hesitated for a minute and looked at both of them, and then he climbed out of the shed, and picked up his bag. He didn't ask what Andrew was doing there, but he could tell that they were both happy to see him. Ginny put an arm around Blue's waist as they walked in the direction of the apartment. As they walked past the railing next to the river, she stopped and led Blue over to it. 'I want to show you something,' she said gently. 'This is where I was standing the first time I saw you. Do you know what I was doing? I was about to jump in, because my life was so miserable, I didn't want to live another minute. All I wanted to do was die in that river, the night before Mark and Chris's anniversary, so I didn't have to live through another one. And then I saw you run into the shed out of the corner of my eye, and after that we went to dinner at McDonald's and the rest is history.

'You don't need to feel guilty about anything, Blue. *Nothing* is your fault. You saved my life that night. I've been paying my dues for the last four years in every refugee camp I could get to. And you saved my life. If you hadn't been there that night, I'd be dead by now.' And then she looked at Andrew. 'And look at all the lives you've changed for the better and the boys you've saved with what you do. I think we're three lucky people who lead amazing lives already.' And then she smiled broadly at Blue. 'And if you ever run away again, I'm going to kick your ass, is that clear?'

He grinned at her when she said it. He knew she wouldn't. 'Were you really going to kill yourself that night?' Blue asked looking serious again, and she looked just as serious when she nodded. Andrew wanted to hold her close to him when she did, but he didn't want to do that in front of Blue. At least not yet.

The three of them walked slowly back to her apartment, and she turned to Blue. 'What do you say we make it official?'

'Make what official?' Blue looked puzzled.

'Would you like me to adopt you?'

Blue stopped walking and stared at her. 'Do you mean it?'

'Of course I mean it. Would I say it if I didn't?'

'Yeah, I'd really like that,' he said, beaming again as he looked at Ginny and then at Andrew. 'Can she do that?'

'It takes a little while, but yes she can, if it's what you both want.'

'I do,' Ginny said clearly.

'Me, too,' Blue added, and Andrew walked them back to the apartment and left them there. He lingered for a minute to say goodnight to Ginny while Blue went to put his things away in his bedroom.

'Thank you for being with me tonight . . . and for everything you said to me,' Ginny said gratefully.

'I meant all of it. You're a very special woman. I hope we get to spend some time together before you go away again.' His eyes clouded as he said it. 'I hate to think of you in those places, in danger all the time.' She nodded, she was beginning to worry about it, too, but that was a discussion for another time. They had covered a lot of ground that night. He bent down and kissed her forehead, and then he left, and Blue went to the kitchen to get something to eat. He was starving, and Ginny walked into the kitchen and smiled at him.

'Welcome home, Blue,' she said softly, and he turned to smile at her and looked like a big happy kid, and his happiness was mirrored by her own.

Chapter 19

Two weeks after Blue ran away for a day, Monsignor Cavaretti called another meeting with Andrew and Ginny. He offered no explanation and there had been no new developments in the case in the past few weeks, and no new victims had come forward. Father Teddy was out on bail, staying at a monastery near Rhinebeck on the Hudson River. And much to Ginny's relief, nothing more had appeared in the tabloids.

Andrew met Ginny outside the archdiocese, and they walked in together. They had had dinner the night before, and things were progressing nicely. His eyes swept her gently as they walked in. A few minutes later they were ushered into Monsignor Cavaretti's private office. For an instant, it reminded Andrew of the hours they had spent together in Rome, having endless discussions about canon law. But the monsignor wasn't smiling as they sat down.

'I wanted to speak to you both today,' he said in a

somber tone. 'As you can imagine, this entire situation has weighed heavily on all of us. These are never happy stories, and everyone involved gets hurt, including the church.' He turned toward Andrew then. 'I wanted you to know that Ted Graham is going to enter a guilty plea tomorrow. There's no point in drawing this out. I think what happened is clear to all of us, and we are all deeply grieved for the children it hurt.' The old priest looked profoundly sympathetic. Andrew was shocked – he had never seen him so humble. 'I want to discuss a settlement with both of you. We have taken this as far up as the cardinal, and to Rome. We would like to offer Blue Williams a settlement of one point seven million dollars, to be put in a trust for him until he reaches twenty-one years of age.' He looked straight at Ginny then. 'Would that be acceptable to you?' He had enormous admiration for what she'd done for Blue, and it showed in his eyes.

She glanced immediately at Andrew, and then back at the monsignor and nodded with a look of astonishment on her face. It was more than she had ever hoped, and it would change his life forever. His education, his sense of security, the options he would have later. Justice had indeed been served. She nodded in grateful agreement, unable to speak. 'Does that suit you, counselor?' he asked Andrew, who smiled at him, and a look passed between two old friends, a look of respect and affection. The end result blessed them all. The church, at

Cavaretti's insistence, had done the right thing for the boy.

'It suits me very well, and I am very proud to have been part of this collective decision that is the right thing to do.' The monsignor stood up. 'That was all I had to say. We'll draw up the papers, and of course there will be a confidentiality agreement to go with it. I think none of us will be well served by speaking to the press.'

Both Andrew and Ginny nodded in full agreement. They all shook hands, and a moment later Andrew and Ginny were back on the street, hurrying away before they spoke. And then he turned to her with a broad grin.

'Holy shit! We did it! Oh my God. *You* did it! Talk about giving Blue an amazing life. You could have just listened to his story and never done anything about it. And instead you had the guts to see it through, and gave him the courage to do it. And this will set the tone for all the other kids Ted Graham abused.' It was one of the sweetest victories of his career, and through it he had met Ginny. The possibilities were infinite now, for all of them. The church could well afford what it was paying Blue. And he would never forget Cavaretti's benevolent hand in it.

They had lunch to celebrate. And Andrew came to dinner that night, and they told Blue. He looked shocked when they told him. He couldn't conceive of having that kind of money one day.

'OhmyGod, I'm rich!' he said, looking at Ginny. 'Can I buy a Ferrari when I'm eighteen?' He grinned at her, and she laughed.

'No, you can buy an education, which is better,' she said sternly, but they were happy for him. He had paid a high price for that money, but it would serve him well, hopefully for the rest of his life if it was well invested, which Ginny knew it would be. It was a lot for him to look forward to and absorb.

She called Kevin Callaghan the next day and told him that there had been a settlement, though not the amount, but she thanked him profusely for the referral to Andrew, which had been exactly the right one. And she told him Ted Graham was pleading guilty that day.

'Excellent.' He was happy to hear it, and he reminded her to call him if she came to L.A. He had realized that he would have a soft spot for her forever. Nothing would ever come of it, but it was nice to dream.

And in November, Ellen Warberg called her from the SOS/HR office. Ginny had been thinking about her job a lot lately. She missed working, and traveling for them, but the job was no longer compatible with her responsibilities for Blue, nor her relationship with Andrew, which was growing day by day, and seemed to be headed in a serious direction, which had taken them both by surprise.

Ginny assumed that Ellen had called her in to discuss

her next assignment, and Ginny knew that she would have to turn it down.

'I want you to know,' Ellen said seriously, as they sat facing each other across her desk, 'that I'm retiring. I want time to do some projects, and travel for myself. I spent years doing what you do, and I've been at this desk now for five years, and I think it's long enough. I wanted you to be the first to know, because I would like to suggest you as my successor, to take my job. I think you'd be great at it, and I don't think being in the field nine months a year, halfway around the world, is what you want right now, so maybe this would work for you,' she said hopefully, thinking she'd have to talk Ginny into it. Ginny wanted to jump up and hug Ellen. It was the perfect solution to the problem that had been tormenting her for months. She didn't want to quit, but she couldn't do her job anymore. But she could do Ellen's. It was tailor-made for her, and she knew the needs and style of SOS/HR inside out.

'I'd love it,' Ginny said, beaming at her, looking as though she'd just won the lottery. Ellen came around her desk and hugged her then, and told her she would be leaving on the first of January. It was perfect in every way. And Andrew and Blue were thrilled when she told them that night. Her days as a nomad had come to an end. They confirmed her new position two weeks later as the director of SOS/HR's main office in New York. It was a prestigious job with a salary to match. She and Ellen had a quiet lunch to talk about it, and she gave Ginny great advice.

After lunch, Ginny went to pick out the Christmas gift she'd been planning for Blue. She bought him a piano and knew it would be the most exciting gift possible, better than a Ferrari. He had wanted his own piano all his life. He was doing well at school, and was preparing for his first recital in December.

It started snowing as she walked home, and it reminded her of the time almost a year before, when she had flown in from Africa one night before the anniversary date she had dreaded, and a boy named Blue had changed her life forever, and she had changed his, and Andrew had helped them. It all seemed like a miracle to her now.

Chapter 20

Blue's fifteenth birthday was the most important one of his life. It was a double celebration. Becky, Alan, and their children had flown in from L.A. And that morning, the entire family and Andrew went to court with Blue, where a Family Court judge asked Blue Williams if he wished to be adopted by Virginia Anne Carter, to which Blue responded solemnly 'I do,' and then he asked Ginny if she wished to adopt Blue Williams, and she said she did. And Andrew O'Connor was the attorney of record. It felt almost like a wedding, which Andrew and Ginny were contemplating as well. But this was Blue's day.

Ginny kissed him when the judge pronounced them mother and son. He had thought about taking her name, but decided he liked his own, which was fine with her. And after the brief ceremony, they all went to 21 for lunch. Later they had dinner at a Japanese restaurant Blue loved. And that night after dinner, they all went back to the apartment, where Blue played the piano and they all sang, and he and Lizzie kept teasing each other about being cousins. He was playing all her favorite songs. Andrew followed Ginny out to the kitchen and kissed her. They turned back to look at Blue for a minute. He had never looked happier. He had finished his first year at LaGuardia Arts and done well, and was getting ready for another recital in September. And Ginny would be there, not in Afghanistan or Africa. Those days were over.

Old stories had ended. New ones had begun. The pain of old memories had begun to dim. New bonds had formed. And new lives had risen from the ashes of old ones. The phrase 'beauty for ashes' seemed apt for all of them. And Ginny reminded Blue that 'nothing is impossible' almost every day. Blue and Andrew believed her and had found that it was true.

Pegasus

Danielle Steel

On the cusp of the Second World War in Europe, Nicolas and Alex are two widowed men raising their children alone. They lead contented, peaceful lives, until a long-buried secret about Nicolas's ancestry threatens his family's safety . . .

To survive, they must flee to America. The only treasures Nicolas and his sons can take are eight purebred horses, two of them dazzling Lipizzaners – gifts from Alex. These magnificent creatures are their ticket to a new life, securing Nicolas a job with the famous Ringling Brothers Circus. There, he and the white stallion, Pegasus, become the centrepiece of the show, and a graceful young high-wire walker soon steals his heart.

But as the years of war take their toll, Nicolas struggles to adapt to their new life while Alex and his daughter face escalating danger in Europe. When tragedy strikes on both sides of the ocean, what will become of each family when their happiness rests in the hands of fate?

A Perfect Life

Danielle Steel

An icon in the world of television news, Blaise McCarthy seems to have it all: beauty, intelligence and courage. But privately there is a story she has protected for years . . .

Blaise's daughter Salima, blinded by juvenile diabetes, lives at a year-round boarding school. But when the school suddenly closes, she returns home to Blaise's New York apartment with her new carer, Simon. As new challenges change the way they see one another, the bond between mother and daughter deepens as never before.

Then Blaise's personal and professional worlds collide, and the well-guarded secrets of her home life are exposed. Suddenly her life is no longer perfect, but real. Can mother and daughter together learn how to face a world they can't control?

Power Play

Danielle Steel

Fiona Carson has proven herself as CEO of a multibillion-dollar high-tech company – a successful woman in a man's world. Devoted single mother, world-class strategist, and tough negotiator, Fiona has to manage a delicate balancing act every day.

Meanwhile, Marshall Weston basks in the fruits of his achievements. At his side is his wife Liz who has gladly sacrificed her own career to raise their three children. Smooth, shrewd and irreproachable, Marshall's power only enhances his charisma – but he harbors secrets that could destroy his life at any moment.

Both must face their own demons, and the lives they lead come at a high price. But just how high a price are they willing to pay to stay at the top of their game?

Winners

Danielle Steel

At just seventeen, Lily Thomas is already a ski champion training for the Olympics, her heart set on winning the gold. But in one moment, Lily's future is changed forever – her hopes for Olympic triumph swept away in a tragic accident.

Her father, Bill, refuses to accept Lily's fate, while her neurosurgeon, Dr Jessie Matthews, is adamant that all hope is not lost. But when Jessie endures a tragedy of her own, her spirit is truly tested.

Then Bill decides to build a rehab facility for his daughter and transforms countless other lives too. But will courage and kindness be enough to make winners of them all?

Get to know Danielle Steel online

Visit Danielle's website to hear the latest news, read Danielle's personal notes to her readers, and sign up for her newsletter at **www.daniellesteel.com**.

You can also find out more about Danielle's two lives in Paris and San Francisco, her family and beloved dogs, and what she enjoys spending her time doing outside of writing on her blog at **www.daniellesteel.net**.

Or join over a million other fans of Danielle Steel at her Facebook page and learn more from Danielle about new releases, news and exclusive content at **www.facebook.com/DanielleSteelOfficial**.